I0691994

Vieux Carré Vengeance

By

Tom Aswell

ISBN: 978-1-7331968-3-3

1

It was early Thursday – twenty-two minutes past midnight to be precise – when the old Chevy Impala pulled up to the gas pump at the convenience store. The car looked as though it was held together with Bond-O and duct tape and its air conditioning had long ago stopped working. A sheet of translucent plastic sheeting, the kind used as drop cloths by painters, replaced the right rear window and it jumped in and out with the heart-stopping thump of the hip-hop beat that sprang in pulsating thuds from the speakers. Bystanders, had there been any at that time of night, would have heard the entire car rattle with each pounding bump of the music, assuming that's what one might choose to call it. Chrome spinner wheel covers adorned the rusted-out car, doubling its NADA book value, underscoring the absurdity of the image.

The store was on Esplanade in New Orleans. Jamal, the driver, exited the vehicle and walked back to the pump where he removed the nozzle as if to fuel the vehicle. A second man entered the store, ostensibly to pay the clerk. Theron, the third passenger in the car, got out, took a quick look around the premises, and lit a cigarette. Both men then just stood looking around the parking lot and watching their companion inside the store.

His name was D'Wayne and he nodded to the cashier as he entered. The cashier returned the gesture as D'Wayne walked to the rear of the store where he removed a beer from the cooler, conducting a visual inspection of the interior of the business as he did so. Satisfied there were no other customers there, he walked to the window and nodded to the others.

That most convenience stores in the New Orleans area are locked at night and serve customers only through a thick glass window with an extendable transaction drawer didn't seem to occur to the three. Nor did the cashier seem to think it odd that a customer would enter to pay for gas but would go first to the beer cooler even as the driver stood outside with the nozzle in his hand, waiting for the pump to be turned on from inside.

D'Wayne approached the counter as the other two men burst through the door, weapons drawn. All three now had automatic weapons aimed squarely at the cashier as a second gunman, Jamal, the driver, yelled for him to empty the cash drawer onto the counter and to move back against the wall behind him. The

1

cashier stood looking at the three, making no move to comply with the gunman's demands. His face was expressionless, revealing no sign of fear or concern for his safety.

"Don't you hear good, asshole?" Jamal, a black man in his late twenties, shouted, waving the .380 caliber pistol near his face. It was evident that he and his companions were impatient and nervous. "I'll blow your goddamned head off if you don't give me the money *right now!*" Jamal shouted.

"I don't think I will do that," the cashier, a native of Sri Lanka, replied.

"You don't think *what?* You gonna die for somebody else's money, somebody who don't give a shit about you? Man, I'll kill yo' towel-head ass right where you standing!" He didn't know a Sri Lankan from an Arab. The clerk could have been Sudanese or Norwegian for all he knew—or cared.

"You cannot kill me again."

"Say *what?! What the hell you talkin' about?*"

"You can kill a man only once and you have already done so."

"Jamal," Theron, said to the driver, "I don't like this, man. This dude looks familiar. Don't he look like the one over on Magazine? Ain't he th' same one?"

Jamal, who stood about six-three and who was the acknowledged leader of the group, shot an uncertain look at the others. "Shut up, goddamnit! That's bullshit, that ain't him! It can't be! He's dead!" Then he turned back to the cashier, shoving the muzzle of his pistol into his throat, just below and to the inside of his jawbone. "Last chance, Abdul. Open the cash drawer or I scatter what brains you got all over the wall!"

"Then you may as well shoot me, for I have put all the money into the floor safe and I am unable to op "

The explosion of the .380 shattered the air, causing both D'Wayne and Theron to jump backwards at the deafening sound.

"As I was trying to explain," the cashier continued, "I cannot open the safe, so you may as well shoot me."

The barrel of the pistol had been pressed against the soft flesh of his throat next to his Adam's apple, yet he was still standing, still talking in the same distinctive Eastern dialect, but there was no blood anywhere – just a gaping hole in the wall behind him. Jamal didn't notice the wall and thought the gun must have misfired, so he squeezed the trigger again and held it down as it roared three more times in quick succession. Now there were four huge holes grouped together in the wall behind the cashier. Still, the clerk stood smiling back at them. "You are not a very good shot, my friend." His grin exposed huge white teeth that flashed, contrasting with the dark brown of his skin.

Jamal and his companions emptied their weapons, filling the air with the ear-splitting roar of gunfire. Plastic shards flew from the wall behind the stoic cashier.

2

"Are you finished now?" the Sri Lankan said. His voice was almost sad. The wall behind him now had multiple yawning holes from the barrage of bullets that had ripped into it, splintering it and tearing it apart. "You seem to be all out of bullets."

In a single, panic-driven motion, all three bolted through the door, arms and legs flailing away like so many windmills. They piled into the Impala in a full-blown state of hysteria. Jamal fumbled with the key. He'd meant to leave the engine running but now he didn't take time to wonder why he'd removed the keys and put them in his pocket during an attempted robbery. Finally, he managed to get the key into the ignition and the old car engine protested and then sputtered to life, the hole in the muffler making it sound louder than it should have. Blue smoke boiled from the exhaust because of a burned engine valve as he left a trail of rubber in the parking lot. With the front end bouncing crazily from worn shocks, he plowed onto Esplanade in front of cars that swerved, honked, and screeched in their efforts to keep from hitting the would-be robbers.

Theron whimpered from the rear seat. A short, stout black man in his early twenties, he had been the one standing outside the car smoking. Now his entire body shook uncontrollably as he tried to light another cigarette. He swore an oath as the lighter fell from his trembling hands. They had driven three blocks without a sound from anyone in the car except for Theron's hysterical mewling when a pedestrian stepped in front of their careening vehicle and turned and faced them. It was the same Sri Lankan store clerk and he made no effort to get out of the path of the Impala. Jamal never had a chance to hit the brakes but miraculously, there was no impact. D'Wayne looked back over his shoulder and saw the pedestrian, still standing in Esplanade but now he was turned toward them as he watched them speed away.

"Jesus, Jamal, that was him, I *know* it was!" screamed D'Wayne, the front seat passenger who had been the first to enter the store. He was sobbing now.

A car pulled alongside theirs. *"Oh, shit, Jamal!"* blurted Theron from the rear seat but only inches from Jamal's right ear. Jamal looked to his left and he slammed on the brakes when he saw the same clerk driving the second car, looking over at them.

"That *was* him!" D'Wayne yelled for a second time, his eyes were wide with fear and his body rocked back and forth involuntarily. "It *is* him!"

"Goddamn right it's him! Where the hell did he come from?" Theron's voice, now a full octave higher than usual – and piercing in its volume – wheezed from the emotional stress that swept over him in a matter of seconds, stress that now aggravated the effects of his chronic asthma. He clutched at his constricted windpipe as his undernourished lungs struggled for oxygen even as the second car disappeared into the night ahead of them. Jamal accelerated in a maniacal effort to catch the second vehicle, much to the displeasure of the other two but it

3

disappeared in traffic. "That was some scary shit, man!" Theron managed to gasp. "How'd he *do* that?"

"I will tell you what is scary, my friend" said a disembodied fourth voice, a voice that belonged to no one in the Impala. "It is scary when one is visited by another who is uninvited and who is unknown."

"Who said that?" yelled Jamal, jerking the wheel as he looked around the inside of the car. He fought to regain control of the faded blue vehicle when it almost ran off the road and as fear welled up inside him. He struggled for his own self-control and to quiet the hysteria of his two passengers even as his own logic, understanding, and courage, already slipping away, now vanished.

"It is I," said the convenience store cashier who was now seated in the front seat between the two black men.

"Oh, *hell* no," shouted Jamal as D'Wayne, screaming, struggled to open the front passenger door of the Impala that was barreling along Esplanade at about eighty miles per hour. A dark, wet pool formed on the seat between his legs as he fumbled with the door handle. Jamal reached down between the seat and door and pulled out a knife that he kept concealed on the floorboard. Holding the knife in his left hand, he lunged across to his right in a continuous motion, taking a wide, arcing swing at the cashier with the razor-sharp blade. The knife – and half of Jamal's arm – went through the Sri Lankan's torso as if it were thin air – which it was – and into D'Wayne's throat, severing his carotid artery and windpipe. D'Wayne's eyes went wide in pain and shock before he slumped down into the passenger seat. Blood pulsated in crimson spurts from his neck, soaking the interior of the car and mixing with air as it bubbled from his mouth and nose. A low gurgle made its way from D'Wayne's throat, but it was a dying gurgle.

"D'Wayne!" Jamal screamed, gaping in horror at his brother's limp body. He turned loose of the wheel at the realization of what he'd done and instinctively grabbed the younger man's shoulders. The old Impala, its front-end alignment shot, and already out of control, lurched into the left lane and into the path of an oncoming garbage truck. In an instant of screaming brakes, grinding metal, and shattering glass, the garbage truck collided with and then rolled over the Impala, crushing the car as well as those inside it. It took over four hours for firemen and police to remove the twisted, broken bodies from the crumpled wreckage. They were so mangled that D'Wayne's stab wound was never detected. Jamal, D'Wayne, and Theron were the only occupants.

4

2

"It was really weird, man," Jim "Tattoo" Reilly explained to the police officers.

He was typical of those who drift into—and out of—New Orleans. An aimless itinerant with no family or responsibilities, he found himself drawn to the dirty New Orleans French Quarter like so many before him. It didn't matter where he came from; he was just like the others who came and went before him. Failing at all else he'd tried, he ended up taking a job at the convenience store to keep body and soul together until he could leave for the next city down the road, probably Houston or maybe Austin. Other than clerking at the store and trying to score a little dope from time to time, he had no life, no ambition, and no future.

"I was comin' outta th' bathroom when I heard voices from up front," Tattoo said. "I started up here to wait on what I thought was customers. That's when I heard this black dude yelling at somebody to empty the cash drawer. He called somebody an asshole," he said. "He acted like he was talking to somebody behind the counter, but there wasn't nobody back there. He was excited, pissed about something, so I just hid behind some boxes and watched as best I could without being seen myself."

"You say there was no one behind the counter?" the officer interrupted. His name was Stuart Wiggins. After twenty-four years on the force, he was still a sergeant – an unhappy sergeant at that. He hated having to deal with losers like Tattoo.

"Nobody. There was just three black dudes and they all had guns. The one who did most of the talking, he was taller than the other two. One of 'em called him Jamal. He told Jamal he looked like somebody on Magazine "

"Who   did?"

"Who did what?"

"Who looked like somebody on Magazine?" Sergeant Wiggins asked, appearing somewhat impatient and more than a little agitated. He couldn't help thinking of the Abbott and Costello *Who's on First?* routine. But then, his mind usually wandered at times like these. He needed any diversion that would help him get through his shift.

"I don't know, man. The guy behind the counter, I guess."

"I thought you said there was no one behind the counter."

5

"There *wasn't*. Nobody was back there, but this guy Jamal, he was holding his pistol up about head high and reaching across the counter like he was pointing it at someone. And he was screaming at the wall, yelling at somebody to open the cash drawer and then, all of a sudden, no warning, he just fires a shot into the wall. Scared th' shit outta me!"

"He fired a single shot?"

"At first, yeah, just one. Then he fired three more shots. But before that, he's yelling and saying he was gonna kill somebody's ass and then one of 'em says to Jamal that he looks like someone over on Magazine and Jamal says, 'that's bullshit,' and then he calls somebody Abdul and says it's his last chance to open the cash drawer or he'll blow his brains out. Right after that, he fires the first shot and then three more."

"Abdul?" *This idiot's just rambling, he's no help at all.*

"Yeah."

"Who's Abdul?" *How long 'til retirement?*

"Hell, man, I don't know. He's talkin' to the damn *wall*. There ain't nobody back there. But then, after he fires three or four shots at the wall, they all three open up. Sounds like a hundred shots going off all at once. Tore th' livin' shit outta th' wall. I'm *prayin'* they don't come back where I am."

"Then what?" Wiggins scribbled on a notepad as Tattoo talked.

"Then all three of 'em run out and jump in their car and they're gone. They almost caused a wreck out on Esplanade when they tore outta here."

"You get a good look at their car?"

"Not really. I stayed in the stock room 'til I could see their taillights when they pulled onto Esplanade. It was an older model car, but I couldn't say what kind."

"Did you see which direction they went when they left?" Wiggins asked.

"Yeah, they turned right onto Esplanade."

"They went east?"

Tattoo Reilly hesitated long enough to get his bearings. "Yeah, that would be east. They turned east."

"What do you think they meant by the reference to Magazine?"

"I don't know unless...."

"Unless what?"

"We got a store on Magazine," he said. "Some dude who works with me here told me once that it was robbed about a year ago and the clerk was killed. I think he said he was from India or somewhere, but I don't think I ever heard his name."

"I don't know that it'll be much help, but I'm going to need you to come back to the stockroom and show me where you were during all this. I need to get your vantage point so I can sorta put all this together for my report."

"I was hidin' behind this stack of boxes, about to shit on myself," Tattoo said.

6

"I'll also need you to come down to the station and give us a statement for whatever good it'll do," Wiggins said. *Where do these stores find their employees?*

The police sergeant, a veteran of dozens of similar investigations, knew it was hopeless, that unless someone walked into a precinct station and surrendered, this case was likely going to be one of hundreds in New Orleans that would remain unsolved. No one was killed, after all, so why pursue it? True, the wall behind the counter had been blown apart, but no money was taken. A few leads would be checked out. He'd interview store executives about the Magazine Street robbery to see if there might be a connection, but it wasn't likely. The clerk was of no help at all with his gibberish about men waving a gun and talking to the wall.

These convenience stores are hit all the time and it was probably just a coincidence that these bungling idiots even knew about the one on Magazine. Probably just an inept attempt at a copycat crime. No use wasting a lot of time and manpower trying to track down the perpetrators of this heinous crime.

When the officers finally left, Tattoo watched them drive away and then went back to plotting ways to score some more crystal meth or, failing that, some pot.

Tattoo was just as repulsive as the felons he battled on the filthy streets of New Orleans on a daily basis, Wiggins thought as he pulled from the convenience store's parking lot into traffic on Esplanade. A native of Mississippi, he had grown to hate the city more with every passing day that he was forced to work among its degenerate, ungrateful vermin. He'd never worked anywhere else, so he had no other cities with which to compare New Orleans so his opinions were at best, subjective. He didn't know, nor did he concern himself with statistics showing New Orleans to be no different than most other inner cities in America. It was all human garbage.

If he wasn't trying to arrest thugs who robbed, raped, and killed innocent people – and the not-so-innocent – only to watch them get off on technicalities or receive only symbolic punishment, he was wasting his career trying to keep drunks from urinating or throwing up in the gutters of Bourbon Street, discouraging women from flashing their breasts for cheap beads at Mardi Gras, or breaking up fights between over-zealous fans during Sugar Bowl festivities or Saints games.

In the end, things were always the same; nothing changed. Even the hookers he arrested every night were right back on the streets the next night for him to arrest all over again. It was a dead-end proposition for an honest law enforcement officer. At times, he'd even wondered how much dirty money he could rat away if he were on the take. Each time he dismissed the idea because he knew he couldn't live with himself as a bad cop and it was a constant source of frustration to know there were so many police officers who shook down the whorehouses, chop shops and drug dealers on a regular basis. New Orleans, after

7

all, is the city that co-authored, along with Chicago, the manual on police corruption.

It didn't help that he was fresh from being cited for contempt of court by a petulant Orleans Parish Criminal District Court Judge who fined him and then subjected him to a humiliating tongue lashing before a courtroom full of attorneys and fellow police officers for showing up in court two hours late. It was only two days ago and Wiggins, still smarting from the embarrassment, was already harboring a deep resentment toward Judge Charles Cheramie.

Wiggins was the arresting officers less than three months before in an ill-advised armed robbery case. A would-be robber, alone and on foot, never had a chance when he held up a fast food restaurant by pointing a .22 caliber pistol at the head of a terrified teenager behind the counter and ran out with all of seventy dollars. When the call came over his radio, Wiggins was barely a block away and soon spotted the frightened robber running down the street and was quick to make the arrest. Despite the positive identification by the employee and the money and gun found in his possession, the robbery suspect decided to plead not guilty and take his chances.

As the arresting officer, Wiggins was subpoenaed to testify at the trial and was en route to court when he spotted a young thug holding a couple at gunpoint in the process of robbing them in broad daylight. Reacting on his police instincts, he momentarily forgot the court date and chased down the gunman and arrested him. He arranged for the couple, Swedes, to come to the police station to give a statement. Then he took the assailant to the station for booking, a process that took nearly two hours.

Many judges have egos that are inversely proportionate to their intellect and Judge Cheramie was irate at being inconvenienced and slapped the contempt citation on Wiggins without bothering to hear his explanation. *What the hell was I supposed to do, look the other way? Bring the prisoner to court with me?* The incident intensified his hatred for lawyers and judges in general and to reinforce his cynical outlook toward a dead-end law enforcement career in a rat hole like New Orleans.

8

3

New Orleans.
The Crescent City.
The Big Easy.

The very name conjures up images unique to this southern Old-World city that rises out of the crescent-shaped basin situated between Lake Pontchartrain and the Mississippi River. There are some more favorable images – like the original trolleys (they're called streetcars by the locals) manufactured by the Perley Thomas Company. The St. Charles line, one of almost forty thousand historic landmarks in the city, is the only place in the U.S. where you can still ride these old rail cars.

New Orleans: beignets, Bourbon Street revelry, Café Du Monde, Mardi Gras parades, Canal Street, crawfish boils, prostitution, jazz funerals, gumbo, NFL playoff futility, crawfish etouffee, street musicians, the Sugar Bowl, booze, oysters, wrought iron gates, shrimp, NBA futility, courtyards, stately old homes in the Uptown district, red beans and rice, and Dixie Beer. All are part of the city's charm. But just as with any city with such a colorful history, there also are scenes that have disappeared from the landscape but which are still held dear by the local citizenry – and some that aren't. Those include the Falstaff and Jax beer breweries, Pontchartrain Beach, WTIX radio station, K&B (Katz & Bestoff) Drug stores with their trademark purple logo, Schwegmann's grocery stores (sold in bankruptcy), reputed crime boss Carlos Marcello, and flamboyant former district attorney and JFK murder conspiracy theorist Jim Garrison.

Then there is the darker side of New Orleans, beginning with its infamous *Cities of the Dead* – cemeteries featuring elaborate granite and cement tombs that stand high above ground in deference to the water-saturated land that lies some three feet below sea level. It was only natural that these eerie graveyards and the practice of voodoo by African slaves imported from Haiti would converge to convey upon New Orleans the unofficial title of America's most haunted city. Founded in 1718, the city has a rich history of voodoo, spiritualism, ghosts, and general tales of the paranormal dating back to legendary voodoo queen Marie

9

Laveau and beyond.

Voodoo is still practiced today and ghosts are everywhere – in hotels, old homes, restaurants, cemeteries, theaters, and even churches, or so the stories go, from former employees of local business establishments, to Confederate soldiers, to children who died tragically. Some others are the ghosts of spurned lovers and tortured slaves. The stories behind them are touching, poignant, tragic, heartrending, and bone chilling. They are stories of love, devotion, and unimaginable brutality. But they wouldn't be ghost stories if they didn't contain bits and pieces of all these ingredients. Perhaps that is what gives New Orleans its charm, its sense of history, its intrigue, its mystique

4

Matt Ramsey was bored. The Baby Cakes, nee Zephyrs, the Triple-A farm club that has been affiliated—depending upon the year—with the Milwaukee Brewers, Houston Astros, Montreal Expos/Washington Nationals, New York Mets or the Miami Marlins, were getting pounded by Oklahoma. The Zephyrs—Matt just couldn't adapt to the new Baby Cakes moniker—moved from Denver to New Orleans – or more accurately, Metairie – in 1993, a few years before Matt came to Tulane.

A native of Farmerville in north Louisiana, near the Arkansas border, Matt quickly learned that New Orleans was a different world from where he'd grown up and he found his refuge in Tulane and Zephyr/Baby Cakes baseball. He owned season tickets and attended every home game that he could. He'd never been to a Saints game and didn't feel he'd missed much. He was in his freshman year at Tulane in 1998 when the Zephyrs, then a Houston Astros farm team and led by Lance Berkman's three home runs in the title game, won the inaugural Triple-A World Series.

This year's team, though, wasn't very competitive. Berkman was long gone, having played his entire career with and retired from the Astros. Other members of the team had moved up or moved on as well, leaving behind inexperienced, less skilled players desperate to follow in their career path. Matt watched with growing frustration as they lost game after game and now he was weary of suffering through the endless string of errors, inflated earned run averages, and deflated batting averages. It was only the sixth inning when he started for the exit.

He didn't need a bad game as an excuse to get home early. He faced a full work day tomorrow, a Friday, and the following week didn't look any better. Clerking for a Louisiana Supreme Court justice is no different than clerking jobs in other states: it involves long hours of research in order to author opinions on writs that justices sign off on as their own work. By its nature, it is a necessary but thankless job.

Because he lived in Metairie, he was home by nine. He tossed his keys and wallet on the kitchen counter, flopped down onto the sofa, and started to turn on the television. He changed his mind and put down the remote and picked up

12

the telephone instead. He needed to get out of town for the weekend and he knew just who to call. She answered after three rings and her voice energized him just as it did each time he heard it.

"Ashleigh. Hi. Am I calling at a bad time?"

"Never," she said. "The game over already?"

"Nah. They were getting their butts handed to 'em again, and since you weren't there with me, I left early."

"I would've gone. You know that. It's just that I have to be in Biloxi by nine tomorrow and I have to be sharp for my presentation."

Matt sighed. "Yeah, I know. Sometimes I wish I'd gone into your line of work instead of law. At least you get out of the office on a regular basis and you're always creating something to help people, to make their lives easier. I just manage to piss off people and make life more complicated for everyone."

"Stop that," she admonished him. "Your job's important. You know I don't hang out with people who indulge in self-pity."

"Speaking of hanging out, what're your plans for the weekend?" he asked.

"Nothing in particular. What do you have in mind?"

"I just want to get out of town for a couple of days."

"Why don't we run up to Covington to see Grandma Rose?"

"That wasn't exactly what I had in mind," Matt protested. "Why there? Can't we go someplace where we can be alone? What's wrong with Destin? Blue water, sand…"

"You know why. I'm the only one left in the family who'll visit her or even talk to her. She's made everyone else mad at her," Ashleigh said.

"That's because you're the only one in the family she hasn't accused of stealing."

"I know. But I love her and someone has to look in on her from time to time. No one else will. Tell you what: go with me to Covington this weekend and we'll get over to Destin later in the summer or for Labor Day."

Matt chuckled. "With you, Ashleigh, I'd even spend the weekend in Chalmette."

"That's what I like in my guy," she laughed. "Devotion, loyalty, and sacrifice in the face of adversity."

Ashleigh Templet, valedictorian of her class at Covington High School, was awarded a Tulane scholarship by her state senator just as Matt's state representative had done for him. Each Louisiana legislator and the New Orleans mayor get a single one-year scholarship to award constituents each year. A political tradeoff that dates back to 1884, the program allows Tulane to gain more than twenty million dollars in property tax exemptions in exchange for scholarships that cost the university less than a million in real dollars. Legislators look good to voters, though, so it continues despite a scandal in the 1990s when politicians got caught awarding scholarships to family members and to relatives

13

of political cronies, proving once again that in Louisiana, some things never change.

Ashleigh and Matt met at a Tulane baseball game when he was a senior and she was a junior and they'd dated no one else since that Friday night. Each seemed to sense when the other needed privacy, which wasn't often. They cherished their time together but could spend hours without talking and still be just as happy. There were occasional nights spent together, but they chose not to make it a permanent arrangement. They'd discussed marriage and knew it was inevitable but neither was in any hurry.

Ashleigh's job took her all over south Louisiana and the Mississippi Gulf coast, where she designed computer applications for a wide variety of clients, from casinos, to oil patch companies in Lafayette, to city, parish, county and state governmental entities. She earned considerably more money than Matt, whose job kept him in New Orleans, though they never got around to discussing who made how much. Somehow, the subject just didn't seem important to either of them.

Her only passion, besides Matt, was her devotion to her maternal grandmother, Rose Melancon, whom she adored. She was once close to her mother Rebecca, but since the rift between Rose and Rebecca and Rebecca's apparent preoccupation with her own interests, Ashleigh had gravitated to her grandmother. As a small girl and later as a high school teenager, she spent as much time at Rose's home as possible. But as her mother and grandmother drifted further apart, Ashleigh was drawn even closer to Rose as the one person she felt she could confide in about all the things girls like to talk about. Rose was always there for her and the bond between them grew stronger after the death of her grandfather Jake twelve years before. Now she visited her aging grandmother whenever she could, even if it meant arranging business trips to take her through Covington.

14

5

The woman walked alone as she made her way up the northern extreme of Canal Boulevard at 11:30 p.m. She wore a short, colorful sun dress that, in the streetlight's glow, gave ample exposure to her long, attractive legs, typical for a hot summer night in New Orleans. Her head was covered by a floppy straw hat that partially obscured her face, but which seemed oddly out of place given the hour. She walked at a brisk pace; oblivious to those she passed on the sidewalk and they to her. So, it was not surprising that she took no notice of the man who watched and walked parallel to her on the other side of the street. What *was* surprising was that he was the only one who saw her.

She crossed City Park Avenue and turned left at the corner and headed west for about half a block, appearing to have no particular destination in mind and in no hurry to get there. Midway down the block she turned right into an old cemetery and disappeared, but only for a moment. It was smaller than the cemeteries that surrounded it. Unlike the newer, more spacious cemeteries nearby, the crypts and copings here were jammed against each other, leaving little room to walk between them. He crossed over at the same corner and fell in behind her. The graves in this cemetery, like all others in the city, rose up from ground level. A full moon kept solitary vigil as it strained to illuminate the silent places of eternal repose, succeeding only in casting long shadows across the ground, giving the cemetery an ominous presence, an eerie *mise en scène*.

Few cemeteries can be called typical in New Orleans where there are generally three types of graves to be found. The most elaborate are mausoleums, ornate structures that feature sealed vaults that may be stacked as many as six high. Some mausoleums may hold the remains of members of a single family, several families, or members of fraternal organizations such as law enforcement officers or firemen.

Single-family crypts are probably the most common of the three types. These crypts generally contain two concrete casket chambers, one on top of the other. Beneath the lower chamber is another, deeper crypt, most of which is underground and enclosed with concrete. After an appropriate length of time, originally one year and one day, but not as long now, caskets are removed from

16

individual chambers and burned. The human remains, usually only bones because the combined heat and humidity in New Orleans expedites decomposition, are either shoved to the back of the chamber to make room for the new occupant or placed in the lower, subterranean crypt where they mingle with the bones of their ancestors, a process known as the *Caveau,* French for cave. This frees the individual chambers to be recycled, thus allowing the tomb to serve generations of families.

The third type is the elevated coping. An elevated coping is constructed of raised concrete walls, either square or rectangular in shape. The coping is then filled with dirt, bringing the earthen level high enough to permit burial in the ground.

He found her standing in front of just such a grave – that of a woman in her twenties whose name, Denise Fleming, and her date of death some fourteen months earlier, were listed at the bottom of a long list of Flemings who had died before her and were interred in this same spot. But it was not the grave that held the man's interest. He was the predator this night and she was his prey. Stealthily, he crept up behind her and threw one arm around her shoulders, holding a knife to her throat with the other. "Make a sound and I'll slice your pretty little head clean off," he whispered through coated, yellowed teeth that had gone far too long without brushing or flossing.

"I have no reason to cry out," was her calm response – *too calm,* he thought. In a sudden, violent motion, he threw her to the ground between two crypts as he unbuckled his belt and unzipped his grimy faded jeans. They fell in a heap around his ankles, exposing pasty white legs that stood in sharp contrast to his filthy, once white jockey shorts as he dropped to his knees beside her. His hot, filthy breath reeked of cheap wine and came in short, excited pants now, heavy enough to almost feel. The sour odor that emanated from his body was no better than his breath, lending evidence that it had been neglected for just as long – or longer – than his teeth.

Rather than making an effort to escape, she instead turned to one side and kept her face toward the ground, refusing for the moment to turn toward him. He was on top of her now, groping, trying to rip away her clothing. But when he reached for her, his hands came up empty. The white glow from the full moon that hung high in the New Orleans sky bathed her form as she now turned to face him. He was not prepared for the horrific creature he saw next.

He recoiled in stark terror at the sight of what was now a skeleton lying on the ground before him. The hat fell from her skull onto the ground and though there was no skin on her bones her eyeballs and her tongue somehow remained intact and now the eyes, glowing eerily red in the darkness, bore in on him and the jaw and tongue moved as she spoke. "Well, here I am, tiger. Take me. You had me once, wasn't I what you wanted? Don't you want me now?"

He tried to scream out, but no sound could escape his throat. He felt his skin go clammy as a wave of nausea washed over him. "Come on, you wanted

17

sex, so let's get on with it," he heard the skeleton taunt him. "I'm ready if you are."

He managed an unintelligible gurgle as he struggled to stand. He had no warning as vomit spewed from his mouth, followed by the familiar sour odor that goes with it and which now mingled with the other foul bodily odors. "Don't you remember me? You knew me last year. You wanted me then. I'm hurt," the pile of bones said, laughing. "You don't seem to be the same man you were then."

He was on his feet now, gasping as he labored for each breath. In less time than it took him to blink and so fast he didn't even see her move, she was standing before him again. The skeleton was gone and in its place was the woman he'd been stalking only moments before. She was a beautiful woman, petite and in her early- to mid-twenties, again wearing her sun dress and floppy hat. She moved two steps toward him and he shrank backward. "Where're you going?" she asked.

He glanced over his shoulder in panic for a split second and then turned back to find himself staring into nothing but the black void of the cemetery darkness that stretched in all directions beyond the moon's less than adequate glow. The woman, his intended victim, was gone now, nowhere to be seen. He spun around in a full circle, trying to locate her, hoping at the same time she wouldn't be there but bewildered at the manner in which she had vanished. "Whaaa...." was all he could manage before he again heard the blood curdling scream he'd heard fourteen months before – just before he'd raped a woman and then stabbed her to death. The scream pierced the still night air and he stumbled backwards, tripping on his pants that were still gathered around his ankles.

His last conscious thought was of the scream. He knew it, recognized it, but he wasn't aware he was only hearing the echo of a long-silenced scream of a dying woman as he lost his balance and tumbled backward. He didn't have time to digest it in his jumbled mind, to put it into a comprehensive form. He just knew he'd heard it before. He kept hearing it all the way down, like some kind of surrealistic dream from which he desperately wanted to awaken. As he fell, the last thing he saw was the luminous glow of the full moon and a wisp of a form that seemed to pass between him and the heavenly white orb, a form that held no physical being. His head slammed against a corner of one of the nearby concrete crypts that rose from the ground as his body hurdled downward with the unrestrained force of a free-fall. His skull split open in a blinding flash of light and he lost consciousness in an instant as the blood gushed from his head and formed a dark pool on the concrete walkway beneath his body that even now was twitching with the dying spasms of one who was mortally injured.

It was several hours before his body was discovered by a cemetery caretaker who arrived at work promptly at 6:30 a.m. Police had little trouble determining the cause of death but they were clueless as to the motive for the homicide and they were largely unsympathetic. Because of the position of his pants, it was finally decided he was killed while struggling against a homosexual rape attempt.

Queers. They got no taste. Look at this filthy bastard. Talk about grave desecration.

They never noticed the name on the marble slab in the coping next to where the man's body was found and even if they had, it was improbable that anyone would have any reason to connect the two.

6

Matt chewed absently on a greasy, spicy thigh as he sat at a downtown Popeye's Fried Chicken. He scanned the police reports in the *Times-Picayune*, the city's once proud but now dying newspaper, as he ate. He rarely read the paper at work, so he usually did his reading during his lunch hour, devouring every word in the police beat reports. For some reason he couldn't explain, he always read the police reports first. Sometimes they were all he read. There were occasions when he wished he had pursued a cool job as a newspaper crime beat reporter instead of opting for a law degree. But then, the realities of newsroom cutbacks, lower circulation numbers and plunging advertising revenue always jolted him back to reality and he was again grateful for the career path he had chosen.

A memory for details can be a remarkable benefit, but it can also be something of a burden and this was one of those times. Two otherwise insignificant stories caught his eye as he took another bite of chicken. He still had a breast and mashed potatoes in the dinner box. He ordered fries but got mashed potatoes, a risk that goes with fast food orders, but today he was too interested in the articles to complain. The first was a four-paragraph story of an apparent botched robbery attempt at a convenience store on Esplanade two nights before.

20

No one was hurt, but the would-be robbers shot up the place before they fled. Police, the story said, were still investigating but they had few leads.

The other story was about a triple-fatality traffic accident, also on Esplanade. Matt noticed the site of the accident was only a few blocks from the store, but he still didn't make a connection between the two even though the names of the men killed in the accident did seem vaguely familiar. The paper said that Jamal Alexander and his brother, D'Wayne Robinson, were in the front seat and Theron Washington was in the back seat when their vehicle strayed into the path of a garbage truck. *I've seen those names somewhere before, but where? Weren't they arrested for something one time? Probably some petty crime, maybe drugs.*

He folded the section of the paper with the stories in it and put it in his inside coat pocket and after emptying the contents of his tray into a trash can, he walked back to his office where a pile of work was waiting for him. He tried to put Jamal, D'Wayne, and Theron out of his mind as he walked, but something kept gnawing at him and he couldn't quite understand why. By the time he'd left his office, packed, and swung by Ashleigh's condo, he'd forgotten the news stories about the bungled robbery attempt and the fatal accident. He was looking forward to spending a worry-free weekend with the woman he loved, even if it was to be shared with her gracious but eccentric grandmother.

He promised himself he wouldn't think about his work – or anything else – for the entire time and that he would devote his full attention to this beautiful woman seated beside him. The half-hour drive across the twenty-two-mile Lake Pontchartrain Causeway brought them into Mandeville and from there it was an even shorter drive to Rose's. A one-time rural, isolated parish on the Lake's north shore, St. Tammany has mushroomed into a thriving bedroom community of professionals who worked in New Orleans but chose to live in the suburbs. Besides the new homes in the subdivisions, there are still many charming older wood frame homes in places like Madisonville, Slidell, and Abita Springs. Rose Melancon lived in one of those in Covington out on LA. 21. At least it was once considered charming. Now, though, early signs of neglect were beginning to appear.

21

7

Ashleigh was dressed in yellow slacks and a white T-shirt. Her dark hair was pulled back in a pony tail that bounced with each step from the open space in the back of her Kelly-green Tulane baseball cap. Though Matt had been here before, he still felt ill-at-ease every time they visited Grandma Rose. There were two reasons for this. The first was the uncomfortable feeling he got when spending the night with his girlfriend in the home of her grandmother. But that feeling of uneasiness was overshadowed by the second, more subtle reason that he found difficult to discuss, even with Ashleigh.

Rose Melancon, who had been widowed for twelve years now, was shunned by her family. Except for Ashleigh, no one visited the eighty-three-year-old woman anymore because of her propensity to accuse visitors of theft. No one in the family had escaped her accusations. No one but Ashleigh, that is. She was so kind, so considerate of Rose, she somehow managed to avoid being pulled into her grandmother's web of suspicion.

Matt trailed a few steps behind as Ashleigh found her way up the walk to Rose's front door. It wasn't easy because the walk was overgrown with azalea bushes that hadn't been trimmed in years. Azaleas bloom for only a short time and the season had already come and gone so there were no flowers, just the bushes leaning out over the sidewalk on each side, sometimes touching each other from across the narrow three-foot width of concrete. An afternoon rain shower, normal for south Louisiana springs and early summers, weighed the azaleas down even more, getting the pair's clothing wet as they made their way up the walk. A calico cat, one of several that Rose encouraged to stay around by feeding them on a regular basis, spotted the visitors and scurried to safety beneath the porch. *Female,* thought Matt as he watched the cat disappear. Almost without exception, tri-colored cats are female. *That means more kittens. Just what Rose needs.*

The front porch was enclosed by rusty screen. She and her late husband Jake once enjoyed spending their evenings together sitting on the porch sipping iced tea and listening to the whippoorwills whistling in the far-off distance. But as subdivisions sprang up around her once rural home, the whippoorwills had been driven away by the ever-expanding suburban sprawl and she rarely sat on

23

the porch anymore. Instead, she was a prisoner in her own home. Her windows and doors were locked and monitored by an electronic security system that she didn't completely trust.

Ashleigh knocked and waited. No answer. She knocked again. Still there was no answer. "She's probably in the back of the house and can't hear," she said as she reached into her purse for her cell phone. She dialed Rose's number and waited. She answered after four rings. "Grandma? It's Ashleigh. We're at your front door." There was a brief pause. "No, this is Ashleigh. Yes, Ashleigh. We're at your front door. Sure, we'll wait." She turned her phone off and turned to Matt. "She was taking a nap, I guess."

After a moment they could hear the beeps that told them Rose was punching in the code to disable the alarm. That was followed by the sound of several keys turning. Finally, the door swung open and Rose, all five feet of her, stood beaming up at them. "Ashleigh, it's so good of you to visit. Come in, come in. You too, Mitch."

"It's Matt, Grandma."

"Of course, it is. Both of you come on in. It's so good to see you." She hugged each of them. "Let me help you with your luggage, Mitch."

"Thanks, Rosie, but I have it. We just have the one bag." Matt laughed to himself at the thought of the frail little woman helping him with their luggage.

As soon as they were inside, Rose busied herself keying in the code to re-activate the alarm system, being careful at the same time to plant herself squarely between the two visitors so they wouldn't be able to detect the number sequence to the code. After that, she re-locked all three deadbolts to ensure everyone's safety.

The air-tight house felt like a sauna. Even in summer, Rose kept a gas space heater going in the bathroom. She kept the flame low, but any extra heat in the sultry, humidity-laden air of south Louisiana summers is redundant. Matt struggled to catch his breath and he could feel his nasal passages slamming shut even as he reached for the bottle of Afrin he always brought with him whenever he accompanied Ashleigh on these visits to Rose's home. The combination of mustiness and heat of her house never failed to aggravate his chronically sensitive sinus condition.

The one occasion that he'd not brought his Afrin was on his first visit. He'd tried to get through the discomfort, but after three hours, he relented and drove to the nearest Rite Aid. Any other time he would have passed a Rite Aid in favor of a discount pharmacy like Wal-Mart but on that occasion, he was desperate. Like a New Orleans native, he resented Rite Aid for having bought out the New Orleans-based K & B (for Katz and Bestoff) drug stores. But relief is where you find it, so he had foregone loyalty in favor of expedience that one time. And about the time he finally accepted Rite Aid, it was absorbed by Walgreen's in another corporate buyout.

24

8

J. François Berthelot, III was upset. One of the more infamous criminal defense attorneys in New Orleans, he was considered a true maverick among legal circles. Not such a maverick, however, that he didn't succumb to the propensity of many lawyers to employ his first initial, middle name, and last name, followed by a Roman numeral, on his letterhead and business cards. Still, he couldn't command social acceptance and that was a constant source of resentment with him.

But that wasn't what upset him on this Saturday morning. He was reading the *Times-Picayune* over his morning coffee. Like Matt, he preferred to read the crime reports, but for very different reasons. Matt read them purely out of curiosity; François was mining the field for clients. He loved criminal defense law. He never even thought of going into civil practice. Lawsuits bored him because they generally dealt only with numbers and non-violent, mundane matters. He preferred the gutter fighting tactics of criminal defense. It was not without its rewards, of course. His clients were from the seamier side of life and though they might not have money to pay his fees, they had the contacts J. François needed for his less well-known but far more profitable activities.

The news today was not good. He had lost another client overnight, his fourth in the past two days. First there had been Jamal, D'Wayne, and Theron and now Deason "Deacon" Watson, who had been found lying on his back in a cemetery, death caused by a blunt trauma to his head. The blow to his head had been suffered, the paper said, when he fell backward onto a concrete crypt in a cemetery. The story added that his fall was apparently caused by his losing his balance when he tripped over his own pants, which, for whatever reason, were draped around his ankles. Police theorized that he'd been the victim of a homosexual attack and that he had fallen in an attempt to escape.

J. François had represented Deacon Watson more than a year before when he had been arrested for a particularly gruesome rape-murder. The victim was a 23-year-old woman who'd moved back to New Orleans from Houston only three months earlier. Denise Fleming was starting over after her divorce. She

25

moved back in with her family and took a job with an auto leasing company at Louis Armstrong International Airport. She was planning to re-enroll at the University of New Orleans when she was brutally raped and murdered, leaving behind a year-old baby girl. J. François, like police, didn't make the connection between Deacon's death and those of Jamal, D'Wayne and Theron.

The attorney had taken the case despite the overwhelming evidence against Deacon. DNA samples taken from the victim's body matched those found on Deacon's body and clothing and semen recovered from her vaginal area also matched Deacon's DNA. It looked like a no-brainer for the prosecution but for the fact that Deacon's was not the only semen found; there was also semen from another, unidentified man taken from the victim's vaginal area. It was not for nothing that J. François cultivated and relished his reputation as a ruthless defense attorney and he found this case to his particular liking. He lost no time attacking the DNA evidence.

Where was the victim found? In an alley? Was she nude? Yes? How long had her body been there before being discovered? Approximately six hours? Who found her? Was it possible someone had found her earlier? Was it possible to plant semen evidence? Not likely? But possible? Yes? Was there other semen DNA taken from the victim? Yes? Whose? No one knows? Isn't that convenient? Was it possible that Deacon had found her and had sex with her after *she was already dead? Really? Did Deacon provide his DNA voluntarily? No? Then why was it taken before he could secure legal counsel?*

The presiding judge didn't like J. François but he also didn't like the idea of any appearance of violations of a defendant's rights. The added discovery that the victim had had sex with someone else or maybe even had been raped by an unknown individual, perhaps after she was already dead, further clouded the issue.

J. François wasn't concerned with attempting to make his client out to be a sympathetic character. It would take more than his considerable legal skills to pull that off. Deacon, with his tattooed arms, long stringy hair, and yellowed teeth, would never be mistaken for a Sunday school teacher. Confusion and doubt in the minds of jurors was Deacon's best ally, and J. François was most adept at creating and exploiting confusion and doubt. In the end, it was that doubt fueled by confusion that won out. Necrophilia may not be the most desirable personality trait for a defendant, but it surely trumps a murder rap.

Members of the jury were unanimous in their opinion of Deason as despicable, low-life pond scum. But agreeing that he was a rapist-murderer was quite a different matter. The seed of doubt had taken a firm hold in the minds of the jurors. Arguments were long and loud in the deliberation room for more than ten hours. It had been a bitterly divided panel of jurors that emerged to grudgingly deliver the acquittal and Deacon walked out a free man – a man no one wanted anything to do with, to be sure – but free nonetheless. Jurors, feeling far guiltier than J. François and his client and more than a little soiled from the

26

experience, diverted their eyes from the anguished faces of Denise Fleming's family as the verdict was read.

J. François Berthelot used similar tactics in the robbery-murder trials of Jamal Alexander, D'Wayne Robinson, and Theron Washington. It is impossible to over-emphasize the importance of doubt in controlling the direction and tempo of a trial. There's nothing more frustrating in a criminal proceeding than for the prosecution to find itself on the defensive. Judges take a dim view of a cop or a prosecuting attorney who hasn't done everything by the numbers. There was no one more skilled than J. François at finding a weakness in the prosecution's strategy and turning it to his own advantage. Jamal, D'Wayne, and Theron had called him in their hour of need and he'd responded.

Once a suspect requests an attorney, questioning is supposed to stop until legal representation is present but police continued questioning each of the three separately without allowing them to engage legal counsel long after each had asked to do so. Moreover, Theron was not read his Miranda rights. The absence of an eyewitness to the robbery and murder of the Sri Lankan clerk at the Magazine Street convenience store further weakened the case against the three.

There was little room for doubt that they were guilty as far as police and prosecutors were concerned. Ballistic comparisons might have matched the bullets in the clerk's body to Jamal's gun – if police had ever found Jamal's gun. François countered by suggesting that someone else used Jamal's gun – if he owned a gun, an accusation that Jamal denied vehemently. And just for good measure, a witness from Lafayette claimed all three were with him the night of the robbery. It was of little consequence that he was a witness of dubious repute; the germ of doubt was planted.

Of course, J. François expected payment from each of his clients, even if it were only payment in kind. He used them as go-betweens for his transactions with crystal meth labs springing up all around and with drug dealers throughout Orleans, Jefferson, St. Bernard, Lafourche, Terrebonne, Plaquemines, and St. John the Baptist parishes as well as with the end users. Deacon, Jamal, D'Wayne, and Theron knew heroin, cocaine, and meth addicts throughout the Crescent City area and they served as the intermediaries for J. François's distribution system – Deacon among the bikers and the other three in the black neighborhoods, particularly the Desire Housing Project. As soon as they were freed, he brought all the free-lancers together under his business umbrella of drugs and prostitution.

J. François also had contacts among the white-collar junkies, many of whom were attorneys. He employed more respectable felons for those clients, getting a substantial markup for higher-quality merchandise in the process. His illicit business practice started small but as his market grew, so did the need for more mules. Thus, it was that he never seemed to take on a client that didn't ultimately turn a profit for him, even if the client couldn't afford his services per se. Instead, the drug and prostitution profits they brought him were credited

27

against their outstanding legal fees. His law practice was the perfect business front through which to launder his illicit but growing enterprise.

Never one to pass up a chance to turn a fast dollar, J. François quickly expanded into illegal bookmaking operations and prostitution. He also recognized early on the profit potential of the bail bond business. All it took was an opportunistic bail bondsman, a handful of cooperative judges who were willing to accept kickbacks disguised as campaign contributions, and willing lawyers who would refer clients.

The bail bond industry in Louisiana, as it is in most states, is regulated by the State Department of Insurance. Bail bonds are, after all, a form of insurance in that a surety, or underwriter, issues a bond that guarantees that a defendant will show up for his court appearance. Should the defendant fail to show for court, the surety company, as the guarantor, is financially obligated to pay the full bail amount but that doesn't mean the system isn't ripe for abuse, especially when one or more of the conspirators are from a corrupt judiciary. A volume-driven, cash intensive industry, the bail bond business depends on a system of checks and balances that for one possessing sufficient skill and enough nerve, is easily circumvented and J. François was just the man for the job.

Most states require a premium of ten percent when bail is set on a defendant but in Louisiana, the premium is twelve or twelve and one-half percent. Accordingly, if bail is set at one hundred thousand dollars, a defendant must pay $12,500 fee to the bail bondsman, or obligor, to get out of jail after his arrest. This payment is non-refundable to the defendant. The guarantor, or surety, receives two percent of the hundred-thousand-dollar bail as its premium for issuing the bond, or two thousand dollars, from the bail bondsman. The local municipality or county (parish in Louisiana) gets another two and one-half percent for administrative costs, and the court gets four percent, leaving the other four percent, or four thousand dollars for the local bail bondsman's profit.

There are basically two ways to beat the system, one of which involves a higher degree of risk than the other. The greater risk is incurred when the bail bondsman, if he is reasonably certain that his client will appear for his court hearing, simply neglects to submit the surety company's two percent premium. This is the less likely of the two scenarios because the prudent bail bondsman usually takes this chance only with clients he trusts – defendants who are arrested for various offenses on a regular basis such as public drunkenness, spousal abuse, or driving while intoxicated. The downside is when a defendant fails to show and the guarantor learns it is on the hook for a bond for which it never received premiums.

The second method is more sinister in that it involves collusion and necessarily involves corrupt judges as well as bail bondsmen who are not above using the justice system to their advantage. A judge may initially set a defendant's bail at a hundred thousand dollars and after the defendant remits the

28

$12,500 to the bail bondsman the judge may say there was a clerical error and bail should have been ten thousand dollars instead of one hundred thousand. The defendant, however, is never told that his bail was reduced and the court then refunds all but $1250 – not to the defendant but to the bail bondsman. The bail bondsman and the judge – and sometimes a lawyer like J. François, who is in on the scam – split the remaining $11,250. The judge's share, of course, is earmarked as a campaign contribution on occasions when it is reported at all. In many instances, the payoff is in cash and goes unreported.

On the surface, it would appear that no one but the judge and the bail bondsman would be required to make such an operation flourish. But attorneys can steer clients in the right direction when it's time to select a bail bondsman. In business, the practice is called a referral. In legal circles, it's just old-fashioned Louisiana collusion, politics as usual, and no was more brazen or more skilled at it than J. François. The system made a lot of money for a few select people not only in New Orleans, but in the neighboring parishes of St. Bernard, Plaquemines, St. Charles, St. James, St. John the Baptist, and Jefferson as well.

CajunAmerica Bail Bonds was a major player and had any good investigative reporters bothered to check records in the Louisiana Secretary of State's Corporate Division in Baton Rouge, they might have learned that CajunAmerica's agent of record and president was none other than J. François Berthelot. If he had learned one thing in his years of practice, however, it was not to be greedy. There was plenty of money for everyone and if someone else wanted in on the action, that was fine as long as he was a rainmaker and not just someone wanting a free ride. More attorneys participating in the scheme meant more referrals and more judges brought into the fold meant more opportunity for all concerned. Everyone wins except the poor sap unfortunate enough to get busted.

Stories abounded throughout the city among outraged honest lawyers— honest being a relative term—about judges who instructed them that if their clients wanted to make bail, they would have to use CajunAmerica Bail Bonds. Otherwise, on more than one occasion, attorneys were told their clients would be unable to post bail. It was flagrant abuse of position and power and it worked – for a while. At first the complaints were quiet and infrequent but they gradually became louder and bolder and were heard more often. Before long, they grew into a steady crescendo that became impossible to ignore.

Benjamin Franklin once said that three people could keep a secret if two of them were dead. Because so many people were in on the bail bond scam—and even more who were not, knew about it—word soon got around about bail bond irregularities in the Orleans Parish criminal district court. Some merely shrugged but prosecutors in Louisiana's United States Eastern District Court began to take notice. The feds sprang into action.

J. François made it a policy to never deal directly with the drug suppliers or prostitutes. He chose instead to use his clients as go-betweens, intermediaries,

29

thus creating a buffer between him and the drug suppliers, bookies and hookers. Nor did he spend time on the internal operations of CajunAmerica Bail Bonds, preferring to leave that to his office manager. With the rash of recent deaths, however, the chain to two important supply lines had been broken. The interruption of his prostitution and drug operations forced him to rely more on CajunAmerica as a means of income. It was going to take time to replace the dead men and to get things back to normal.

Because he dealt with such unsavory characters, J. François was aware that he was always just one deal gone wrong from finding his life in peril. For that reason, he always carried a .380 automatic – much like the one Jamal used – in his briefcase, except when he was in the parish prison visiting clients. In prisons, everyone was run through security checks but in courthouses, attorneys were usually waved through. He threw the paper onto the table and gulped down the remainder of his coffee. He grabbed his briefcase and headed for the garage of his home in a middle-class Kenner subdivision. He refrained from flaunting his wealth, choosing instead to live a modest lifestyle while moving his money offshore in regular increments. There would be ample opportunity to enjoy the fruits of his labor upon his retirement to Aruba, Grand Cayman, or Cozumel in a few more years. For now, however, J. François needed to fill in some unexpected gaps in his business organization. A man had to make a living, after all, and there were others who depended on him for their livelihood. He had responsibilities.

He started the three-year-old Nissan Altima and backed out of his driveway, closing his garage door as he did so. Even though it was Saturday, he drove to his office. There was work to be done.

On the other side of the street, federal agents waited in a nondescript white SUV until they were sure he was gone before they entered his home to install court-approved electronic eavesdropping equipment. It was the same type equipment they had installed earlier in the homes and offices of three Orleans Parish criminal district judges as well as the offices of CajunAmerica Bail Bonds. It was the first legal step in what would soon become a far-ranging federal investigation into the New Orleans area bail bonds business as well as the practices of several sitting judges and scores of attorneys. It soon became known as Operation Dishonor.

9

The roots of New Orleans paranormal mysticism are firmly embedded in the tradition of Voodoo. Dating back thousands of years, the practice of Voodoo was brought to the New World by slaves, who were introduced to the Catholic faith but who continued to practice their native religion in private. Voodoo made its way to New Orleans in the early Nineteenth Century when French slave owners and their slaves were expelled from Santo Domingo (modern day Haiti) during Touissant L'Ouverture's 1791 Haitian revolution, according to one version of the story. Once in Louisiana, the native Caribbean island culture dovetailed easily with Catholicism to create a hybrid form of Voodoo called Hoodoo. The religion, enhanced by Voodoo priests and *zombie* drugs, was practiced by slaves and free blacks alike.

No study of New Orleans Voodoo would be complete without acknowledging the undisputed *Queen of Voodoo*, Marie Laveau. Born in 1794 in Santo Domingo to a white father and a free black woman, her arrival in New Orleans was first recorded in 1819 when she married a free black man, Jacques Paris. He died seven years later and she then lived with Christophe Glapion, a veteran of the Battle of New Orleans, and they had a daughter, named Marie Laveau Glapion, among their fifteen children. Christophe died in 1835.

A hairdresser by trade, Marie Laveau converted to Voodoo in 1826, the same year her first husband died, and she proceeded to elevate the religion to an art form in the Crescent City. Her hairdressing business allowed her to gain access to many of the more fashionable homes of New Orleans. She explained her unusual knowledge of people and events by claiming to have special *psychic* powers but the truth was that her access to the pillars of New Orleans society allowed her to listen to her customers and employees and thus develop a sophisticated intelligence network so that she knew details of virtually everything that went on in the city.

Despite the strictly segregated culture that was characteristic of southern cities like New Orleans at the time, she soon established herself as a force with which to be reckoned. Integrating Voodoo and Catholicism in such a creative manner, she is credited with changing Voodoo into much more than mere African superstition. She pulled off the unlikely feat of placing the Virgin Mary

31

as the central figure of Voodoo worship. She conducted worship services in Congo Square, now Louis Armstrong Park. Adding to her almost supernatural hold over believers in New Orleans was the fact that so few people knew of her death in 1881 that her daughter, also named Marie Laveau, was able step in undetected and to continue her mother's traditions for several more decades.

Marie Laveau is buried in St. Louis Cemetery Number One, Crypt Number Three and even today, many of the faithful remain convinced that she returns to life once a year from her grave to lead believers in a spectacular Voodoo ritual of worship on St. John's Eve, June 23. Some claimed to have seen her ghost in the cemetery, recognizable by the *tignon,* a seven-knotted kerchief worn around her neck.

10

Josie Arlington and the prestigious Metairie Cemetery also occupy a historic place in New Orleans ghost folklore. Metairie Cemetery (Lake Lawn Metairie today) was organized in 1873 to cater to the city's elite. It represented the epitome of influence and social prominence, right down to its classic Victorian design. Understandably, it created quite a scandal when the city's most colorful and notorious madam decided she wanted her remains interred there.

For the twenty-year period from 1897 to 1917, New Orleans was known as the home of America's largest red-light district. City officials, acknowledging they could not rid the city of prostitution (Mayor Martin Behrman famously said of efforts to outlaw prostitution, "You can make it illegal but you can't make it unpopular), decided the next best approach was to segregate it from the rest of New Orleans society. Alderman Sidney Story fathered the plan to create a district for the sole purpose of establishing control by licensing prostitution. Much to his consternation and embarrassment, the district was named *Storyville* in his honor.

Storyville in turn made Josie Arlington, also known as Josie Deubler, a very rich woman as proprietor of the finest brothel in the district. Her whorehouse featured the most beautiful women in the city, fine liquor, great food and even exotic drugs. The women, clad in expensive French lingerie, hosted the crème de la crème of New Orleans society – doctors, city officials, politicians, bankers, lawyers, and judges – men who would never acknowledge Josie in public. Because of this, she never quite attained the one thing she most desired in life – social acceptance. Her money and charm carried no weight in the upper circles of New Orleans society so she decided what she could not have in life she would have in death. To the horror and disgust of the city's upper crust, she elected to be buried in Metairie Cemetery.

To that end, she purchased a plot on a small hill in the cemetery and had constructed an appropriately red marble tomb, topped off with two blazing pillars. A bronze statue ascends the steps of the tomb holding a bouquet of roses in the crook of her arm. Designed by distinguished architect Albert Weiblen, the mausoleum cost Josie a small fortune but the ensuing scandal made it worth every penny to her.

33

But shortly after the tomb was completed in 1911, weird stories started making the rounds. Curiosity-seekers who visited the tomb one night claimed they saw it burst into flames before their eyes, the red marble shimmering with fire and tongues of flame appearing to crawl over the surface. Literally overnight, the cemetery was overrun with people wanting to witness the bizarre event for themselves.

Josie died in 1914 and was interred in her now-infamous "flaming tomb." Sightseers continued to report the glowing tomb and some claimed to have seen the statue on the front steps move. Two cemetery gravediggers told anyone who would listen – and there were plenty – that the statue left her post and moved around the tombs. They claimed to have followed her one night, only to see her suddenly vanish.

The story of the flaming tomb has been kept alive for many years, largely by tour guides who certainly have the motivation for doing so. Some more rational explanations said the perceived movement by the statute was an illusion, caused by a nearby streetlight that would sway in the wind.

11

Hurricane Katrina was not the first time New Orleans was flooded. Much of the city was inundated by Hurricane Betsy in 1964. In the aftermath of Betsy, two looters approached a New Orleans home by boat, entering the house through a window. In the darkened home, two large Dobermans waited quietly until the men were inside and then sprang to the attack. One of the looters got out alive but suffered extensive lacerations. His accomplice was not so fortunate; he was killed. That's why some residents of high crime areas keep dogs in fenced-in yards. Sometimes they're Dobermans or German Shepherds. Others may simply be mongrels, but they all have one thing in common: they're vicious and they don't like trespassers.

Now, more than forty years later, Lenny Stevens stalked his prey in one of those neighborhoods. He watched the six-year-old boy intently as he played alone on the sidewalk. He first saw him two days before and returned the next day and again today. The boy played alone each time and there were no adults on the hot, deserted street in this old section of the city.

As darkness approached, he maneuvered his beaten-up van into a parallel parking spot a few feet from where the boy was playing. He was careful to leave ample space in front and behind his vehicle so as to allow his quick re-entry into traffic on the residential boulevard. Lenny watched and waited. He'd done this before – seven other times, in fact – but had been arrested only once. He was strong then; he stood up under questioning, admitting nothing, never revealing where he'd disposed of the boys' bodies.

He knew J. François Berthelot by reputation and he called him and a defense strategy was soon formulated. No witnesses had seen the actual abduction. That was good. Someone had spotted the van in the neighborhood, but he didn't see the driver's face. The only witness, an elderly neighbor, said he became suspicious when he noticed the van come down the street several occasions within a short period of time – about forty-five minutes – so he tried without success to get the license plate number.

He'd sworn under oath that it looked like the same vehicle when shown a black and white photograph of Lenny's van. *But did he see the little boy abducted? Had he seen the boy in the van? For that matter, had he seen the*

35

accused driving the van? Had he gotten the license number? Each question drew a negative response and the witness was unable to provide the color of the van – just that he thought it was dark blue…or maybe black. The seed of doubt was again planted. The old man was no match for the legal dexterity of J. François who could smell fear and hammered each of those points home in the same ruthless manner that had long ago become his trademark. The acquittal didn't come without a price. Lenny had contacts in the homosexual community, especially transvestites. In the world of sexual perversion, there is a market for just about everything and J. François knew those who had certain special sexual proclivities, so it was an easy decision to move in on the lucrative homosexual prostitution market in the French Quarter and Lenny became his pimp.

But now Lenny was not pimping for J. François. He was stalking a small boy for his own sick, twisted needs. He was parked only a few feet from the boy, who continued to play alone, oblivious to his surroundings. Lenny waited a few more minutes for total darkness. He wasn't worried about the boy going inside because he'd observed him two straight evenings and he'd remained outside until well after nine each night.

When he decided he had sufficient darkness to conceal his actions, he exited on the passenger side of the van and opened the sliding side door about two feet. Then he turned back toward his intended victim. Less than a dozen feet away, the boy, his back to Lenny, sang a child's song to himself. In three long strides, Lenny was directly over the boy. He looked around one last time to be sure no one was watching and then he struck.

In a move that he'd repeated seven times before, he reached his left arm around the boy's waist and simultaneously clasped his right hand over his mouth, lurching backward toward the van at the same time. This time, though, he felt no resistance. In fact, he felt nothing but air. He stared for an instant at his empty hands and then looked up to see the boy, still playing, still singing the same song to himself. Lenny moved a step forward and repeated his gestures but again came up empty. "What th' hell ?" The boy had moved again, this time about six feet ahead and now he was turned, facing Lenny, and laughing. Bewildered, Lenny lunged at the boy. The boy made no attempt to move away, but again, Lenny grasped only air and he stumbled and fell face down on the sidewalk. He pushed himself up on one elbow in time to see the boy approaching him, smiling.

Lenny changed his mind in an instant. Now he wanted nothing to do with this apparition. He got to his feet and took two or three steps backward and turned around to flee only to find the boy standing in front of him again, still smiling and still approaching. His extended hand held a toy, which he offered to Lenny.

"What *are* you?!" Lenny screamed. *"Get away from me!"*

Still the boy walked toward him, or rather appeared to float toward him. His feet didn't seem to be touching the sidewalk and now Lenny could swear he could see through the small body. He thought he could make out the sidewalk

36

and the bordering grassy area through the image of the boy's body in the only illumination, that of a nearby street light. In full panic, Lenny wanted only to get away from this boy, or whatever he was, as fast as humanly possible. Trouble was, the boy now stood between him and the van. And Lenny wasn't particularly eager to challenge the pint-sized obstacle. He made a choice and bolted for a nearby yard.

The decision to leap over a four-foot chain link fence and to attempt to run through the neighborhood yard wasn't a choice based on sound logic. The moment he cleared the fence, he was greeted by two pissed off pit bulldogs who were extremely agitated at having their sleep interrupted. The first animal to reach him went straight for his crotch. The final comprehensible image to register on Lenny's brain before unspeakable pain turned out the lights and he crumpled to the ground was that of seven young boys standing on the sidewalk, looking back at him in calm, almost eerie silence.

In that instant, Lenny's last dying thought was that a mist of serenity seemed to envelope the boys. In the approximate time it would have taken the dogs to devour a couple of pounds of raw hamburger meat, Lenny's face was mangled beyond recognition and his body more resembled fresh road kill than a human being. The gaping hole opened in his groin area left important organs strewn across the yard and one testicle was never found. Every drop of blood in his body either soaked into the grass or was licked up by the dogs after they'd inflicted their carnage. Slimy red saliva drooled from their mouths.

Police had no idea why Lenny jumped the fence into the yard. An old wino who witnessed the events unfold from a block away said he saw Lenny groping crazily at the air and then fall to the sidewalk. He thought Lenny was suffering from delirium tremens, the D.T.'s. Authorities seized and destroyed the dogs over the angry, but futile protests of the owner who felt the animals were merely protecting his property from criminals.

37

12

Rose was in her element as she went about entertaining her guests and fussing over them Friday evening. Saturday morning, she picked up where she'd left off. She made every effort to make Matt and Ashleigh feel comfortable while in her home. It was an unusual way for a dating couple to spend a weekend but Matt knew how much Ashleigh loved her grandmother. And it was evident in the old woman's face that she cherished doting on them as much as they enjoyed the attention. Ashleigh cooked for all of them and she washed, dried, and folded clothes. After that, she vacuumed Rose's house over the old woman's protests that guests shouldn't be expected to do household chores.

But most of the time was spent just sitting and listening to her talk about family and of years too far gone for Matt or Ashleigh to remember – years that had turned into history long before either of them was born. Rose's eyes misted over more than once as she spoke of Jake and of her four daughters. All but one of the daughters – Ashleigh's mother – moved out of state many years before and seldom even called their mother, much less visited. Rose had come to terms with her family's estrangement but it did nothing to lessen the pain and there were times – times like this – when it showed. Ashleigh did what she did best during Rose's periods of melancholy: she made herself available and she listened.

Ashleigh's mother, Rebecca Templet, left in tears when Rose accused her of stealing a gold necklace from her mother and vowed not to visit her mother again, a promise she'd kept. Rebecca's pride wouldn't allow her to take the initiative to repair the damage and Rose was still convinced that her daughter had taken the necklace. Never mind that it showed up three weeks later in a vase. Never mind that everyone in the family assumed Rose had placed it there for safekeeping only to forget where she'd hidden it. As far as Rose was concerned, Rebecca had sneaked back into her house and returned it. She couldn't bring herself to admit to her own forgetfulness at hiding the necklace in the vase and to apologize for her false accusation.

The incident tore at Ashleigh's emotions, causing her many sleep-deprived nights as she agonized over the wedge driven between her mother and grandmother. She loved her mother, but she refused to abandon Rose. Rebecca understood and respected her daughter and never tried to sway Ashleigh or to do

39

anything to turn her against the older woman. That made it somewhat easier for Ashleigh to cope with the situation. Besides, Rebecca, divorced from Ashleigh's father, was eager to move on with her life. Ashleigh was a big girl now and could take care of herself. Sometimes Ashleigh was the more mature of the two and her mother more often than not assumed the role of the confused child.

Matt and Ashleigh slept in the front bedroom. About 1:30 Saturday morning Matt got up to go to the bathroom. Too much coffee at night does that. The bathroom was adjacent to Rose's bedroom in the rear of the house. He found the door to the hallway that led into the bathroom was closed. He turned the doorknob but it refused to open.

Why is the door locked?

Seeing a light under the kitchen door, he knocked softly.

He waited and hearing nothing, knocked again. "Come in," came Rose's reply. He opened the kitchen door to find Rose applying Noxzema Cold Cream to her face. She looked up and saw him. "Oh Mitch, are you thirsty?"

"No, ma'am, you locked the hall door and I can't get into the bathroom."

Her mouth fell open. "Oh, my goodness, I didn't mean to do that. I guess it's just a habit. My bedroom's right off the kitchen, so I lock that door and the hall door because of people breaking into the house. It keeps intruders from getting into my bedroom from the rest of the house and keeps me safe." She walked around through her bedroom door and into the hallway where she unlocked the door from the inside for Matt. He walked past her into the bathroom and she went back to the kitchen table and her Noxzema.

When he exited a few minutes later, she called out from her bedroom. "Are you okay, Mitch? Is your stomach upset?"

"No, ma'am, I'm all right."

"Are you sure? I've got some medicine if your stomach's upset."

"No, I'm fine."

"Well, I thought your stomach might be upset. You sure it's okay?"

"Yes, ma'am, I just had to pee," Matt said, embarrassed now.

When he got back to the front bedroom, Ashleigh was laughing. She'd heard the exchange. "I can't believe she's still up at this time of night," she said.

"She couldn't have been applying cold cream all this time," Matt said. "What do you think she's doing?"

"She's probably been hiding stuff half the night."

"From whom?"

"Probably from us, *Mitch,*" she said, giggling at her grandmother's insistence at calling him by the wrong name.

The next morning, Rose accosted Ashleigh as she came out of the bathroom. "Is your stomach upset, Ashleigh?"

"No, Grandma, I'm fine."

40

When she got back to the front room, she and Matt started making the bed. "Somebody's going to have to get an upset stomach just to keep her happy," she said. She had long since learned it was easier to laugh at Rose's idiosyncrasies than to try to make sense of them. She had grown accustomed to laughing often.

After breakfast, her grandmother brought out a box of ancient snapshots, most of them black and white pictures of family members standing together in front of Rose's house, statelier and fresher then than now. Ashleigh didn't know many of them, but she took the time, as always, to look as if she were interested. There were obligatory shots of Rose and Jake holding a baby, its identity known only to Rose, in front of the family car, a nineteen forty-something black Plymouth. "This is Cherie," Rose said, extending a weathered old snapshot to Matt. "She's my oldest daughter, Ashleigh's aunt. She lives in Springfield, Missouri." Matt took the photo and tried his best to foster a look of rapt interest, as if the photos meant something to him, as if he knew the people staring back into the camera. Ashleigh looked at him and flashed a knowing smile. Rose, if she caught the private joke between them, didn't let on.

"I had a lot more pictures, but somebody came in the house and took them."

Matt looked up. "Somebody stole your photographs?" he asked.

"Oh, yes, they're always coming in here and stealing things. Last month, they came in and stole my Fingerhut catalogue that I had hidden in the freezer."

Matt chanced a puzzled look at Ashleigh who guessed his unspoken question. "Grandma has an old freezer on the back porch she uses as a safe," she offered by way of explanation. "It's unplugged. It's only used for storage."

"Yes," Rose said, "I have a key so I can lock it. I keep my valuables in it, but they got in it somehow. They took a brand-new card of bobby pins, too. They picked the lock, I guess. I change the locks but they keep getting into the house."

"Who is 'they'?" Matt asked, wondering at the same time how a Fingerhut catalogue or hair pins could be considered valuable enough to keep under lock and key. He stole another look at Ashleigh. Her smile was now gone, replaced by a look of concern for the old woman's mental state.

"Whoever's coming in the house," Rose answered in a flat, matter-of-fact tone as if anyone with a lick of sense should have known the answer. "They're always coming into my house."

"How long have they been doing that?"

She looked up at the mantle. Matt followed her gaze to an innocent-looking cherry wood box. The box measured about ten inches long by six inches wide by four inches deep. "It started right after Jake died," she said. "Twelve years ago."

"Grandma had Grandpa cremated," Ashleigh said in a quiet voice. "Those are his ashes."

41

"He told me before he died he wanted to be cremated and to have his ashes scattered over his vegetable garden," Rose continued. "It just sickened me to have him cremated instead of buried like he should have been, but that was his wish. I just couldn't bring myself to scatter his ashes in the garden, though, so I keep them up there. I guess it's my way of keeping him close to me."

Ashleigh, having heard it many times before, knew the story by heart. Silence enveloped the room for a few moments before Rose returned to the subject of petty theft.

"Somebody, whoever it is, was in the kitchen just last week sometime during the night," she said. "They stood over the sink and ate grape jelly. I found some of the jelly in the sink the next morning. I even tested them a few weeks ago. They've been stealing my underwear so I took some and hid them in the fig bush in the back yard one night. I went back out there at two o'clock in the morning to check on them and they were gone."

"Grandma," Ashleigh said, taking Rose's hand in hers, "you mean to say you actually hid your underwear in a bush in the back yard and then went out in the middle of the night to check on them?"

"Why, yes. I was testing them, like I said."

"What if you'd fallen down out there and hurt yourself?" "Then I guess I'd have just been there for a while, wouldn't I?"

"Grandma, you can't be doing things like that. It's dangerous. If something happens, you need to be near a phone so you can call someone."

"It can't be any more dangerous than having people come into my house all the time. They even show home movies on the wall at the foot of my bed at night."

"Home movies?" Matt repeated.

"Yes, of Jake. I recognized him. He just walks back and forth in front of the bed. I wish you and Mitch could just stay here with me all the time. I bet Mitch would find out who it is and stop them."

"Matt, Grandma. His name is Matt."

"It's okay," Matt said to Ashleigh. "I don't mind. Rose, have you ever seen anyone in your house?"

"No, I've never seen anyone. They're very good at not letting me see them."

"Don't you think it's a bit unusual that someone's been breaking into your home for twelve years and you've never caught them?" Matt asked.

"No, I don't. Like I just told you, they're very careful."

"How do they get into your bedroom if you keep the hall door and kitchen door locked?" he asked, remembering his attempt to get into the bathroom the night before.

"I don't know. I told you, I've never seen them."

42

"Has anyone in your family tried to find evidence of break-ins?" he asked.

"I can't ask any of my kids," Rose said. "They think I'm just a crazy old woman. Well, I may be old, but I'm not crazy." Neither her voice nor her expression revealed any emotion. She appeared to have accepted the fact that unknown intruders were now a fact of life – her life, anyway. She attempted to change the subject.

"Did you two sleep well last night?" she asked with a mischievous twinkle. "Or did you sleep at all? You know, I'm all the way in the back room and you two are up here in the front bedroom and I can't hear a thing. That's a damned shame, too."

Matt was embarrassed at the old woman's candor about their implied sex life, but Ashleigh was accustomed to it and just laughed. "Grandma, you're something else, you know that? How old do you have to *be* to stop thinking about sex anyway?"

"I don't know sweetheart. You're going to have to ask somebody older than me."

That remark even elicited a grin from Matt and Ashleigh laughed aloud. "We're going to have to fix you up with a young man, Grandma."

"He *better* be young. I don't want an old man. I'd probably kill an old man." Then she turned to Matt. "You know, Mitch, you're the first young man Ashleigh ever brought here to meet me. I think she has awfully good judgment, for what it's worth."

"Well, that's a relief," Matt said, smiling at Ashleigh. "It's always good to know where you stand." It was Ashleigh's turn to be embarrassed. She could only smile.

Just as quickly, Rose returned to the subject of the uninvited guests in her home. "Maybe you and Mitch could spend your weekends here and help me find out who's coming in here and taking my stuff. You're the only ones I can trust."

Ashleigh thought her grandmother was just lonely for companionship and that this was a ploy to get them to visit more often. Matt, however, thought he perceived a hint of desperation in her voice. "Do you have any idea who might be doing this?" he asked.

Unaccustomed to having someone humor her, she jumped at the opportunity to name a suspect.

"I believe it might be the boy who comes out here to change my locks."

"What do you mean, Grandma?" Ashleigh asked, puzzled. "You've changed your locks?"

"Seven times this year," Rose said. "I have three locks on the front door, three on the back door and a lock on every window, Seventeen I believe. That makes how many locks in all?"

"Twenty-three," Matt said. "Twenty-four, counting the freezer lock. You've changed Twenty-four locks seven times this year?"

43

"Yes, because they keep getting in. It has to be the boy who changes the locks. "Unless Rebecca's got copies of the keys," she added, looking at the floor as she rubbed her gnarled hands. Matt noticed how twisted and knotted her fingers were. *Arthritis.*

"Grandma," Ashleigh said, coming to Rebecca's defense, "I don't think Mom would do that. She hasn't been here in ages."

"Then it's that boy at the hardware store who changes the locks for me. He's keeping copies of the keys and he's the one coming in here."

"He'd have to learn twenty-four new key-lock combinations every time he changed locks to be able to get in and out quickly," Matt said. "How would he know which keys match which locks?"

"And how would he know to come in the front when you're in the back rooms and in the back when you're in the front room?" Ashleigh asked.

Rose just looked at the two as if the obvious answer had somehow eluded them. "He just knows, that's how," she said. "You don't know half of what goes on here." "They drink my tea, pour my milk down the sink, eat my food, move things around and just plain steal things. There're new clothes I never even got a chance to wear before somebody stole them."

Ashleigh put her arms around her grandmother's shoulders. "Well, we're here now, Grandma. No one's going to steal anything from you this weekend."

"Don't be too sure about that. They can get in and out of here and we'll never know it. They've even stood outside my bedroom window at night and watched me when I undress."

"You've seen them?" Matt asked.

"No, but I've investigated around the outside of the house during the day. And I've seen where they trampled the grass down when they were standing outside my window. I think they may have been taking video tape of me."

It surprised Matt that an eighty-three-year-old woman would know enough about electronic technology to be knowledgeable about the videotaping process, but that did little to dispel his skepticism over the veracity of that dubious claim. It was just too much of a stretch to think that anyone would video recorded a frail, elderly woman as she disrobed and such likelihood would have required far more credulity than he was willing to concede. *There's not enough Jack Daniels in the world....*

"I think I'll take a walk around outside and take a look around," he said, starting towards the door.

"Wait, I want to go with you," Ashleigh said, just as eager to get out of the stuffy house even if it was only for a few moments. "I need some air," she said as she stood to follow him. She hoped the two of them might take a short walk while outside.

"Just a minute," Rose said. I have to disable the alarm." She again positioned herself between them and the alarm keypad so as to prevent either of

44

the two from discerning the number sequence for the alarm system. Matt smiled to himself.

Outside Rose's bedroom window, Matt and Ashleigh observed that the grass was indeed flattened and the dirt bordering the grass was packed down as well. "Something's been here, all right," Matt said.

"Who could it have been?" Ashleigh asked. For a moment, she believed Rose.

"Well, from the looks of it, I'd say it was a large dog just trying to find himself a little shade so he could sleep. He made his bed here."

"How do you know that?" Ashleigh asked, clearly puzzled at his simplistic explanation as she examined the spot at her feet.

"You forget I'm an old country boy. I grew up in Farmerville and believe me, that's country. We lived way out, toward the little community of Truxno. That's rural, even by Farmerville standards, and we had about a half-dozen dogs. I know their habits and believe me, dogs in Covington aren't that much different than dogs in Farmerville."

"Are you going to tell Grandma that?"

"I have to tell her something and I'd rather try to put her mind at ease than give her something else to worry about," Matt said. "Yeah, I'll tell her it was a dog."

"I don't think it'll make any difference either way," she said. "Grandma's going to believe what she wants to believe, no matter what you or anyone else says."

Matt took her hand in his and they walked back to the front door only to find it locked. They'd been outside no more than ten minutes and Rose already had re-locked the three deadbolts and keyed the alarm.

Ashleigh knocked. "Grandma, it's Ashleigh. We need to get in."

From inside the house, they could hear the beeps as Rose punched in the code and then turned the keys in the three deadbolt locks. "Just a minute, dear."

45

13

Saturday night in the New Orleans French Quarter is not all partying and good times. It has its dark side, a lesson that many tourists have learned the hard way after walking down the wrong side street by mistake. There is a certain element of the New Orleans night life that depends on these miscalculations. Sometimes the locals make absurd attempts at subtlety by approaching a tourist and "offering" to shine his shoes for twenty dollars or sometimes even as much as fifty dollars. It makes little difference if he is wearing sneakers; the prudent tourist will quickly agree to the shoe shine and hope the thugs will let him go his way physically unharmed after he pays.

Others, though, are not so charitable. Lives come cheap to them. All they want is money with which to purchase meth or crack cocaine and a live witness is a potential liability. Often, no provocation is needed for a perpetrator to kill his victim in a street robbery in the New Orleans French Quarter. William "Billy Boy" Borque was such a criminal who lurked in the shadows of the side streets while waiting for the right person to come along.

It was around 11:30 when the middle-age man veered off Bourbon Street and headed toward the Mississippi River along Toulouse Street. Billy Boy watched as the unsuspecting sightseer walked in his direction. This was where he usually waited for his targets. Typically, they would have seen enough of Bourbon Street for a while and now wanted to walk over to Café Du Monde on Decatur for coffee and beignets. Billy Boy fidgeted as he waited in a doorway. He eased the knife from his pocket and waited. When the tourist, a small man who appeared to be in his late fifties or early sixties got even with the doorway, Billy Bob thrust the knife into his gut and forced the blade upward so as to inflict as much damage as possible to the man's abdominal area. The maneuver usually meant a quick, silent kill.

But as he lunged, something wasn't right. The knife – and Billy Boy – kept going, carried forward by the momentum of Billy Boy's skinny frame as he pushed off hard with his feet to give the maximum leverage to his attack. It might have worked except for the fact his intended victim was no longer there and with no resistance to push back against the knife blade, Billy Boy sprawled in an awkward manner on all-fours onto the sidewalk. The knife fell from his hand as

47

he tried to brace himself against the fall and it skidded about six feet before coming to rest next to the gutter with the stale vomit and urine deposited by pedestrians who'd passed that way hours and even days before.

He scrambled on his hands and knees to retrieve the knife and then jumped to his feet. The tourist was still walking toward Decatur, appearing to be unaware of the attempt on his life. *Jesus! How'd I miss him?* Billy Boy closed the gap between them in hurried strides, reached around the man with his right arm and brought the knife back in anger across his throat in a sweeping motion intended to decapitate the unsuspecting sightseer. Instead of achieving its goal of mortally wounding the man, however, the knife just swished harmlessly through the air. Billy Boy pulled the blade back with so much force, in fact, that he came very close to slashing his own face when it again failed to encounter any resistance from his intended victim.

He was baffled at his inability to carry out his objective. It was such a simple thing to do; slit the man's throat, grab his wallet as he fell and be on his way by the time his victim hit the sidewalk. The procedure was normally such a routine matter for one with his street smarts that he should have been making a buy from his supplier before the body could grow cold. But now two savage attempts to take out one weakling victim had failed. He had to try again; a man had to make a living, after all. With a desperate effort, he tried to plunge the knife into the man's back as he walked away. He lunged so hard that he again fell down, snapping the knife blade in two on the cement as he did so.

This time, the tourist stopped and turned around to face his adversary. "You're losing your touch, Billy Boy," he said. "You were much more efficient the last time. But perhaps you don't remember me. I'm Steven Olsen from St. Paul. We met here a little over a year ago. But you did the job with just one thrust then."

Billy Boy's eyes widened in fear – utter, unrestrained fear.

"Let me help you up so you can try again," Steven Olsen said, taking a step toward his attacker and extending his hand. Billy Boy shrank backwards on the sidewalk and blanched. His bowels released and simultaneously, a warm, moist feeling ran down his thighs as the stench filled the air. He looked back over his shoulder toward Bourbon and then toward Royal and then made his decision. He darted to his left to get around Steven and into the middle of Toulouse Street where he broke into a dead run toward Royal. As he approached Royal, he looked to his right and thought he saw a shadow floating along the sidewalk. It appeared to him to have the general shape of a human being, but then it was gone. He was still looking for the shadow when he got to Royal. He never saw the taxi traveling along the street as he hurtled headlong into its path.

At that moment, a mule-drawn carriage belonging to a carriage tour company was parked just ahead and to the right of the taxi, waiting to take on passengers. Though the taxi wasn't traveling at an unreasonable speed, the vehicle struck Billy Boy with sufficient force to send him tumbling into the hind quarters of the mule that, until that moment, appeared content with its existence which consisted of nothing more than pulling lazy, gawking tourists around the French Quarter. The unexpected jolt of Billy Boy's flying body surprised the mule and, out of instinct, he did what mules do best.

In a single, blurred movement that seemed far too quick for the heretofore indolent beast, his hind quarters bolted up and his rear hooves lashed straight out behind him once, then twice. The first kick caught Billy Boy in his lumbar area, destroying a kidney and spinning him in mid-air even as the second kick caught him squarely in the left temple. The impact of a mule's kick can be quite lethal if the animal's aim is good – or lucky, as was the case on this occasion. The mule was still kicking and jerking the carriage violently when Billy Boy's limp body hit the pavement and lay still, blood oozing from his mouth. It took several minutes for the carriage driver to get the mule calm enough for others to pull Billy Boy from between the mule and carriage.

"Call 911!" someone yelled.

The carriage driver, an old black man, with solid white hair and beard and dressed in a tuxedo, spats, and top hat, was busy holding the bridle and trying to bring the mule under control. He looked over at Billy Boy. "Ain't no use callin' 911," he said, shaking his head slowly. "You may jes' as well go on and call th' morgue. That man's daid. Mule caught him square in th' hed." The irony in the manner in which one of J. François's human mules was killed by the four- legged variety was lost on those who witnessed the gory sequence.

49

14

Steven Olsen, or at least the one who said he was Steven Olsen, was right; Billy Boy had killed a Minnesota tourist more than a year before on Toulouse, between Bourbon and Royal. Police had apprehended Billy Boy soon after the murder based on a tip from a man who'd seen him walking on Toulouse and Royal streets in a less-than-casual manner that appeared strange to the observer. It just wasn't the way a regular person, tourist or local, would walk in the French Quarter, he'd told police. It seemed almost *too* casual. The witness, Dr. Wayne Specht, a psychologist from Lincoln, Nebraska, was in New Orleans for a convention. He observed that the man seemed nervous, looking over his shoulder several times toward Toulouse from which he'd just emerged. He got a good look at Billy Boy, making a mental note of his height, weight, and the clothing he was wearing. Then, more to satisfy his own curiosity, he walked down Toulouse until he found the still bleeding body of a dying Steven Olsen.

Dr Specht came back to New Orleans for Billy Boy's trial but he didn't anticipate the grilling or the verbal abuse to which defense counsel J. François Berthelot, III subjected him.

Had you been drinking that night, Dr. Specht? How much? Do you consume that much alcohol as a normal routine? No? Well, is it possible that you'd had enough to drink that your judgment may have been impaired? I didn't ask you to reiterate your qualifications, sir. We've already stipulated to that. I asked if it were possible that you were impaired. No? You say you walked down Toulouse and found Steven Olsen's body, is that right? Did you see anyone else? Oh, just some people at the other end, near Bourbon. I see. Well, would it be possible that one of those people may have killed Mr. Olsen? Could it have been possible that my client had witnessed the murder and in a moment of panic, fled out of fear for his own life? If my client killed Steven Olsen, where was the knife?

J. François knew, of course, that the answer was there were none. Whoever killed Steven Olsen was probably careful to wear gloves to avoid leaving fingerprints. But no gloves were found in the possession of Billy Boy Borque. Nor was the murder weapon ever found. They were in a storm drain somewhere beneath the French Quarter streets. In fact, whoever killed Steven Olsen didn't even bother to take other valuables. His wallet was on the sidewalk, emptied of cash but still containing all his credit cards. *My client is no saint, to be sure. He may be a petty thief, but that doesn't make him a murderer. He's always broke, so if he'd killed Mr. Olsen, why wouldn't he take his credit cards?*

J. François argued with a passion on behalf of all of his clients and Billy Boy was no exception. The eyewitness who'd seen him exit Toulouse onto Royal was all the prosecution had and his testimony was circumstantial at best. He'd not actually seen Olsen killed. No one had. No one saw Billy Boy commit any crime, certainly not murder. The jury had little to go on to return a guilty verdict and the jurors knew it. The trial ended in a hung jury and the district attorney's office, realizing it had a dog of a case, dropped the case. Billy Boy walked out of the courthouse a free man and J. François had another runner for his ever- growing enterprise.

15

Now, though, J. François was angry as he read the Sunday *Times-Picayune* over a cholesterol-laden breakfast of scrambled eggs, bacon and toast. He gulped his coffee in frustration. This was getting out of hand. Since Thursday night, he'd lost six good men. It couldn't be just a random thing, he knew that. He'd seen the movie *Star Chamber* and he wondered if there might be someone out there exacting his own brand of demented vigilante justice. The thought frightened him. *What the hell was going on out there?*

Somebody was killing all his clients. The papers said they were all accidental, but that's bullshit. He didn't believe in coincidences and he sure as hell didn't believe six of his clients could be taken out in a matter of three days in a series of unrelated accidents. It didn't matter that a witness half a block away saw Billy Boy flailing away at thin air in the shadows of Toulouse before he bolted into the path of the taxi. Strange behavior, to be sure, but there had to be a reason for it. It would just require some digging.

He made a decision at his breakfast table to launch his own investigation to ferret out this evil person as soon as his next trial in nearby St. John the Baptist Parish was finished, before, if possible. There was even some preliminary work he could do before the trial started in a few weeks. *It could be some self- appointed executioner who works in the courthouse. It's probably some over- zealous sheriff's deputy. I'm gonna have somebody's ass over this.*

53

16

They finished Sunday breakfast of oatmeal, bacon, orange juice and coffee and now Ashleigh was cleaning up the dishes as Matt threw clothes into the suitcase in preparation for their return to Metairie. Rose was standing next to Ashleigh, keeping her entertained with old stories about long-dead relatives whom Ashleigh had never known.

"Do you need money for groceries, Grandma?" Ashleigh asked as Matt came back into the kitchen. "Matt can go to the store for you."

He walked up and put his arm around Rose. "We've got plenty of time; we can run to the store and get your groceries for you," he said. "Better yet, why don't you come with us so you can get what you need before we go?"

"I would, but they'd just come in and steal it," Rose said without looking up. "They took three slices of bread just this past week."

"Bread? They took bread?" Matt asked.

"Sure. But if you could run to the store, I need some toilet tissue, a package of purple hull peas, and a few other things. I'll try to hide them so no one can take them." Then she stood staring at the kitchen table for several moments without speaking.

"What's wrong, Grandma?" Ashleigh asked.

"I put a brand-new box of Kleenex on the kitchen table just last night and now it's gone," she said, her voice filled with disgust.

"No, Grandma, I saw you take the box into your bedroom last night," her granddaughter said.

"Really? I don't remember doing that."

Ashleigh started for the bedroom door to retrieve the Kleenex box. She should have known better. No one entered Rose's bedroom, not even Ashleigh, who now found her path to the bedroom door blocked by Rose who'd moved faster than Ashleigh thought possible. "That's okay, I'll look for it," she said disappearing into the room for a few moments. She re-emerged empty handed. "Well, it's not in there. Somebody took it."

Ashleigh tried to dismiss the matter as she continued washing dishes. When she was drying them, she picked up a boiler, wiped it dry and reached down to the left of the sink to open the cabinet to place the pot in its proper

55

location. As she did so, she saw a package of bacon inside the cabinet, on the shelf. She picked it up and showed it to Matt. "Grandma put the bacon in with the pots and pans," she whispered. She walked over to the refrigerator and opened the door to place the bacon in it. She stopped short and then reached in and removed the box of Kleenex. "How'd this get in here?" she asked.

Rose, who was sitting at the table now, turned and saw Ashleigh holding the box. She exhibited no surprise at the discovery. "I guess they brought it back sometime during the night and put it there."

A mixed feeling of sadness and helplessness, washed over Ashleigh and Matt picked up on it in an instant. He walked over to Ashleigh and held her to him as she stared out the kitchen window. "She's getting worse," she said under her breath to Matt. They sneaked a look at Rose and saw that she'd turned back to the table, her back to them, and was straightening the sugar bowl and a small jar of jam on the table, aligning them for no particular reason other than to keep her hands busy. She appeared to have put the Kleenex matter behind her.

Then she remembered the groceries. "I forgot to make you a list," she said, looking in her huge purse for a paper and pen. She kept all her valuables in the purse and she had her right arm through the strap at all times, never setting the purse down, not even in her own home.

With painstaking effort, she printed out a short list of items for Matt to purchase at the store. He took the list from her. "Be right back," he said, heading for the door.

"Wait," Rose called after him. "I have to disable the alarm for you."

It didn't take him long to complete the list and to pay the clerk $18.72, including the price of a Sunday *Times Picayune*. He had a paper at his condo in Metairie, but he thought he would let Ashleigh drive back and this would give him a chance to check out the news before he got home.

He knocked hard several times on the door when he returned because Rose had re-set the alarm and locked all the deadbolts. They couldn't hear him back in the kitchen because Rose had turned the television on to a church service and he didn't have his cell phone. He was forced to return to his car where he laid on the horn until the front door was finally opened. Ashleigh was laughing when he entered with the Wal-Mart bags and placed them on the kitchen table.

"How much do I owe you?" Rose asked as she reached into her purse. "Not a thing, Rose. Strangest thing, Wal-Mart was giving stuff away today."

"I know better than that," she said. Where's the receipt?" She dug through the bags until she found it and then counted out $18.72 in exact change and pushed it across the table toward him.

"Rosie, I'm not taking your money. You put us up two nights and fed us, so I'm not about to take your money."

"You certainly are, Mitch. I'm always happy to have you young folks here and I don't want you thinking you have to buy my groceries. I'm not a charity case yet."

"Well, consider it our contribution to the upkeep anyway," he said, refusing again to take the money.

"Well, I'll just put this money up in a safe place so I can buy some food next time you two come visit." With meticulous care, she then stacked the seventy-two cents in change on top of the bills, which consisted of a ten, a five, and three one-dollar bills and pushed the stack to the center of the table.

Ashleigh gave Matt a knowing look that he failed to comprehend. Then she walked past him into the front bedroom and retrieved their bag. When she re-emerged, Matt and Rose were standing together in the living room. "Well, Grandma, I guess we'd better be going. We'll be back in a few weeks. You take care of yourself."

Once again, Rose positioned herself between them and the alarm keypad as she disarmed it for them to leave. They hugged her and walked out. Ashleigh turned back to Rose. "I'll give you a call when we get home to let you know we made it," she said.

"All right, honey. You drive careful, now." She stood in the door and waved to them until they were out of sight.

They hadn't traveled a mile when Ashleigh sighed.

Matt looked up from the newspaper. "What's the matter?"

"You know she's going to hide that money and forget where she put it."

"You think?"

"Oh, yeah. When she dies, we'll have to go through every book and magazine in that house to be sure she hasn't stashed money between any of the pages. Did you see how she kept her keys pinned to her clothes all the time?"

"No, I didn't."

"She has her purse on her arm and her keys pinned to her clothes. I don't know what will happen if she has to go to the hospital. The first surgical procedure they'll have to do on her is to remove the keys and purse and that won't be easy."

She continued talking for several miles onto the Pontchartrain Causeway and Matt tried to listen as long as he could, alternating his gaze from her face to the miles of uninterrupted water on each side of the causeway. South Louisiana is as flat as any place on earth and it was impossible to see land in any direction from mid-span as the water extended all the way to the horizon. After a while, Ashleigh grew tired of talking about Rose and Matt soon returned his attention to the newspaper and he immersed himself in the police reports. Two stories caught his eye right away.

The stories were about two more men who had been killed over the weekend. One of those, a man named Lenny Stevens, 39, had entered a yard in a residential neighborhood where two dogs attacked him and mauled him to death.

A witness said he'd seen Lenny walking erratically just before he vaulted a chain link fence into the yard where the dogs were. There were few other details available, police said.

The other story was about a character named William "Billy Boy Borque, who was killed in a freak accident when he was kicked in the head by a mule on Royal Street after first having been struck by a cab. The taxi, the story said, knocked Borque into the rear of the mule that was used to draw tourist carriages through the French Quarter and the mule had then kicked him to death in a startled reaction.

The stories noted that each of the victims had extensive police arrest records, mostly for minor offenses. No mention was made of their murder acquittals.

Again, just as with the story about Jamal, D'Wayne, and Theron, Matt had a strange feeling he'd seen the names before. *That's five since Wednesday night. What's going on here?* While visiting Rose, he had missed the story about Deacon Watson. He turned to the sports section and saw that the Baby Cakes had dropped two straight in its weekend three-game series. The third game was today. But he couldn't concentrate on baseball; he went back to the stories about Lenny and Billy Boy. *I know I've seen those names before.*

That was his last lucid thought during the drive. The gentle rocking motion of the vehicle and the whining drone of the tires on the pavement, interrupted by the rhythmic thump of the tires over the bridge's expansion joints soon combined to lull him to sleep. For the remainder of the ride home, the five fatalities were temporarily pushed from his mind, only to be replaced by subconscious visions of far more grisly deaths he'd read about years before and which only now resurfaced in his subconscious mind.

As the miles fell behind them, a surreal story unfolded in his subliminal state, a story too eerie, too bizarre, and too grisly to be true – but it *was* true and almost two hundred years later remains as much a part of the New Orleans legacy as Bourbon Street and Mardi Gras.

17

If any New Orleans structure ever earned the title of most haunted building in the French Quarter, it was the Lalaurie House at Royal and Governor Nichols streets. Dr. Louis Lalaurie and his wife Delphine purchased the Creole mansion at 1140 Royal in 1832. The gracious building complimented the beauty of Madame Lalaurie and her stylish soirees that catered to New Orleans society's upper crust, right down to the china and silver, which were consistently sparkling clean and polished. Only the finest cuisine available in the city renowned for its food was good enough to be served at her parties. Hand-carved mahogany doors opened into bright parlors illuminated by hundreds of candles in magnificent chandeliers. The floors were adorned with imported Oriental rugs. Madame Lalaurie was one of the most beautiful and intelligent women in the city. An invitation to a social event at 1140 Royal Street was a thing to be cherished. In addition to enjoying a reputation for hosting the most lavish parties, she was also noted for her well-behaved slaves. Everyone envied the Lalauries for their elegant lifestyle.

That was the public side of Madame Lalaurie. The private side, the dark, evil side, was that of a woman so inhumane in the treatment of her slaves as to defy description. It was enough that she kept her cook chained to the fireplace in the kitchen, but when a twelve-year-old slave girl named Leah caught a snag while brushing her mistress's hair, Delphine Lalaurie chased the frightened girl to a third-floor rooftop where the girl lost her footing and plunged to her death. A neighbor witnessed the incident and reported it to authorities who promptly seized all the Lalauries' slaves and re-sold them, fining her a mere three hundred dollars in the process. Not one to admit defeat so easily, Madame Lalaurie prevailed on friends to purchase the slaves and sell them back to her and for a while everything returned to life as usual.

But then, credible stories about the mistreatment of the slaves began to make their way around New Orleans. Whispered conversations persisted about how the Lalaurie slaves seemed to come and go on a regular basis; stable boys disappeared never to be seen again and maids were replaced with no explanation. The first ominous indication that the Lalaurie name no long held sway over Crescent City society became evident as the first few party invitations were

59

declined. Then dinner invitations were ignored and finally, the family was simply shunned by former guests.

Finally, in April of 1834, it all came crashing down.

A fire broke out in the Lalaurie kitchen – started, it was claimed, by the cook who could no longer endure the wretched treatment of Madame Lalaurie. The flames swept through the house. After the fire was extinguished, slaves directed firefighters to an attic crawlspace. The door was bolted and locked from the outside but screams and moans could be heard from inside the door. A battering ram was used to open the door and as soon as veteran firemen entered the room they began vomiting from the stench.

Inside were more than a dozen slaves, victims of crude and unspeakably horrid medical experimentations. All the victims, male and female, were naked and those not on tables were chained to a wall. A woman who had somehow managed to free herself from her shackles bolted past her rescuers and plunged through a window to her death. Other women had their stomachs cut open and their intestines wrapped around their waists. One had her arms amputated and her skin peeled in a circular pattern. Another was locked in a dog cage. When she was removed from the cage, rescuers found all her joints had been broken and reset at odd angles. She more resembled a crab than a human. One woman had her mouth stuffed with animal excrement and her lips sewn shut. Yet another, a man, looked as though he had been subjected to a crude sex change operation. Other men had their fingernails ripped off, eyes poked out and genitals removed.

The horror chamber discovered by the firefighters had human body parts scattered around. Heads and human organs were thrown in buckets. Some of the human souvenirs were found placed on shelves along with whips and paddles. One man found hanging in shackles had a stick protruding from a hole that was drilled in the top of his head. The stick was to *stir* his brains. Some had their mouths pinned shut and their hands sewn to various parts of the body. Many had been dead for some time and others were unconscious. Those still conscious begged to be killed so their misery could be ended.

Word of what the firefighters had discovered swept through the city and an angry rope-carrying mob soon gathered outside the *Maison Lalaurie*. Most of them had been guests in the house at one time or another and they were outraged at what they had learned. As they screamed for vengeance, a carriage burst out of the gates and into the crowd. It disappeared from sight and the Lalaurie family was never seen again. Rumors persisted that they fled to the north shore of Lake Pontchartrain, settling in the Covington-Mandeville area.

The haunting started right away. Many people claimed to hear screams of agony emanating from the vacant house at night and some said they saw apparitions of slaves walking on the balconies and in the yards. Some New Orleanians refused to walk on the same side of the street when passing the mansion. Others avoided the block altogether and the house remained vacant for forty years. It was opened as a home to Italian immigrants but families began

60

claiming to have seen a large black male walking the balcony covered in chains and blood. A mother of twin babies said she awoke in the middle of the night to discover that a sock had been stuffed into the mouth of one of the babies. Animals were found decapitated in the courtyard. Despite the crushing need for housing for the influx of Italian immigrants in the late nineteenth century, the house was soon vacated, shunned even by the homeless newcomers.

One enterprising businessman tried to open a furniture store in the building only to enter the store one morning to find urine, feces and blood covering his entire inventory. He cleaned up the mess, ordered new furniture, and sat up all night with a shotgun to catch the vandals. The following morning, he found the furniture had been destroyed again, though no one had entered the building. He closed the building. It re-opened later as the *Haunted Saloon*, but no one would patronize the bar and it, too, soon closed and the building again remained vacant for many years.

After falling into serious disrepair, it was eventually renovated into apartments. When workers replaced floor boards in the third-floor slave quarters, the skeletons of seventy-five slaves were found. They had been buried alive; the screams and moans heard in the early weeks after the fire turned out to be real. Neighbors, thinking the cries to be ghosts, never made any attempt to save the unfortunate victims.

The discovery did little to assuage the fears of the locals that the old house was haunted.

18

Matt awoke when Ashleigh pulled into her condo driveway. "We're here," she said as she brought the car to a stop. He sat staring straight ahead for a moment, trying to understand why people dream the things they do. The dream and the reality of the details troubled him as they walked together to her door. Matt carried the suitcase into her house still preoccupied with his dream of the horrifying events of 1834 and wondering why the human mind responds to buried memories that otherwise would have been long forgotten.

"I think I'm going to take a long, hot bath and go to bed," Ashleigh said, breaking the silence.

"Yeah, I'm kinda tired, too. I think I'll go on home. I'll call you tomorrow, okay?"

"I'm counting on it, big guy. I owe you a weekend in Destin. Thanks for going with me to Covington."

Matt smiled and kissed her. "Glad to do it. Rose is a sweetheart, but she's got some issues."

"I know. Talk to you tomorrow. Good night." She closed the door as Matt walked to his car.

Back at his own house, he stopped to pick up the Saturday and Sunday issues of the *Times-Picayune* from his driveway. Once inside, he went through the Sunday edition one more time to see if the local edition had any stories in the police beat that weren't included in the state edition, which goes to press earlier in order to get the paper to the outlying suburban areas on time. He didn't see anything that grabbed his attention. But when he opened the Saturday paper, he sat down when he saw the name of Deason "Deacon" Watson. He was *certain* he knew that name; you don't forget a name like Deacon. He read about how Deacon's body had been found in a cemetery. The 42-year-old man, the story quoted police as saying, had apparently fallen and struck his head on a concrete vault in the cemetery. The fact that his pants were around his ankles led police to believe he was involved in some type of homosexual encounter at the time.

"Jesus," he said aloud. He read the story again and then retrieved the Sunday paper and re-read the stories about Lenny and Billy Boy. He looked around the kitchen and swore to himself. "Damn!"

63

He dove to the garbage can under the sink and dug into it for the Friday paper, hoping he'd brought it home with him from work. He pawed through the eggshells, and an empty orange juice carton until he found the paper. It had coffee grounds on it, but he brushed them off, walked to the table, and began turning through the paper until he found the stories about the botched convenience store robbery and the deaths of Jamal, D'Wayne, and Theron in the wreck. He found a pair of scissors and clipped all five stories.

He knew where he'd be spending his lunch hours during the coming week.

19

Matt had clerked for State Supreme Court Justice Thomas Gravois for four years and liked his job despite its demands on his time. He liked being on the cutting edge of important decisions handed down by the court on civil and criminal matters. Most of the time, when he drew the assignment to write the opinion, Judge Gravois was in the majority. But on a few occasions, he'd had the privilege of writing a minority opinion for the judge. He secretly enjoyed writing those more than majority opinions because it seemed that minority opinions were more candid, more critical of the majority opinion, and more passionate even though Louisiana Supreme Court decisions are written before it is known which opinion will represent the majority and which the dissenting one.

Both the Orleans Criminal Court and the Louisiana Supreme Court are only a few blocks off Canal Street, but they are about twenty blocks apart because they are at opposite ends of Canal. The Louisiana State Supreme Court is located in the 300 block of Loyola Street and the Orleans Parish Criminal District Court is located in the 2700 block of Tulane Avenue at the corner of Broad. Tulane, also called U.S. 61, was once the only major route between New Orleans and most of the rest of the state. That was before the interstate highway system.

If Matt had reason to visit the criminal district court in the course of his duties, it would not have been quite so inconvenient for him to conduct his research. As it was, his work was largely confined to the Supreme Court building and there just wasn't enough time to do what he wanted to do during his lunch hour. He could have asked a couple of paralegals he knew to do his legwork for him, but this was too important to trust to someone else with no real interest in the facts. There was no way he could risk important information in the records being overlooked by someone else. Besides, conducting personal research for him was not part of their job. He would just have to request a few days of vacation so he could take his time conducting his research.

He pulled the chair out and sat down at his computer. If he was going to do this in just a couple of days, he would have to be methodical about his research so as not to waste any precious time. He was growing more excited by the minute with the prospect of the work that lay before him. He didn't know where it would take him, but he couldn't wait to get started. Something about the

65

violent deaths of the six intrigued him. He knew there had to be more to the stories than just what he'd read in the newspaper.

What if I do find something significant? What am I going to do with it? Who can I tell? What will I tell them? If I find something really weird, who'll believe me?

He continued to wonder about the deaths as he lay in the darkness of his room before sleep finally overcame his conscious thoughts. *Could the deaths have been deliberate and made to appear accidental? Could they have been the work of a single person on some twisted mission of revenge for something the victims had done? Why would I even think that? I don't even know for sure that they* did *anything.*

The next sound he heard was his clock radio beckoning him from his bed at six a.m. Why was it that morning drive radio personalities always seemed to be just too damned happy?

20

J. François had long since archived his files on his now-dead clients, so he paid a visit to 2700 Tulane and went right to the clerk of court's criminal archives basement office. He requested the files on each man and deposited them on a nearby table and started to work. He was meticulous in his research, looking for anything that might provide a clue to the untimely deaths of the six. Jamal, D'Wayne, and Theron had each been tried before the same judge, Lyle Bergen, but that was only because it was a single trial for the robbery and murder of the convenience store attendant. Lenny also was tried before Bergen, but Deacon, and Billy Boy each had a different judge, so he dismissed that as a possible connecting factor.

He next checked to see which prosecutors from the district attorney's office had tried the cases to see if there was a common thread. There was none; all the prosecutors were different except, again, in the case of the convenience store trial. A team of four attorneys had led the prosecution in that trial, but none of them had participated in any of the others. He'd felt that was the case before he started poring over the files, but he just wanted to satisfy himself that he'd remembered correctly. Nor was there any connection between families of the victims. One was a Sri Lankan named Rijah Mulaquah and another was a tourist from Minnesota named Steve Olsen. The nine-year-old boy named Chad Moran and the lone woman, Denise Fleming, were the only local victims but there was no known connection between those two.

Denise, who had only recently moved back to the city, was from a middle-class family and was planning to return to school when she was raped and killed. Chad Moran's parents were divorced and his single mother lived in a blue collar mixed neighborhood. She was forced to work two jobs to make ends meet and was at her second job, as a barroom waitress, when Chad was abducted, raped and murdered.

He first put in a call to his contact at the parish prison to see if any of the six men had ever encountered each other in jail or, more important, if any of them had made any common enemies while incarcerated prior to their trials. Because the four crimes occurred in different areas of the city and at different times, he had no reason to suspect any link between the actions that led to their arrests and trials,

67

so he didn't pursue that angle. Instead, he worried and fretted over the volumes of legal documents while self-inflicting a severe case of eyestrain and frayed nerves as he pored over pages of useless indictments, arraignment, and trial records that offered up no clues.

The trail had grown hopelessly cold unless his contact at parish prison could come up with something. It wasn't until he noticed employees preparing to shut down the office that he realized he'd been there all day. It was 4:25 and the clerk's office would be closing at 4:30. He had worked right through lunch without realizing it and now he felt the pangs of hunger and the frustration of having come up empty in his frantic search. For the first time in his professional career, despite all the threats from the law and order freaks over his representation of those accused of heinous crimes, he felt genuine concern for his safety and he found himself looking over both shoulders as he exited the basement of the courthouse and walked to his car two blocks away. He looked all around once again before he squeezed his portly frame into the Altima.

Once in his vehicle, he turned on his cell phone and a message popped up that he had a new voicemail. He pressed the key to play the message and heard the voice of his parish prison employee friend. "Fran, I ran down that information you gave me and came up with nothin'. I ran the names of those who were in here when your boys were and there's only four still in here and they say they never saw or talked to any of them in jail. One of the guys I talked to says he once lived a few blocks from this guy Theron, but that he never saw him in prison. Sorry I couldn't be more help, man. Call me if there's anything else."

J. François Berthelot cursed under his breath as he erased the voicemail and slammed on his brakes to keep from rear-ending another car stopped at a red light in front of him. He kept glancing from side to side until the light changed. He was certain that the traffic light sequence was somehow a conspiracy to make him stop so some unknown avenger could take out his next victim. It seemed to him now that he caught more red lights and interstate congestion than he ever had before on the drive home. He was a nervous wreck by the time he pulled into his garage. He killed the engine and leaned back in the seat, closing his eyes for just a minute to ease the tension. Tomorrow was another day and he had to decide where he'd start his search for answers.

He reached for the remote attached to his sun visor and closed the garage door before he exited his car to open the door leading into his kitchen. As he tried to insert the key into the lock, he glanced back one more time and he felt the blood run ice cold in his veins. Standing behind his vehicle was the faint image of a young woman. Before he could focus on her, however, he caught a movement to his left, on the far side of the Altima. He saw what appeared to be a foreigner, an Indian, perhaps. The keys fell from his hands as his knees almost gave way. He looked down just long enough to retrieve his keys. When he looked up again, an middle-age man had replaced the Indian and a small boy was now standing where the woman had been only seconds before. Neither of them moved

69

and no words were spoken. They just seemed to hover there as they looked at him – expressionless, emotionless wisps of chilling surrealism.

More terrifying than the sudden appearance of the eerie visitors, other than the fact they'd managed to get inside his locked garage, was that even though he could make out their images, he could still see through them – as if they were there, yet somehow weren't, like some kind of cruel, demented fog. His mouth fell open and he tried to scream out, but no sound came from his throat other than a couple of choked gasps. Shaking uncontrollably, he somehow managed to get his key in the lock and opened the door just as the images disappeared altogether. He half stumbled and half fell into his kitchen and slammed the door behind him and locked it. Sweat poured from his face as he stood and stared at the door leading to the garage for several minutes before he dared move.

He was afraid to shower lest the sound of the running water might prevent him from hearing intruders in his home. He didn't turn on the television for the same reason and dinner was out of the question. Who could eat after witnessing what he'd just seen? For that matter, there was no way he could sleep, either. It was going to be a very long night. He chose a spot in his living room where he could see the front door, the door leading to the garage, and the door that led to his patio. That, he decided, would be his best vantage point. He opened his briefcase, removed his .380 automatic, and sat wide eyed for the next thirteen hours.

21

"Three days?" Judge Gravois said, looking up from a writ application the Supreme Court was considering. The plaintiff had applied for the writ after his multi-million-dollar award was overturned in a major bodily injury lawsuit. The defendant, the State of Louisiana, had been sued over catastrophic injuries to a fourteen-year-old boy when the vehicle in which he was riding was hit by a drunk driver. The drunk, whose blood alcohol content was .27 percent, over three times the legal limit, was speeding when he blew a clearly visible stop sign, rendering the young boy a quadriplegic. His parents, devastated as any parents would be, also sued the manufacturer of the car in which he was riding and the car dealership where they'd purchased the vehicle, alleging safety design deficiencies. They sought damages for pain and suffering on the boy's behalf, past and future medical expenses, and loss of consortium for the parents.

For some reason, it's not considered a conflict of interests in Louisiana for a member of the legislature, elected to protect the fiscal interests of the state, to serve as plaintiff attorney in lawsuits against the state. Thus, it was that the plaintiff attorney in this matter enlisted the services of a state senator as his co-counsel. It was a calculated move; the plaintiff attorney was white but the plaintiffs were black, the jury was predominately black, and the state senator was black.

The trial jury, incredibly, found the state to be one hundred percent liable for nearly fourteen million dollars in damages even though it was revealed at trial that it was the offending driver's third DWI conviction. The state filed an immediate appeal and a three-judge appeals court panel reversed the decision in a two-to-one decision. A re-hearing was granted and a five-judge panel ultimately reversed the decision by a three-to-two vote, finding the drunk to be one hundred percent negligent for the collision. The plaintiffs applied for writs to the Supreme Court.

Every major daily newspaper in the state and many television stations had picked up the story. Each news outlet, it seemed, had an opinion. Pressure was applied in a not-so-subtle fashion by certain members of the Louisiana Legislature, particularly through the untiring efforts of the state senator/co-counsel who worked hard at the trial and wasn't one to watch quietly as his

72

efforts went for naught. He could almost taste his share of the fourteen million from the state treasury and he was lobbying hard to protect his interests and, in the process, those of his clients – if not those of the state.

So, it was understandable that this was a closely-watched case and one that the Supreme Court would have to consider with all due political consideration, the law itself notwithstanding. Judge Gravois was counting on Matt's assistance in drafting an opinion on the volatile matter of weighing the rights of a deep-pocket defendant against those of an innocent juvenile who would spend the rest of his life in a wheelchair and who would require twenty- four-hour assistance for every routine chore – eating, bathing, and using the bathroom. It was just the kind of case state Supreme Court justices dreaded. Their decision would be subjected to criticism no matter which way they ruled.

The procedure for the Louisiana Supreme Court's handling of writs is very different than that of the U.S. Supreme Court. The nine-member U.S. Supreme Court, when it decides to hear a case, grants of a writ of certiorari. Arguments are heard and the court makes its decision. If the Chief Justice is in the majority, he makes an assignment to one of the majority justices to write the majority opinion and the senior justice in the minority assigns the dissenting opinion to a minority justice. If the Chief Justice is not in the majority, the most senior justice in the majority assigns the opinion and the Chief Justice assigns the dissenting opinion to another minority justice. The Chief Justice may assign the writing of the opinion – majority or dissenting – to himself, but usually the court's caseload and the specialization of each justice is taken into consideration when opinions are assigned.

In Louisiana, however, each of the seven justices receives a copy of a writ application but it is assigned to an *original* justice and a *duplicate* – or *alternate* – justice on a random basis. The *original* justice reviews the application and makes his or her recommendation by memorandum to the other six justices on whether or not to grant the writ. Should the *original* justice be unable to participate because of a conflict of interest or some other personal reason then that duty falls to the *duplicate* justice.

If any of the other six justices should disagree with the recommendation, the application may be held over for further consideration as a courtesy to that justice. Once a writ is considered by the court, the *original* justice circulates his final recommendation to the other justices. Each justice who agrees with the recommendation signs at the top of the memorandum and each one who disagrees signs at the bottom. Only then does the *original* justice know whether he will be writing the majority or dissenting opinion. His or her opinion does not change; only the status of majority or dissenting opinion does. Thomas Gravois was the original justice for this application.

"Matt, this is a terrible time to be taking off. I really need you for this writ decision. I'm recommending that we deny writs. I believe the appellate court was right in its findings, but I still don't know yet whether that's going to be the

73

majority of dissenting opinion. Either way, you're going to have to write it and I'll have to take the heat. What do you need the time off for?"

Matt couldn't bring himself to divulge his reason for wanting time off. "It's a personal matter, Judge, and I'd never ask off if it weren't important."

"I know that, Matt. You're very dependable. I don't question that. It's just the timing of the request. It could really put us in a bind. What days do you need?"

"Wednesday through Friday. I'll work late today and tomorrow to get as much work done as possible."

"You're not running off to get married or something silly like that, are you?"

Matt laughed. "No, sir, nothing like that. But if I ever do, I'll ask you to officiate."

Judge Gravois laced the fingers of his hands together behind his head as he leaned back in his oversized desk chair. "Well, Matthew, I guess you aren't being unreasonable. Get as much work off your desk as you can before you leave."

"Thank you, sir."

"And, Matt...."

"Yes sir?"

"Say hello to Ashleigh for me and give her a big hug."

"I will. Thanks again."

22

It was not a good day for J. François Berthelot. He appeared in court looking disheveled, unshaven, his eyes swollen and red. His unkempt appearance and preoccupied demeanor were in stark contrast to his usual dapper dress and obsessive attention to details. To those around the courthouse who knew him, he seemed nervous, at times disoriented, far from the smug, confident lawyer they all knew. He fumbled through his opening statement on behalf of a man accused of killing a neighbor over a barking dog. J. François and his client both knew the killing was over a drug deal gone bad, but they stuck to their story of the barking dog. Now, after innumerable delays, the matter was going to trial and for the defendant, the timing couldn't have been worse.

J. François had been known to lose cases before. He gave his best efforts only on behalf of those who would later be joining his other business ventures – hawking recreational drugs, bookmaking, and prostitution. In cases of clients reluctant to commit to post-trial participation in the enterprise, well, J. François would defend them, but fees were due up front and they shouldn't expect miracles. They usually regretted their decisions.

The scuttlebutt in legal circles had more than a half-dozen judges deeply involved in what had become the worst kept secret in the courthouse. That would have provided a convenient explanation for many of the criminal trial outcomes had an explanation been necessary. J. François, however, preferred to think that his dramatic courtroom victories were the result of his brilliance and hard work. To a great extent, it was an accurate self-appraisal; he was a skilled – some would even say brilliant – attorney.

But today was different. This client, Chet Voitier (pronounced *Vo*-shay), was already a part of the J. François enterprise, having successfully retained the lawyer's services in an earlier felony case. Chet was an important conduit in the network that supplied generous supplies of methamphetamines to clients, many of whom earned their livelihoods in the Orleans Parish Courthouse. Several distinguished members of the New Orleans bar thus were surprised – and concerned – to see J. François struggling with so much at stake.

Word ran through the courthouse, leapfrogging from corridors to offices to courtrooms to rest rooms that he was floundering. The courtroom began filling

75

with lawyers who had a lot to lose. They were worried to see the great J. François fall on his face on behalf of a client he had personally groomed. A couple of judges even managed to drop by, unprecedented in just about any courthouse anywhere. They watched for a while, said nothing, and then left. *What's going on, here? Is J. François throwing the match? If so, why? Doesn't he know the client could start screaming if he suspects a double cross? This could be embarrassing.* It wasn't long before an informal, six-lawyer oversight committee was assigned to monitor the trial on a rotating basis. Each attorney reported that their colleague appeared nervous, often stopping in the middle of grilling a witness to glance around the courtroom and visibly flinching every time the door to the courtroom opened, frequently losing his train of thought, uncharacteristically having to fumble for words.

Several judges held an emergency caucus of their own. *Maybe we should call J. François in to find out what's going on.* In the end, though, they decided to do nothing for the time being. There would be ample opportunity to take decisive action if it should become necessary.

23

Matt got started two days later than J. François and like the attorney, he spent most of the first day, Wednesday, in the criminal clerk's office examining the trial records of the six dead men. He was surprised to see that each of the men had been represented at trial by J. François. It was an interesting discovery, to be sure, but one to which he attached no immediate importance. He took copious notes on each trial record. He didn't think he would ever need all the information he wrote down but he had learned in his first-year law school class years ago that it was better to err on the side of caution.

Beyond their common defense counsel, there was little to distinguish the cases from hundreds, even thousands of others in the files that occupied the rows of dusty files in the clerk's archives. The files were computerized upstairs in the clerk of court's office but he preferred to hold the actual papers in his hands. Their cases were tried before different judges at different times. He read each file thoroughly, looking for that elusive bit of information that might be the key to the inexplicable deaths. Matt and J. François weren't the only ones who were curious about the deaths. After Matt had pored over the files for several hours, a clerk of court employee made his way to a telephone somewhere in the back. He punched in a phone number and spoke for just over a minute before returning to work in the file room.

Upstairs, a criminal court judge who had reason to worry – did. He hung up his telephone and immediately picked it up again. Even as the judge was placing his call, Matt finished his note taking and prepared to leave. As he walked out the door, he was nearly run over by a burly deputy sheriff who was in an apparent hurry to get inside the office. "Excuse me," Matt said as they passed. The deputy ignored him.

Matt read his notes at home that night in an effort to make some sense of the mysterious deaths of six men whom he believed had left society better off for their having died. At a quarter past ten, after he'd lost count of the cups of coffee he'd consumed and the number of times he went over his notes, he decided to get some rest and get off to an early start on Thursday. *Why do I even care about these men? They were low-life criminals who most likely deserved what they got.*

He knew why, of course. He long ago became hooked on crime stories and these had a common thread other than J. François as defense attorney and their subsequent and sudden, violent deaths. He was convinced of that, and he knew he wouldn't rest until he knew what it was that linked them. *What am I overlooking? There's something I haven't discovered, but what?*

Then something clicked in his mind. He got up, turned off the lights and walked into his garage. By 10:30 he was driving to the convenience store on Esplanade. He had found nothing in the trial records that shed any light on the deaths, so he thought he'd try to talk to Jim "Tattoo" Reilly.

The hour was late, but he didn't want to waste any time. Besides, Jim Reilly had been working the late shift when he said the three entered the store the night they were killed. After talking to him, if he could get him to open up, he would next try to find the witness who saw Lenny Stevens just before he vaulted himself into the yard guarded by the pit bulldogs. Then he would attempt to find the last man to have seen Billy Boy Borque before he pissed off the mule on Royal Street. There was no known witness to Deacon Watson's last moments on earth, but he'd check around the neighborhood anyway. *Who knows I just might get lucky.*

24

Wednesday was even worse than Tuesday for J. François. Chet Voitier, having lost confidence in his legal counsel, was demanding a new lawyer. J. François and the defendant argued in sufficiently loud whispers as to be audible over the entire courtroom, prompting the presiding judge to inquire if there was a problem. "No, Your Honor, just a little misunderstanding," J. François answered even as he and Chet returned to flailing their arms in the air in an animated discussion before a throng of lawyers, paralegals, and law clerks.

By now the number of spectators had grown as the story of the infamous defense lawyer's impending meltdown made its way out of the courthouse and into the coffee shops and private offices of criminal lawyers all over the city. Those with no conflicts on their calendars made it a point to attend the trial that any other time would have attracted only a handful of onlookers at most. Side bets were made on the outcome. The smart money was on J. François, based largely on his stellar track record. But this case was different. It'd been days since he'd slept, shaved, or showered – and it showed.

He still wore the same rumpled suit that now reeked of soured sweat that clung to his body in the stifling New Orleans heat and humidity. It's the same heat and humidity that swallows a man's entire body until it stifles his very will to breathe, only to be followed by the afternoon showers that leave clouds of steam rising from the sidewalks. It was as if the heat had gotten to J. François's brain itself. He bordered on incoherence as baffled lawyers exchanged puzzled glances.

The presiding judge spent most of his time studying J. François's every nuance, every movement, in an effort to determine if the lawyer might be sampling more of his own product than usual. There were a number of times over the first two days that he considered ordering a mistrial and calling J. François into chambers for a good, old-fashioned judicial ass-chewing. Even members of the jury, unfamiliar as most of them were with criminal trial proceedings, knew something was askew. *This ain't like the lawyers on television at all.*

The smart money lost; J. François and Chet went down in ignoble fashion. The jury took less than an hour to return a unanimous guilty verdict of second-degree murder. Even on the worst of days, J. François would have been

80

expected to get no worse than an involuntary manslaughter conviction. But it was no contest this time and the spectator attorneys filed out of the courtroom in perplexed silence following the verdict, each consumed with his own thoughts about what they had just witnessed. *What the hell just happened? Has he lost his touch? The media are going to love this.*

Three judges convened in chambers when the work day came to a close and the Scotch flowed freely as they discussed their options. "This could get ugly," said Judge Lyle Bergen. "We need to get J. François in here and find out what happened."

"We don't want to over react," said Charles Cheramie, a veteran of over twenty years on the bench. "It could've been just one of those weird occurrences that happen."

"Bullshit," said Judge Ray Sonnier. "Did either of you see how he looked, how he was dressed? That wasn't J. François. He was sputtering up there, for Christ sake, talking gooneybabble. This isn't just some 'weird occurrence.' Something's wrong. Something's going down that we don't know about and it could bite us all in the ass."

25

Matt pulled up to the gas pumps at the Esplanade Avenue store at quarter past eleven. He inserted his Visa card and filled the tank and then walked up to the window. The clerk eyed him the same indifference he showed all his customers. "Help you?" he asked through the round speaker in the inch-thick glass. He had yet to slide the cash drawer out, choosing instead to wait and see what this customer wanted.

"Jim Reilly?"

"Who wants to know?" was the cautious response. He eyed the patron with a measured combination of curiosity and suspicion, wondering how he knew his name.

"My name is Matt Ramsey. I'm an attorney and I'd like to ask you some questions about the shootings that occurred here a few days ago."

"I got nothing to say to no lawyer. I done told the cops everything I know."

Matt was holding one of his business cards in his right hand. "I'm sure you have. I'm not looking to sue anyone. I just want to ask you some general questions."

Jim Reilly pushed the cash drawer out far enough for Matt to place his card in it and then he pulled it back in. He picked up the card and examined it as if he expected it to tell him the winning Powerball numbers. "So, what do you want from me?"

Matt studied Jim Reilly and noted that he appeared to be in his late twenties or early thirties, was thin, even frail, and the vacant stare in his eyes told Matt there was little that could jar him emotionally. He had seen it all and even the recent shooting at the store didn't particularly scare him, just made him a little warier. Both arms and the back of his neck were covered with tattoos – body art, they called it now. Matt hoped that Jim wasn't stoned at the moment so that his memory might be clear if he chose to talk at all.

"Is there any way you might let me in so we don't have to talk through this glass?" Matt asked.

82

"No way, man. Regulations. But I tell you what: I'll come out there as long as we don't have any customers. I need a smoke anyway and I like to smoke outside. But if somebody drives up, I hafta get my ass back in here, okay?"

"That's fine."

Jim retrieved a package of Marlboro lights from beneath the counter and unlocked the door, let himself out, and re-locked it. He stood facing Matt as he lit his first cigarette. "Jeez, it's hot out here, even this late at night. What's on yer mind, pal?"

"Those three men who shot up the place were killed in a bad accident on Esplanade just a few minutes after leaving here, did you know that?"

"Not when I talked to the cops. I found out later. Why? What's that got to do with what happened here? The accident was just one of them bullshit things that happen, wasn't it?"

"I really don't know for sure," Matt said. "But did you know they'd just been acquitted of charges that they robbed and murdered a clerk at your Magazine Street store a little over a year ago?"

Jim removed the cigarette from his lips and looked at Matt. "No shit? They did that? They the ones that killed that Indian fella?"

"Sri Lankan, actually."

"Whatever. They did that for sure?"

"Well, like I said, they were acquitted, but most likely it was them."

"How'd they get off?"

"Slick lawyer."

"Figures. So, what you're tellin' me is they was gonna rob this place and most likely kill me? Thanks a lot, pal. You just made my night."

"I can't say that for sure, but they did seem to follow a pattern, except for the part about them shooting up the wall behind the register. Can you fill me in on that?"

"Look, man, I'm gonna do something that's against the rules and I could get fired for it, but I'm gonna let you come inside. I don't like it out here much all of a sudden."

Jim locked the door behind them and turned to point to the wall. "They still ain't fixed that damned wall. It gives me the creeps ever time I look at it. It coulda been me standin' back there. Look at them bullet holes. They're all right about chest and head high. They'd a cut me in half."

"Where were you, Mr. Reilly?" Matt could understand why Jim didn't like to smoke inside; the rank odor of stale cigarette smoke in the store was stifling, causing him to want to hold his breath for the duration of his visit. He knew the foul smell would permeate his clothing and he also knew now that his clothes had an appointment with the dry cleaners awaiting them first thing tomorrow.

"Name's Jim. Friends call me Tattoo. I guess you can see why. I was in the back, takin' a piss in the rest room. It's back there next to the stock room.

Actually, I was outta the bathroom and on my way back up front when I heard 'em. This one guy, he seemed to be the leader, was wavin' a gun around and yellin' an' shit. I ducked down behind some boxes back there. There was two stacks of boxes and they was about a inch or so apart, so I looked between th' boxes."

"Could you see anything?"

"Oh, hell yeah, everything. This guy who I said was the leader, one of the others called him Jamal. He says, "Jamal, this guy looks familiar." Said he looked like the dude over on Magazine Street."

"Who did?"

"I don't know his name, one of the robbers, man." "No, not him. Who looked like the guy on Magazine?"

"That's the weird part, man. There wasn't nobody up there 'cept the three of them. I don't know who they was talkin' about."

"But Jamal was talking to someone else, whoever it was?"

"Seemed to be. Yelling for him to empty the cash drawer or he'd blow his damn head off. He was even holding his gun sideways like some kind of street gangsta. Dumb-ass way to hold a gun, if you ask me."

"Did you hear anyone talking back to him?"

"No, but they sure seemed to hear somebody. Jamal acted like he was having some kind of discussion over whether or not he was gonna hand over the money and that's when the other one said he looked like the guy on Magazine. Man, I sure didn't know they were talking about that Zirluk....what did you say he was?"

"Sri Lankan. Sri Lanka is an island nation off the southern coast of India."

"Yeah, whatever. Well anyway, Jamal fires a couple shots at the wall at or this person he thought he was talkin' to, or whatever. Anyway, it was just a few seconds after that that all three of 'em emptied their guns at their imaginary friend. Shit, it sounded like th' world was comin' to a end. I jus' ducked down and stayed down 'til I heard 'em burning rubber when they was leaving. Then I went up front and called the cops. There was blue smoke in the air and you could smell th' gunpowder. Them guys meant business, all right. I'm jus' glad I had to take a whiz when I did."

"So, they were talking to someone, but no one was up there?"

"Yeah, I think they musta been stoned. They had to have had some good shit to get that messed up. That's why I don't screw around with nose candy. I stay with pot. Ain't gonna be shootin' up nobody's store on pot. I might get a little hungry, but not violent. That jus' ain't my style."

Tattoo was lying and they both knew it.

"Had anyone been in the store just before they came?"

"Nah, I don't think so. Actually, I was supposed to have had the door locked like tonight, but I had just had a smoke break and forgot to lock the door

84

behind me when I came back inside 'cause I had to piss. Almost got fired for that, too. But unless somebody came in while I was in the pisser, nobody else was here, jus' them three."

"Jim, I really appreciate your help. Thanks for talking to me."

"What do you think was goin' on? You got any ideas?"

"Not a one, but thanks again."

"Here, let me unlock the door so you can get out. Thanks for comin' by man, I enjoyed the company. If there's anything else, jus' come on in."

"I will," Matt said as he exited the store for his car, thankful to be outside again and breathing the New Orleans version of fresh air, the quality of which was only somewhat better than the interior of the convenience store.

26

It was well after midnight by the time Matt left the dingy store and headed west on I-10 to his home in Metairie. The traffic had thinned out, making the drive easier but traffic congestion was not on his mind. He kept going over his conversation with Jim Reilly, trying to connect the dots, to interpret the meaning of the events of that early morning nearly a week ago. It made no sense. Three men talking to a wall and then emptying their weapons on it just wasn't rational – unless they were hallucinating. He made a mental note to check with a friend with the New Orleans Police Department to get the results of toxicology tests on Jamal and his two cohorts.

They'd have to have been stoned out of their minds to stand there and talk to a wall and then shoot it up – unless they really did see something, or someone. But what? Or who? Who did they think they saw? It's highly unlikely that three stoned men would somehow share the same hallucination. One of them said somebody looked like a guy on Magazine. Who *did? And why Magazine Street? The company had a store on Magazine and there'd been a clerk killed there in a robbery a year before, and these were the same three who were tried for that robbery-murder. There had to be a connection between this incident, the three dead men, and the Magazine Street robbery, but what was it? Could it be that one of them thought he saw someone who looked like the attendant who was killed on Magazine? Why would he show up in the Esplanade Street store over a year after being killed? And* how? *Why am I even* asking *this?*

He was still trying to put everything together when he pulled into his drive. For just a moment, he tried to remember details of the drive home and was surprised that he could recall nothing about the trip. *Damn! This crap is really getting to me.* Then it was back to the baffling matter of trying to sort out everything he'd heard tonight. His thought processes continued unchecked through his shower and later as he lay in his bed before sleep finally pushed the maddening thoughts from his mind, if only for a few hours. He began rehashing the information when he awakened the next morning.

The pieces of the puzzle were just as jumbled as he played with his cereal and drank his coffee and orange juice. Today, he would call his friend at the Central Evidence and Property Division to put in his request for the

86

toxicology test results and to get the name of the witnesses who saw Lenny Stevens and Deacon Watson just before they were killed. Then he would travel to the neighborhood to try to locate the witness.

There've got to be some answers that can tie all these dead people together.

The thought occurred to him as he shaved that he was going to great lengths to solve a mystery about people he didn't know and that in all reality, meant nothing to him.

Why am I even wasting my time on this?

He knew why, of course. What had started as a case of simple curiosity was now an obsession. Something very strange was taking place and he was now at a point where he had to know the answers, if for no other reason than to satisfy his own morbid curiosity. There was some unknown but common thread connecting all these deaths, he knew there was, and it wasn't just J. François. He needed to know. He had to. He wouldn't rest until he knew what was going on.

27

As was feared by those who had reason for such concern, Chet Voitier did not take losing well. He was supposed to have been protected by the enterprise. The trial was to have been a formality; an acquittal perhaps, but surely no worse than an involuntary manslaughter conviction with a token jail term or even a suspended sentence. Instead, he was headed for the Louisiana State Penitentiary at Angola just about an hour up the Mississippi River from Baton Rouge. Angola, its annual prison rodeo notwithstanding, is no picnic.

Chet still didn't know what had happened, why the trial had gone the way it had, except that J. François had performed nothing like he had in his first trial. That time, he dazzled the jury, danced circles around the prosecution – with the help of a friendly judge, of course, who invariably ruled in his favor on all motions. This time he'd been little more than a dancing clown, one whom even the judge could not help. Like all the lawyers and judges who came and went during the trial, Chet was at a loss to understand why everything had gone south. Unlike the lawyers and judges deeply involved in the enterprise, he was the only one going to prison.

Perhaps. Perhaps not.

The prosecution wanted to make a deal.

It was time to talk.

The situation was a paradox of sorts; any discussion with Chet about cooperating with authorities necessarily would have to include J. François as his legal counsel. It is forbidden for prosecutors to discuss any aspects of a legal proceeding, civil or criminal, with any party who is represented by legal counsel ex parte, that is, without including his attorney in the negotiations. To do otherwise would be to risk having any deal negated by the courts – and to have sanctions imposed on prosecutors. So, J. François was brought in to advise his client. His advice was straightforward, to the point, even urgent. This was not a time for mincing words. Too much was riding on this.

"Chet, you can't do this. You've gotta trust me."

"I did trust you and look what it got me."

88

Chet pushed his chair back from the table and wrinkled his nose at his attorney. "Damn, man, when's the last time you had a bath? You smell like soured milk."

"I've been going through a rough time, but never mind that now. Chet, you've gotta think this through," J François said, looking around the room as if he expected someone to suddenly burst in. "If you talk, you won't walk out of here alive. I can promise you that. That's not a threat; it's way outta my hands now. You gotta keep your mouth shut. I'm filing an appeal next week; it's going to be all right."

"I don't know, man. Things ain't the same now. You ain't the same. I'm heading to Angola and you and your lawyer and judge and crooked cop friends are gonna stay here and it's gonna be business as usual for you."

"Don't talk, Chet. I'm warning you."

"Yeah? Well, you need a strong dose of mouthwash to go with your bath."

J. François was sweating profusely now and each breath was a labored wheeze. He glared at his client for a full minute without speaking. Then, he grabbed his briefcase and started out of the room. He stopped at the door and turned back to Chet. "You're making a huge, huge mistake, my friend. Don't say I didn't warn you."

In his car, J. François could feel the noose tightening and there was nothing he could do about it. He needed a shower but most of all, he needed sleep. He took fresh cloths when he left his house the day before because he didn't intend to return any time soon. He found a hotel and checked in. He requested and got a corner room on an upper floor overlooking the French Quarter. Upon entering what would be his new home for at least the next few days – he didn't intend remaining in one place for very long – he peeked out the window to be sure he was not followed. Then he closed the curtains and locked the door. Only when he was satisfied that he was alone, did he strip off his clothes and step into the shower. The water felt wonderful as it peppered his face and cascaded down his filthy, flabby body, washing away the grime and the sweat. He watched in silent fascination as the water and soap bubbles disappeared in a circular motion into the drain and he felt as if he was watching what was left of his career and his life itself being pulled down into the abyss of the tiny whirlpool.

The water was steaming hot, even more so than the summer heat that baked the city outside his room and when he finally emerged from the shower, the entire bathroom was filled with a heavy fog and the mirror was coated with a thick film of condensed moisture. The scene was another perfect metaphor for the fog in his brain and the perception void that had enveloped him, blunting his thinking processes over the past several days.

Despite the overwhelming heat in the tiny bathroom, J. François felt an eerie cold tremor run through his grotesquely overweight body and he could feel

89

the thick black hair on his back standing on end, defying the sticky, heavy humidity.

28

"I've got tickets to see *The Producers* at the Saenger tomorrow night," Ashleigh said Thursday morning. "You free to go?" Matt loved Mel Brooks and he thought he needed a break. He'd heard good things about the play.

"Sure, I'd love to," he answered. I'll pick you up at six and we can eat dinner first and then catch the play. I've read some excellent reviews on it; it should be good."

Matt had been so involved in his quest to find answers the previous evening he forgot to call her so he did so when he finished his breakfast. She knew he was involved in some type of mission so she wasn't upset that he hadn't called. They had long since moved past that stage of their relationship. "What about lunch today?" she asked. "We could meet somewhere downtown if you have time."

"You got yourself a date," he answered. The agreed upon a small, hole-in-the-wall restaurant just off Canal Street near her work. Matt said he would call for her at her office and they could walk to lunch.

As soon as he hung up, he grabbed his keys and was out the door. There was work to be done. In his car, he called Rob Jenson, his friend at the police department. He told him about the six fatalities he was investigating. He then asked for assistance in identifying the witnesses who'd seen Lenny and Billy Boy. "I also need the results of the toxicology report on Jamal Alexander," Matt said. "Jamal was the driver of the car in which those three men were killed in Esplanade last week. If they took blood from the other two, I'd like to have those test results, too. Their names are D'Wayne Robinson and Theron Washington."

"I doubt they took blood from the other victims if investigators knew for sure they weren't driving," Jenson said. He'd worked in the department for a number of years and was familiar with procedure. "If there was a question of who was driving, they'd probably run tests on the others. I'll get you a copy of the accident report, too, just in case you need it. You need copies of the fatality reports on the other three?"

"Sure, that'd be great."

"You got it. I'll have 'em later this morning."

92

"I'm having lunch with Ashleigh downtown. I'll swing by right after that and pick them up," Matt said.

"See you then," Rob said.

Matt thanked him and disconnected the call. He stayed on I-610 as it split off to the left from I-10, forming a bypass that allows eastbound motorists to avoid the congestion of downtown New Orleans. It re-connects to I-10 several miles later on the eastern end of New Orleans and continues on to Mississippi, Alabama, and Florida. But Matt didn't stay on 610 long enough to hook up again with I-10. Instead, he exited onto City Park Avenue and made his way to one of several cemeteries that are located in that section of New Orleans.

He chose the cemetery where they'd found the body of Deacon Watson. He parked and walked around until he spotted a caretaker. He walked up to the man who was busy pulling weeds from around one of hundreds of above-ground vaults. His shirt was drenched with sweat in the hot June sun. The faded blue shirt was long-sleeved despite the heat and humidity.

The man didn't look up as Matt approached. He was accustomed to people visiting gravesites and had long ago lost interest in them or in the tourists who seemed to come through more out of morbid curiosity than out of respect for the dead. His main concern was nighttime visitors who periodically desecrated the graves, seeking skulls or other artifacts for satanic worship rituals, a practice that had been increasing in regularity at an alarming rate. He was genuinely frightened of those people, but because they generally raided the graves at night when he wasn't in the cemetery, he exhibited no outward sign of concern as Matt walked toward him. When he was six feet away, Matt stopped. "Excuse me, sir. I wonder if you could help me out."

Only then did the man look up. He appeared to be in his sixties and was small, almost frail. He had a gray moustache and long strands of gray hair fell from beneath a floppy brown hat he wore to protect himself from the unmerciful summer sun – the same reason he wore long-sleeved shirts. He looked up at Matt without speaking. He puffed at a pipe that was clenched between his teeth and wisps of smoke drifted upward and disappeared into the muggy air.

Matt waited for him to respond but when he didn't, he continued. "I'm trying to get some information on the man who was killed here last week."

Only then did the man remove the pipe that he now held in his right hand. His left hand still held a handful of weeds he'd just snatched from the parched earth. "I done talked to the police. What's your interest? You a lawyer or an insurance adjuster?"

"Well, as a matter of fact, I am an attorney, but I'm not here in that capacity. I just need a little information."

"You ain't suin' th' cemetery, are you?"

"No sir, on my word as a gentleman."

"Thought you said you was a *lawyer,*" the caretaker deadpanned.

93

Matt had to laugh at that. "Yes sir, that's right, but I'm not that kind of lawyer. I'm not here to sue anybody, I promise."

"What do you need to know?"

"For openers, I'd like to see where he was found."

"You *are* talkin' 'bout that pervert they found with his britches down, ain't you?"

"That's correct. Deason Watson."

"You know they called that freak Deacon?"

"Yeah, I know. Can you show me where they found him?"

"Actually, *I'm* th' one that found him. Had his britches down around his ankles, th' damned pervert. How'd he get a name like Deacon?"

As they walked, the old man introduced himself. "My name's Ben Price, what'd you say your name was?"

"I'm sorry," Matt said. "I don't think I introduced myself. I'm Matt Ramsey," he said, handing Ben one of his cards.

Ben studied the card for a moment. "Louisiana Supreme Court? Th' Louisiana Supreme Court interested in this guy?"

"No sir, this is something I'm pursuing on my own time. The court's got nothing to do with it."

"You know this weirdo?"

"No sir. I'm just conducting some research, kind of a hobby of mine."

"You got a strange hobby. You need to take up chess or dominoes. Well, here it is."

They were stopped in front of a grave marked *Denise Fleming*. Matt saw the name on the coping's marker and his double take was right out of a television sitcom. The only thing missing was a mouthful of water to spew out.

He'd read the newspaper clippings and the court trial records so often that he made the connection between Deacon and Denise in an instant. He felt almost as if he knew her. *Jesus, that's who Deacon was accused of raping and murdering. What the hell's going on here?* He was so engrossed in this newest bit of information that he almost didn't hear Ben Price as he continued his narration. "They didn't mention it in the paper, but somebody threw up right over there," he said, pointing to a spot about six feet from another crypt. Matt looked and could barely make out the faded blotch on the concrete.

"Threw up?"

"Yeah, vomited. I saw a pool of dried vomit on the concrete a few feet from the body and I noticed bits of vomit around his mouth and nose. I'm pretty sure it must've been him that threw up just before he died. Served him right, th' pervert."

Matt had not expected to find someone with such keen observational powers and he was thankful for his good fortune. Ben was right; nothing of the vomit was in the newspaper accounts of Deacon's death. *Maybe it'll be in the report that Rob's getting.*

But what intrigued him the most was that police had failed to notice the name of Denise Fleming on the grave marker where Deacon was killed. He knew there was no reason for authorities to make the connection unless the investigating officers also knew of the link between the two. He debated whether or not to tell police of what he'd found but thought better of it. *What would I tell them? There's no way they'd believe it was anything other than a coincidence. Hell,* I'm *not convinced it was anything else.*

Still, the unlikely discovery caused an unfamiliar sense of anxiety. *What had lured Deacon to the gravesite of the person he was accused of killing over a year before? Was it morbid curiosity or had it been something more sinister, more diabolical? And did that rendezvous lead to his death?*

He was still visibly shaken when he called at Ashleigh's office for lunch. She noticed that he seemed distracted. "What's wrong with you?" she asked over her grilled chicken salad. "You don't seem yourself today. Is anything wrong?"

He stopped and turned to her. "Ashleigh, I'm going to tell you what I've stumbled across and I don't want you to think I'm crazy, o.k.?"

"Sure. What's going on?" she asked, taking another bite of her salad.

He told her what he'd found as she continued eating. He spent so much time talking that he ate little of his meal. She didn't speak until he was finished.

"Know what I think?" she asked. She wasn't smiling or eating now.

"You *do* think I'm nuts, don't you?"

"Well, I do wonder what draws you to these kinds of stories. But no, I don't think you're crazy. I think you may be delving into areas that could be dangerous and I wish you'd take it a little more slowly. Please be careful."

"Delving into dangerous areas? What does that mean?"

"I'm not sure, but I don't believe in coincidences. You believe these cases might be related and I think you may be right. But we don't know *how* they're related and I'm afraid that might be where the danger is. That's the unknown in this equation and the unknown can be very unpredictable and very dangerous. That's what I mean by dangerous areas. Just please be careful, that's all I'm saying."

95

29

J. François slept late in his hotel room. It was the first real sleep he'd had in days and he'd showered the night before, so he was in decent shape. Fresh clothes almost restored him to the J. François of old. But he was still nervous, jumping at every sudden noise or unexpected movement. He had a good case of hives starting in his abdominal area that produced huge, red, ugly splotches and he kept scratching his stomach as he drove to his office where he checked his messages.

He found more than thirty messages on his desk, his e-mail, and his telephone voicemail. Almost all of them were from the same three criminal court judges in the courthouse. The messages were urgent, almost shrill, in their tone and they all demanded an immediate conference in chambers. Most of the messages were from Judge Charles Cheramie, the senior of the three, so J. François called him first – after locking the door to his office.

"Where the hell have you been?" demanded Judge Cheramie when he picked up.

"I got some issues going on in my home so I stayed at a hotel last night. I had my cell phone on, why didn't you call me on it?"

"Because I don't trust the goddamn things, that's why. I've seen too many stories about cell phone calls being intercepted up by third parties and we can't risk that. You need to get in here right away so we can talk."

J. François walked into Judge Cheramie's chambers forty-five minutes later. He found Judges Ray Sonnier and Lyle Bergen sitting across from Cheramie when he entered. Neither of the judges was smiling. He took considerable pride in being able to read the faces of potential jurors but now as he tried to decipher the mood of the room, he found it difficult, impossible even. *What the hell's going on here?*

"Come on in and sit down," Judge Cheramie said.

J. François found his way to a chair and eased his hefty frame into it. "What's up?" he asked, forcing a smile as if it might lift the somber mood.

"Your client's dead," Judge Sonnier said, looking directly into J. François's eyes.

J. François felt the blood drain from his face. "Dead? Which client?"

"Chet Voitier."

"No way! You gotta be kidding! What happened?"

"We're not quite sure. He was found hanging in his cell this morning. It happened sometime last night. But our question to you is did he talk first? We heard rumors that he was going to flip. Did you talk to him?"

"He hadn't talked when I left him yesterday. I advised him not to talk to prosecutors." He didn't tell them the details of his last meeting with Chet.

"Well," Judge Cheramie said, "unless he gave a sworn statement, anything else he might have said would be hearsay. Even a deposition wouldn't be as bad as any personal testimony he might have given. But you know, none of this would ever have come up if you hadn't screwed up his case the way you did. What the hell came over you?"

"I told you, I have some issues at home that just came up."

"These issues – did they make you wear the same clothes for three days and go without bathing and without sleep? Hell, J François, you're not married, so what issues could be that serious?"

"I'm not at liberty to divulge that information at this time, judge. I'm going to have to ask you to trust me that they are that serious."

"Serious enough that you had to move out of your house? J. François, you live alone. Is your house *haunted?*" asked Judge Bergen.

J. François didn't know if the judge was being facetious or if he was serious. He swallowed hard before answering. "I… I'm not sure."

"Not sure if your house is haunted?" bellowed Judge Sonnier. "J François, have you lost your mind? You actually believe your house might be haunted?" All three judges were laughing. But they were nervous laughs nonetheless.

"All I know is I saw something in my garage the other night that I can't explain, J François said. "I'm not sure who – or what – it was, but it was damned sure *something* and I'm not spending another night in that house."

Judge Cheramie wasn't laughing anymore. "Well, J François, we don't give a rat's ass about your poltergeist or whatever it is in your house. What we do care about are our careers and our good standing in the community. You better hope to God that your boy Chet didn't give any statements to anybody before his *suicide.*"

To J. François, it seemed Judge Cheramie placed a little too much emphasis on the word *suicide,* causing him to wonder if Chet's death indeed *was* indeed a suicide or if someone had been making sure he wouldn't testify. There were sheriff's deputies and jailers in his enterprise. He decided it might be best if he never knew the answer.

30

As promised, Rob had the reports ready for Matt when he came by the Central Evidence and Property Division on Broad Street. "Not a whole lot to see in these reports," he said when he handed them over. "I was wrong; they tested all three and all of 'em had traces of meth."

"Methadone?"

"Nope, methamphetamine, the latest drug of choice. In Thailand it's called yaba. On the streets of this country, it has several names: chicken feed, crink, crystal meth, hot ice, ozs, meth, peanut butter, to name just a few. But they only found traces, not enough to affect them. But when you first ingest it, it kicks ass."

"Tell me about it," Matt said.

"I know you've heard of meth labs," Rob said. "They're springing up all over the place, faster than law enforcement can keep up with 'em. They're easy to set up and just as easy to move if the heat gets too intense. You can't set up a meth lab just anywhere; the chemical odors give you away. You have to be out in the country where there're no neighbors. They're real popular with biker gangs. It can keep you going without sleep for days. The biggest tip-off is people buying an extraordinary amount of decongestants and antihistamines. They're the main ingredients in producing meth."

"So, you're telling me there wasn't enough meth in their system to account for them holding a conversation with a wall?"

"Not at the time they were killed. There were just small, almost insignificant traces. If they'd been tested several hours or maybe the day before, you might've had a different picture. They might've been talking to God."

"What the hell could they have been talking to in that store?"

"Or who?" Rob said.

"What?"

"No, who?"

"Right."

Matt took the reports that were in a large brown envelope. "Everything you asked for is in there," Rob said. "The accident report on those three and the individual incident reports on each of the others are all there."

98

"What about the reports on the murders of Rijah Mulaquah, the Sri Lankan, Denise Fleming, Chad Moran, and Steven Olsen?"

"Technically, they're supposed to be open files, still under investigation, since the acquittals of our friends here, and not available to the public. But I got you what I could. I hope it helps."

Matt thanked Rob and drove to a downtown parking lot and walked to the Café Du Monde on Decatur Street. He was only a few blocks from where Billy Boy Borque was kicked to death by the mule. He found a table and pulled his file out of the envelope. A Vietnamese waiter took his order for coffee and beignets while he read. There wasn't much in the report he didn't already know except for the name of the lone witness who'd seen Borque just before he went into his spasmodic fit and then ran onto Royal street into the path of the taxi. Thinking he would find the name of some long-gone tourist, he was surprised – and gratified – to learn that the witness was a bouncer at one of the Bourbon Street clubs who was taking a smoke break around the corner on Toulouse Street.

He stuffed the report back into the envelope, drank his coffee and finished his beignet. With the envelope under his arm, he walked down Toulouse to Bourbon and found the club. He half expected it to be closed in mid-afternoon, but again luck was on his side. The manager was behind the bar and a black man was mopping the floor. "We're not open yet," the manager said as he continued stacking glasses behind the bar in preparation for the night rush of tourist business.

"I'm not a customer," Matt said. "I'm looking for someone, I think he's one of your bouncers."

"Bouncers come and go. He in some kind of trouble?"

"No, no trouble, I just want to ask him some questions." He gave the manager one of his business cards.

The man looked at the card and put it into his shirt pocket. "You suin' somebody for something?"

Strange, Matt thought, how the first reaction to seeing an attorney's business card was to ask if someone was getting sued. *No wonder people hate lawyers.*

"No, no one's getting sued. I'm just following up on a police investigation from last week."

"All my guy did was to break up a fight between a couple of tourists and I tossed both of 'em. We don't want trouble here. That runs off business and I make my living from bringing in business, not running it away."

"This isn't about a fight or anything that happened in the club here. I'm looking for Fred Bishop."

"He'll be here in about a half-hour. I'll let him decide if he wants to talk to you or not. In the meantime, what're you drinking? It's on the house."

"Bud Light," Matt said. "Thanks." He picked a table where the cleanup man had already mopped and sat down where he could see the entrance. He

99

pulled out some more of the files that Rob had given him and started reading the report on Borque.

He wrote notes and sipped his beer as he read. He was almost finished with his beer when a large, muscular man who looked to be in his mid-twenties walked through the door. His head was shaven and he wore a diamond stud in his left ear lobe. A clean white tee shirt was stretched tight across his broad shoulders in its effort to cover the massive frame. A Fu Manchu mustache further enhanced a menacing appearance. He never noticed Matt in the corner as he exchanged greetings with the manager. He couldn't hear their conversation at the bar, but he could see them talking and the large man turned and looked in Matt's direction. The manager handed a pair of Bud Lights to the larger man who then walked over to Matt's table. He placed one of the bottles in front of Matt and held the other as he sat across from him.

"You looking for me?" Fred Bishop asked.

Again, Matt thrust a business card at the man. "Yes sir, I'd like to ask you some questions if you don't mind."

"I don't mind at all." He was smiling at Matt. "I'm Fred and you can ask me anything you like. I got nothing to hide unless there's a woman looking for me."

Matt laughed politely at Fred's attempt at humor. *Everyone's a comic.* "You're not going to ask me if I'm suing anyone?"

"Doesn't matter to me, long as you aren't suing me and I figure you wouldn't be talking to me if you were suing me. Isn't that unethical, or something?"

This guy knows his way around better than most.

"You're right. Besides, I'm not suing anyone. You were working last Saturday night, weren't you?"

"I work every Saturday night. It's our busiest night. Oh, this is about that freak that hauled ass down Toulouse Street and got kicked to death by the mule, isn't it?"

"That's right," Matt said, relieved that he'd found someone who wasn't reluctant to talk to him.

"Yeah, I was working. I've already talked to the police but what do you want me to tell you?"

"Just tell me what you saw."

"Well, that's easy enough. I go on break at 9:30 every night. Last Saturday was no different. I don't like to hang out on Bourbon because there's so much traffic and so many weirdoes. I see it all the time when I'm working. I want it a little quieter when I'm on break, so I always walk around the corner to Toulouse where there's less foot traffic. I can enjoy a quiet smoke there and still keep an eye on the crowd.

"I'd just seen this guy lookin' around like he was nervous or something. He headed down Toulouse just before my break. A few minutes later, I'm having a smoke and I looked to my right and saw him lunge out of a doorway and fall flat on his face. He was holding a knife and it fell out of his hand. He scrambled along the sidewalk, grabbed the knife and got back on his feet and took two or three steps away from me, towards Royal, and acted like he was grabbing someone from behind. He brought the knife across in front of him. If he'd been holding somebody, he'd have cut his throat. Instead, he damned near sliced his own throat open when he brought the knife toward him. I mean, he was acting like a damned crazy man. I was afraid he was gonna hurt himself so I took a few steps toward him. Then he ran three or four steps away from me and lunged again with the knife. He fell down again and this time he broke the knife blade.

"Then, as he got up, he took a couple of steps backward, toward me. He looked over his shoulder in my general direction. I don't know if he saw me or not, but then he ran out into the middle of Toulouse and toward Royal. That was the last I saw of him. I heard about an hour later that someone had been killed by a mule on Royal Street. I didn't know until the police came around that it was him.

"That's all you saw?"

"That's it."

"It sounds like he was trying to attack someone," Matt said.

"Looked like it, too," Fred Bishop said.

"Did you know that he'd been tried and acquitted of stabbing a Minnesota tourist to death on Toulouse Street just over a year ago?"

"No shit? This same guy?"

"Yes, the same guy."

"He killed a guy on Toulouse a year ago? *Stabbed* him?"

"That's right. At least he was indicted for it. He was tried and acquitted about two months ago."

"Holy shit. Man, it looked just like he was acting it out all over again. He looked just like he was trying to stab somebody that wasn't there."

Somebody that wasn't there.

The words reverberated in Matt's mind.

First Jamal, D'Wayne, and Theron were seen screaming at a wall, demanding that it open the cash drawer just before they riddled the wall with gunfire.

Then Deacon Watson gets killed mysteriously right in front of the grave of the woman he was accused of raping and murdering more than a year before.

Now, Fred the bouncer was saying he saw Billy Boy acting as though he were stabbing *somebody that wasn't there* – in the same location where he'd been accused of committing just such a robbery-murder within the same approximate time frame, only a year earlier.

This is getting just too weird. Who the hell is going to believe this?

101

He placed both hands on the table and mentally ran through the information he'd just heard from Fred. Finally, he stood and extended his hand to his host.

"Mr. Bishop, I really appreciate you taking the time to talk to me."

"Anytime, pal. Kinda strange, huh?"

"Very."

Matt thanked him again and walked back to his car in the commercial parking lot. He had another stop to make just off the northern end of Canal Street. He was looking for an old wino named Woodrow "Woody" Russo and it was about the right time of day.

31

J. François drove slowly past his house en route to the hotel where he was staying. Everything appeared normal, but he made the block just to be sure he wasn't followed. Satisfied, he edged up the driveway and into his garage. Just as before, he lowered the garage door with his remote control before exiting his vehicle. Holding his key in his hand, he approached the door to the kitchen as quickly as he could. He glanced back once more before disappearing into the house. Nothing. Relieved, he closed the door behind him and locked it before heading down the hallway to his bedroom.

He wasn't staying long; he only wanted to retrieve some clean suits, shirts, and underwear and some toiletries. Then it was back to the hotel where he felt safer with people around him. The last thing he wanted now was to be alone. The sightings of those four people, whoever they were, had him frightened out of his wits, but now the implied threat from the judges hovered over him like so many vultures waiting for him to die. He'd half expected to see a sheriff's department cruiser following him to his house. When that failed to materialize, however, he found it did little to calm his fears. He had no idea what he would do if someone did fall in behind him. He knew he wasn't going to outrun anyone in the Altima.

He peeked through the front window for any sign of a strange vehicle on his street. Seeing none, he made his way back into the garage with an armload of clothing. He threw the bundle onto the back seat and almost dove behind the wheel, shutting and locking the door as he did so. He looked around once more before hitting the remote and waited as the garage door started its upward journey. He was watching the door disappear in the top of his rear-view mirror when his heart almost stopped. His temples pounded as the blood raced through his veins at a dangerous pace. His skin became instantly clammy and cold.

He found himself staring at the translucent figures of four people, or beings, standing just outside the garage, immediately behind his vehicle. Even though he could make out the driveway and street behind them, he still could see the distinct images of a young woman, a small boy, a middle-aged man, and a small dark-skinned, foreign man. They were back.

104

Having already shifted into reverse and without a conscious thought, he gunned the engine, trying to stomp the accelerator through the floorboard. The sound of screaming rubber filled the garage as he plowed backwards in a frantic effort to run down the four uninvited visitors. He slammed on his brakes as he exited the garage and the car bounced and lurched at an angle across his front lawn and continued skidding almost to the edge of the street before stopping. The maneuver left deep ruts in the yard but he didn't care.

His breath was coming in short, pained gasps as he looked to see if he'd injured or killed any of them. Instead, he saw that the figures had not moved from their positions except that they now had turned to face him. *How'd I miss them!? Jesus, they were right behind me!* He felt his chest tighten as panic gripped him like a vise. He gunned the motor again and jerked the Altima into drive and he careened down the wide street, blowing through a stop sign just as a Kenner police patrol unit was approaching the intersection. The patrol car fell in behind him, lights flashing and siren whooping. J. François shot a look in his mirror and swore an oath. Then, he realized he was in a densely populated area with plenty of witnesses. He was actually relieved as he pulled into a convenience store parking lot and exited his vehicle.

"Keep your hands where they can be seen at all times," the officer said over his public-address system, prompting onlookers to attempt to see what dangerous criminal had been apprehended. J. François did as he was told, grateful to have real people around him – even if they were people he didn't know and even they were gawking at him.

"I need to see your license and vehicle registration," the officer said as he approached. "Do you know you were speeding and that you ran a stop sign?"

"I'm sorry, officer. I wasn't paying attention," J. François said. He thought about the .380 automatic inside his briefcase that lay on the front passenger seat.

The officer glanced at the name on the license and at J. François. "Are you J. François Berthelot, the attorney?"

"Yes, I am," said J. François. He thought he saw the glimmer of a smile flash across the officer's face.

"You live near here?"

"Yes, just two blocks from here."

"Why were you speeding and why did you run that stop sign?"

"I told you, I wasn't paying attention. My mind was on a trial I have coming up."

The officer got on his radio and called in J. François's license plate and driver's license numbers and waited. He was disappointed to learn there were no outstanding tickets or warrants for J. François, who was universally despised by law enforcement officers, even those assigned to traffic. "Is the address on your license correct?" he asked when he returned to J. François's vehicle, hopeful that

105

he might have yet another violation for which to cite the infamous criminal defense lawyer.

"Yes, I live at 1136, two blocks back that way, like I said."

"I'm going to have to cite you for speeding, running a stop sign, and reckless operation of a moving vehicle," the officer said.

"Aren't you being a little redundant with the last one?" J. François said with a slight trace of sarcasm in his voice.

"If you have a problem with the citations, you have the right to plead not guilty in traffic court." The officer fought hard to suppress a grin as he wrote the tickets.

J. François, in an ill-advised moment of cockiness, attempted to belittle the officer when he asked in his typically sarcastic manner, "Have you gotten your quota for today?"

But the officer was more than up to the challenge: "Two more today and I get a free toaster," he said without looking up from his ticket pad.

J. François, seething, considered taking the officer's name and badge number but thought better of it. *He'd probably love to tell all the other cops at roll call about how he pissed off J. François Berthelot.*

He wanted to tell the officer about the four apparitions he'd seen outside the cruiser, but he knew no one would ever believe him. It's never a good thing for an attorney to lose his credibility. Instead, he took the citation from the beaming officer, shoved it into his shirt pocket and returned to his vehicle.

"Have a nice day, sir," the traffic officer said.

"And you likewise, officer," J. François replied with all the pseudo courtesy he could muster. He squeezed his massive frame behind the wheel and pulled back into traffic, making sure to use his turn signal as he did so.

32

The extreme northern end of Canal Street and the bustling downtown stretch between the Mississippi River and I-10 might just as well be in two different worlds. The downtown stretch is always crowded with tourist traffic but the street changes its appearance radically on the north side of I-10 where it quickly deteriorates into an odd mixture of run-down, working-class residences and small businesses, many of them neighborhood bars. It seems to be an area of town forgotten by zoning laws. Matt began his search in one such tavern near the intersection of Canal and North Carrollton Avenue.

He started near where Lenny Stevens was killed. His plan was to hit every bar in the area by going up and down every street that ran parallel to Canal and then, if need be, to walk each street that crossed Canal. He would keep working in this pattern throughout the area until he was satisfied that he'd done everything possible to find Woody Russo, the last person to see Lenny alive. He figured he would have to return on Friday to continue his canvassing but once again, he got lucky.

The sixth neighborhood bar he entered was typical of others in the neighborhood. It was small, dark, with a row of vinyl-covered booths along one wall and a row of stools along a dingy bar. A juke box stood in the corner, but the clientele weren't here to hear the music. They wanted one thing: alcohol, be it beer, wine, gin, or cheap whiskey. Two filthy restrooms, one for each gender, were at the far end of the bar. The men's bathroom sink had rust stains that streaked down its interior from the iron in the tap water. The pipe joints and faucets were caked with green corrosion from years of neglect. The toilet was no better; it barely held any measurable quantity of water and it could only gurgle in protest when flushed with the loose handle. Matt knew all this because the filthy rest room was his first stop when he entered the bar, necessitated by his having purchased a beer at each of the previous five bars. He exited the rest room feeling dirtier than when he'd entered and then walked up to the bar and sat down on one of the stools. The bartender, who appeared to be every bit as old as the bar itself, hobbled over to Matt. "Welcome to Pop's. I ain't seen you in here before. What you drinkin'?"

108

Matt thought for a second. He'd had Bud Lights at the other five bars, but he now was deep in blue collar New Orleans. "Dixie," he said, ignoring advice from his college days about mixing brands. It was something about taste buds that he'd long forgotten.

Dixie, one of the South's last regional breweries still operating, is indigenous to New Orleans. It was a micro-brewery before they became fashionable. When the Dixie Brewery opened in the Crescent City in 1907, there were several breweries in New Orleans, including the Jackson Brewery, which made Jax Beer, and the Falstaff Brewery. The Jackson Brewery shut down in 1974 and Falstaff in 1978. Remnants of the old Falstaff Brewery still stand in the city's old brewery district just a few blocks from the Dixie Brewery.

Dixie, out of necessity, switched to non-alcoholic beverages during prohibition, but by 1934, it was again turning out its unique product that features a distinct juniper aftertaste as the result of its being aged in cypress barrels. Many New Orleans natives would never consider having a crawfish boil with any beer other than Dixie.

"Why don't you try the Dixie Blackened Voodoo?" the bartender said, already reaching for a bottle. Dixie, fighting its way out of a 1989 Chapter 11 bankruptcy, introduced the Blackened Voodoo Lager the following year and it became an immediate hit. It was so popular, it helped the brewery open up new markets and by 1992, Dixie had exited Chapter 11 and was profitable again.

"Why not?" Matt said, smiling at the bartender-turned-huckster. *This guy missed his calling; he should've been a vinyl siding salesman.*

"I'm Pops. Here ya go, a Dixie Blackened Voodoo," he said as he placed a chilled bottled and a frosted mug on the bar in front of Matt. "What brings you here?" There was only one other customer in the place, so the bartender, thankful to have someone to talk to, took the initiative of striking up a conversation.

"My name's Matt. I'm looking for somebody," he said, tilting the mug as he poured the Blackened Voodoo slowly to keep the beer from foaming over.

The beer was a dark reddish-brown, almost black, with a tan head. Matt noticed the head didn't last long, and he could detect the strong presence of hops and a sweet, malt-toasted aroma. He took a long, slow sip of the beer and noted that it reminded him of stout with a predominantly malt-like flavor with hints of caramel. He detected a nice fizzy carbonation that complimented the deep flavor. "This is pretty good," he said.

The bartender was pleased; he had made a new friend. He leaned on the bar and grinned at Matt. "Glad you like it. Who you lookin' for? He got a name?"

"Yep, his name's Woody Russo. Know him?"

"Yeah, I know him. What th' hell you want with Woody? He's never sober."

"I need to ask him some questions about a guy who was killed by some pit bulldogs."

109

"Oh, yeah. That happened right down the street. Woody still talks about it every night. He drives us crazy with his story. It's like he's obsessed with the blood and gore. He never changes a word; he remembers every detail."

"He comes in here?"

"Every night. Everyone likes Woody. He's got money, but the regulars here all buy him a few rounds every night anyway. Sometimes, when he's real drunk, he'll buy a round. If you're looking for him, he's over in the corner booth, next to the juke box."

Matt spun around on the stool and saw an old, grizzled man he took to be in his seventies sitting alone, nursing a drink, probably gin, Matt guessed – incorrectly, he would soon learn. He dropped a five on the bar. "Thanks, Pops. I appreciate the help."

He walked over to the booth and stood next to it a few seconds. "Mr. Russo?"

The old man looked up at Matt, trying to figure out who this strange man was who knew his name. "Yeah? Who're you? What do you want?"

He didn't sound too friendly. "My name's Matt Ramsey. I'd like to ask you a few questions about Lenny Stevens."

"Okay, I can do that. What you want to know?"

Matt almost volunteered that he was an attorney so Woody could ask him if he was suing somebody. But Woody just didn't really seem to care. Matt decided people like Woody and Fred Bishop, who had nothing to lose, weren't concerned about being sued. He seemed to enjoy telling the story, according to Pops, and he was now ready to tell it again to a total stranger. Woody was none too discriminating.

"Can I buy you a drink?" Matt asked before Woody settled into his narrative.

"Sure, how 'bout some whiskey?"

Matt waved at Pops and the bartender responded by pouring a shot without waiting for the order. He knew from experience what Woody was drinking.

He might have money, but why waste it when someone else was buying?

"I seen this guy you talking about. They tell me his name was Lenny. Anyway, I seen him circle the block a couple times in this old van. Then, about the third time around the block, he stops and parks and gets out."

Pops placed the whiskey on the table in front of Woody and another Blackened Voodoo in front of Matt and Matt gave him a ten. "Keep the change," he said.

"Thanks, Matt," Pops said, picking up the bill and heading back behind the bar.

"Where was I?" Woody asked.

"Lenny had just parked his van," Matt said.

110

"Oh, yeah. He parks his van and gets out on the passenger side next to the curb and opens the sliding door on that side. Then he acts like he's grabbing somebody, but if that's what it was, it wasn't no regular-size person."

"What do you mean?" Matt asked.

"He bent way down, like he was grabbing a kid or a small animal, but there wasn't no kid or animal nowhere around. There wasn't nobody. He done that twice and then he just kinda dives onto the sidewalk. He just lays there a second or two before he gets up and stumbles backwards a few steps. Then he whirls around back toward his van and hollers out, 'What are you? Stay away from me!'"

"'Stay away from me'?"

"'Stay away' or 'get away,' I'm not quite sure about that part. A car passed on the cross street behind me and I couldn't hear him so clear. Anyway, it was then that this guy, Lenny, turned and just jumped over that fence with them dogs and they just tore into him. I ain't never seen nothing like what I seen that night. I was walkin' toward him all along and when I seen th' dogs, I ran up there as fast as I could, which ain't too fast at my age. By th' time I got to the fence, he was already dead. They just ripped him open like he was a paper sack full of meat.

"I thought he had th' D.T.'s, the way he was acting before he jumped in the yard," Woody said. "I've seen drunks with th' D.T.'s before and he was actin' just like 'em. You shoulda seen him. He was just grabbing at thin air, like he was grabbing at someone or something small, but there wasn't nobody or nothin' there," he said, repeating himself.

Grabbing at someone small, but there wasn't nobody there. First Fred the bouncer and now Woody the wino. Matt felt sweaty and when he looked, there were goose bumps on his arms. "Did you know Lenny was a pedophile?" he asked Woody.

"A what?"

"A pedophile, a child snatcher. He had been arrested and tried for abducting and killing a nine-year-old boy last year."

"No kidding! Really? He killed a kid?"

"Well, he was charged with it, but he was acquitted."

"I'll be damned. I knew it looked like he was trying to grab somebody short."

Woody's pretty lucid for a wino.

Matt's eyes dropped to the Dixie bottle that he was turning in his hand and his gaze locked on the *Blackened Voodoo* label. *Voodoo. Black magic. Ghosts.*

111

33

For reasons he didn't fully understand, J. François felt a strange sense of calm he hadn't experienced in almost a week. He had a trial to prepare for in Edgard in St. John the Baptist Parish, just upriver from New Orleans and he was looking forward to getting to his office so he could get back to work.

There were eight messages from the judges on his cell phone when he finally remembered to turn it on. His receptionist, Sandy, handed him a dozen more when he strode into his office. All the messages were the same; the judges wanted to meet with him immediately to discuss matters of grave importance. He tossed the written messages that Sandy had given him into the waste basket and deleted the cell phone voice mails. He was in no mood to talk to the judges just yet. *Those idiots will talk themselves silly if I humor 'em. If they gotta talk to somebody, let 'em talk to each other.*

He smiled to himself as he settled in behind his desk, wondering as he did so if either of the three Orleans Parish judges had enough clout to get his tickets fixed in neighboring Jefferson Parish. He promised himself a long vacation to clear his mind when the trial in Edgard was over. Until then he had no intention of talking to the judges. *I'll call 'em later. I've got too much to do to be worrying about those dumbasses.*

J. François made up his mind – again – that he would not go back into his house for the foreseeable future. He took up permanent residence in the hotel where he hoped there was sufficient activity to discourage any unwanted visitors. He picked up enough clothes on his last trip home to keep him presentable in the courtrooms where he practiced. He never dined alone for fear the four might drop in on him.

He may have lost his last case and the three judges might be nervous and upset with him, but he still had work to do. He had a big case involving the brutal murder of a seventy-eight-year-old Edgard priest by a young punk named Deke Morgan who wanted to take the priest's car. There had been no reason to kill him; he could easily have taken the vehicle without so much as a protest. At his advanced age, Father Theo Jeansonne didn't even drive anymore. His housekeeper ran all his errands for him. He was planning to give the car, a seven- year-old Oldsmobile with just 11,000 miles on it, to one of his great-nephews.

112

Deke, stoned on crack cocaine, was unable to comprehend the meaning of moderation or compassion. He pummeled the old man mercilessly with an aluminum baseball bat far beyond the point necessary to kill him. The entire community of Edgard was enraged and the good people of St. John the Baptist Parish wanted blood. They weren't going to settle for anything less than the death penalty for this lowlife. The district attorney, of course, was doing all the political posturing expected of him.

It was just the kind of case to bring out the best in J. François and he was eager to get back in the swing of things. He was determined he wouldn't blow this case the way he had that of Chet Voitier. The upcoming trial was just what he needed.

34

Matt kept turning the bottle in his hand, reading the words *Blackened Voodoo* over and again. It was his fifth beer, so his thinking wasn't as clear as it might have been. Woody, on his fourth shot of whiskey, courtesy of Matt, was just as fuzzy with his thinking. He stared at Matt, wondering in turn why he kept looking at his beer bottle.

"You know anything about voodoo?" Matt asked, staring at the amber bottle.

"Huh?"

"Voodoo, black magic, paranormal events. You know anything about that?"

"Nah, just enough to know it's all a bunch of hooey. Why?"

"No reason, just wondering," Matt answered, pocketing one of the beer bottles.

Woody watched, a bit curious. "You collect beer bottles, or somethin'?"

"No, not really. I just want to follow up on something. Mr. Russo, I really appreciate your help. Can I buy you another drink before I leave?"

"Anytime, son. And hell yes, you can always buy me a drink."

Matt made his way to the bar where he ordered another whiskey for Woody and settled up with Pops. He left a ten-dollar tip on the bar and drove home. Pops, elated over the rare tips, told Matt he was welcome back any time, any time at all.

He seldom read his e-mails and he spent even less time on the internet. It was something he had learned he could live without. But now he was eager to conduct his own research to determine if he could get to the root of the series of violent deaths in New Orleans. He was glad he had a fast access modem instead of the slower dial up.

He logged on and did a Google search on *voodoo*. He got more than five million hits, many of those duplicates, but he needed only a few to get an idea about what he was looking for. He was surprised to learn that voodoo was not indigenous to New Orleans as he had always assumed. An offshoot of one of the world's oldest religions, its name can be traced to an African word for *spirit* and it

114

is believed to have started on that continent long before the time of Christ, as far back as 10,000 years ago. The practice of present-day voodoo was introduced to the New World in Haiti during the colonization of Hispaniola by the Europeans. African slaves brought to the Caribbean nation were baptized into the Catholic Church but because Christianity was so disorganized during the early part of the Nineteenth Century, the slaves generally adhered to their native faith, but practiced it in secret.

When the Haitian government officially sanctioned voodoo as a religion, it cleared the way for its practitioners to perform baptisms and marriages. Slaves spread the practice throughout the southern U.S. Many thousands of Haitians continue to practice voodoo today. Matt was also surprised to learn that voodoo is considered to be a practical religious faith and that it plays a vital role in family and community. It teaches that a person's ancestors are a part of the spirit world. He read the last part again: *a person's ancestors are part of the spirit world.* He printed that page and read further.

He downloaded several web pages on voodoo before he moved on to searches on ghosts, poltergeists, haunting, black magic, and paranormal activities.

35

"Matt, you can't be serious!" Ashleigh held her glass of wine suspended between the table and her mouth, incredulous at what he was telling her and yet wanting to laugh at the same time. But she knew he wasn't joking.

They were in Brennan's on Royal Street for dinner before heading to the Saenger to catch the performance of *The Producers*. Matt chose the restaurant for reasons other than its fine food. He wanted to delve even further into the mysterious deaths and he was explaining his evolving theory to her. "I'm dead serious," he said. "Ashleigh, there've been six violent deaths in the past week and every one of the dead men had been tried and acquitted for murders. They were all represented by the same lawyer."

"I know. You told me that before but couldn't that just be a coincidence?"

"I thought you didn't believe in coincidences."

She looked away for a moment and then turned back to Matt. "I don't," she said.

"Well, if it makes you feel any better, I thought the same thing, but there's a common thread besides the same attorney. In the first one, three men tried to hold up a convenience store. The store clerk was in the back and he said they were talking to someone who wasn't there, someone they apparently saw behind the counter. They died a few minutes later in a car wreck. Then, another one was killed in front of the grave of the same woman he was accused of raping and killing. There were no witnesses to that but two men saw the other two just before they died and they seemed to be flailing away and grabbing at something
– or someone – that wasn't there. They all said the same thing: there was *someone who was not there.*"

"That just doesn't make any sense."

"Yes, it does," he said, measuring his words with care now. "New Orleans has the reputation as the most haunted city in the U.S. I spent all day on the internet and I found out that some of the best-known businesses in New Orleans have histories of ghosts and hauntings. The Hotel Monteleone, just up the street, has documented at least five ghosts. A paranormal research team has identified four ghosts in the LePavillon Hotel. Muriel's Restaurant has reported

117

three known ghosts. The Le Petit Theatre has three ghosts. There're others." Matt went down the list, clicking off names of places that he'd memorized: The Cabildo, Arnaud's Restaurant, Antoine's Restaurant, Court of Two Sisters, the Omni Royal Orleans Hotel, the Andrew Jackson Hotel, the Bourbon Orleans Hotel, and Lafitte Guest House.

"And then there's Brennan's," he said, looking across the table at Ashleigh.

"What do you mean? Here, in Brennan's? Right here?"

"Yep, three ghosts right here, all former employees. One of 'em was a slave named Percy. He was a caretaker here. Another one was a Dutch chef named Paul Blange. When he died, they put a restaurant menu and a knife and fork on his chest. The third ghost was the wine master. His name was Herman Funk and he made the restaurant's wine cellar among the best in the world."

"Three ghosts in Brennan's?" Ashleigh repeated. "Jesus." Without moving her head, her eyes darted left and right and then up, toward the ceiling. "That gives me the willies. What're they doing here? Do they scare customers?"

"I don't know but that's what I've been trying to tell you. There's a lot of history in this town to back up the ghost theory. A lot of it is just hype to pump up the tourist trade, but I believe there's something connecting these deaths besides their lawyer."

"Anything else?"

"Yeah, there is. You ever hear of Marie Laveau?"

"Sure, who hasn't?"

"What about Delphine Lalaurie?"

"Who?"

"Delphine Lalaurie." Matt told Ashleigh the story of the Lalauries and their torture chamber. As he laid out that story, he explained the connection between Delphine Lalaurie and Marie Laveau. He told her that Madame Lalaurie was a contemporary of Marie Laveau and was a regular customer of the voodoo princess/hairdresser. He wove his story carefully, leaving out none of the grisly details about the Lalauries and when he finished, Ashleigh rubbed her palms across her forearms briskly as if she were cold.

"God, Matt, why're you telling me this? I'm trying to eat a steak. I'm glad I don't like them rare. That's the goriest, sickest story I've ever heard."

"Now, here's a weird twist: The Hotel Monteleone, the naked slave woman, the Lalaurie house, and Brennan's are all on Royal Street. No real significance, but interesting, I thought. I'm sure that's just a coincidence."

"*What* naked slave woman?"

"I'm sorry. I forgot to tell you about her. There was a slave woman who was having a relationship with her master and wanted to marry him. He told her if she'd spend a night naked on the rooftop of his home on Royal, he'd marry her. Apparently, he had some kind of warped sense of humor. Anyway, one night while he played chess with a friend she climbed out onto his roof naked, but

118

because it was on a cold December night, she died from exposure. Since then, two ghosts have been seen at the house. One is the nude ghost of the slave woman and the other is a man seated by a window, playing chess all alone." He leaned back in his chair and took a deep breath when he finished telling the story.

"God, I've got chill bumps," Ashleigh said. "These are good stories to tell out in the woods some dark night around a campfire, like the one about the hook in the car door handle, but not over dinner in a restaurant like this. Besides, what do all those stories have to do with these scum bags getting killed?"

"I think plenty," he said, leaning forward again. "That's why I want to try a little experiment to test my theory." His elbows were on the table, his face only inches from Ashleigh's. He waited for her to ask and she didn't disappoint him.

"What kind of experiment?

Invoking every New Orleans ghost story in his repertoire, Matt outlined his plan as Ashleigh picked over her food, her appetite now long gone. She never interrupted him but stared wide-eyed at Matt as he laid out every detail of his scheme. Even when he was finished, she still could only stare at him in rapt disbelief. Until now, she never once in her life seriously considered the possibility that ghosts could inhabit her planet.

36

"I'd like for the two of us to pay another visit to Rose tomorrow afternoon so we can make a proposal to her," Matt said to Ashleigh.

They were walking north along Canal Street, on their way to the theater. The downtown New Orleans area was bustling with activity, as always. It was nothing like the Mardi Gras season of course, or Jazz Fest at the Fairgrounds for that matter, but it was New Orleans and the city attracts tourists from all over the world. They weaved their way in and out of the crowd and Matt tried to imagine how a salmon must feel when it swims upstream to spawn. Their conversation wasn't as intimate as it had been in Brennan's because they each had to concentrate on not running into other pedestrians.

"Grandma Rose? Why? What kind of proposal?"

"I want to set up some video surveillance monitors so we can find out what's happening in her house."

Ashleigh stopped in her tracks and turned to Matt. "You want to do *what?*"

"I want to set up some monitoring equipment. She said she wished we lived in Covington because she thought we'd find out what's going on. Well, we don't live there but this could be the next best thing and maybe we can try to find out what's happening."

"What are you going to tell her? Are you going to tell her you're doing this because you got curious about six low-life murderers getting killed? Matt, you can't do that; it would scare her to death."

"No, I'm not gonna tell her that. I'm not *that* insensitive."

"But that *is* why you're doing it, isn't it?"

"Well, I'd be lying if I didn't say it had occurred to me, especially after what I found out about ghosts in New Orleans. If there are ghosts here, there's no reason there can't be at least one in Covington. That's where the Lalauries ran to, remember?

Ashleigh flashed a mischievous smile and looked up and down Canal. People continued walking past in each direction, none of them paying any attention to the couple engaged in conversation on the sidewalk. "Is that what you believe, that there're ghosts in New Orleans who're killing your guys?" The question did catch the ear of one middle-aged black man and he turned and looked at them, but continued walking, looking back at them occasionally until other pedestrians obliterated his view.

"I'm not sure what I'm saying. Something's or someone's certainly killing them or causing them to kill themselves. And something's also going on in Rose's home."

"That's what she says. But the whole family thinks she's just chronically absent-minded. Nobody takes her seriously. She's just getting old."

"But what if she isn't, Ashleigh? What if we found out there really is paranormal activity? That would vindicate her and don't we owe her the chance to find out?"

"What if we do set up video equipment and it turns out that she's the one who's hiding her stuff from herself and she's just forgetting where she put it? What would that do to her self-esteem, her frame of mind? She'd be shattered, devastated."

"I don't know. Why don't you be the one to ask her before we set it up? Make sure she considers all the options and understands before we do it."

"That's the only way I would agree to this. I just don't want to hurt her. I couldn't do that to her. What time do you want to leave?"

"As early as possible, but first I have to go to Best Buy and get the equipment. Call her first to let her know we're coming."

They were walking past an elderly black man who was playing a beat up old trumpet. The horn didn't even have a flanged bell on the end of it, just a shorter-than-normal tube with a jagged end. The music was that of a rank amateur, but he was an upbeat street performer and on the ground at his feet was a battered brown hat turned upside down. In it were a few dollar bills and several coins. The neck of a wine bottle protruded from his jacket pocket. Cheap wine, Matt noted absently.

He made eye contact with Matt and lowered the horn from his lips. His face split into what otherwise would have been a toothless grin but for a single upper tooth.

"What happened to the bell of your horn?" Matt asked. "It's not beveled."

"I cut it off."

"Looks like you chewed it off."

"What's your lady's name?" the old man asked, changing the subject from the battered old horn he'd retrieved from a trash bin to the couple standing before him.

"Ashleigh."

"Assley. That's a mighty sweet name and that's a mighty sweet-lookin' lady you got. She look *awful* sweet. I got a song jus' fo' her. He raised the horn to his mouth and started belting out *Ain't She Sweet* as best his limited talents permitted. Matt grinned back at him and dropped a five-dollar bill in his hat and

122

the two started walking again. The old man called after him. "You believe in Jesus?"

Matt turned back to him. "Sure," he said.

"What yo' name?

"Matt."

"Matt, I'm Jesse. I'm gon' pray for you and yo' lady Assley. You be sho and pray for Jesse, you hear?"

"I will, Jesse. I sure will," Matt answered.

"We both will, Jesse," Ashleigh said. "Thanks so much for the nice song."

"That was a *sweet* song, jus' fo' a sweet lady."

They had walked only a few feet when they heard him call out to another man. "What's yo' lady's name, Mister? She looks *awful* sweet. I got a special song fo' her...."

The sounds of the old trumpet faded behind them as they laughed and continued on toward the Saenger. The heavy summer air soon forced them to slow their pace or risk having their clothes soaked with perspiration by the time they got to the theater.

They both enjoyed *The Producers*, but they were each preoccupied – for different reasons – with the next day's visit to Rose. Ashleigh was burdened with the fear that somehow the experiment might serve the wrong purpose, might put the old lady in a bad light, even humiliate her. Matt was excited at the possibilities that he might be on the cusp of some startling new discovery that paranormal researchers had pursued for years on end but which he had somehow managed to stumble upon by accident. They laughed in all the right places during the play, but their minds were far away from the Saenger.

Elsewhere in the theater, Judge Charles Cheramie sat beside his wife. She was enjoying herself, oblivious to his inattentiveness just as she was oblivious to anything that did not enhance her social standing in some manner. He felt the walls closing in on him and fellow judges Lyle Bergen and Ray Sonnier, along with half a dozen New Orleans police officers and sheriff's deputies, judges from neighboring parishes, and a host of esteemed members of the New Orleans bar. He was not in a laughing mood. Too much was at stake for his attention to be held by some inane diversion like a Mel Brooks play. His jaw was clenched tight and he was grinding his teeth, something he did when under extreme pressure. The entire side of his face ached but he was unaware of that, too.

123

J. François had better get his act together or the enterprise will be forced to take drastic measures it found distasteful. It wasn't something any of them looked forward to doing and it wasn't something either of them would do themselves. If it became necessary to initiate such a desperate plan, it would have to be delegated to someone else. That, of course, meant one more person would be a party to the inner operations of the enterprise, another undesirable prospect. As a contingency, the three judges were privately screening candidates to carry out whatever assignment might become necessary against whomever stood in the way of the enterprise's operation and their freedom.

Judge Cheramie was still thinking about J. François and measures that might be taken to remove any unfortunate person who might pose a potential threat. *Why are we even thinking about this? This is madness.* Business is business, however, and there were times when drastic measures were necessary to preserve the status quo.

He could barely recall any of the scenes from *The Producers* as he stood with the audience for the actors' curtain calls. He applauded and for all any observer might think, he had enjoyed the comedy as much as anyone else in the audience. Even the man sitting behind him during the play, the man working an undercover detail and who had never taken his eyes from the back of Cheramie's head, had no hint of the judge's mental distractions as he, too, stood and applauded the actors as they bowed to the audience. *He's one cool bastard, I'll give him that.*

Slowly, Judge Cheramie and his wife made their way out of the crowded Saenger. As they spilled into the spacious foyer, the crowd thinned out with some of the patrons exiting through the side doors. Judge Cheramie spotted J. François and their eyes locked as the lawyer walked directly toward the judge. "Judge, how good to see you tonight," J. François said. "Did you enjoy the play?" He thrust his right hand toward Cheramie and the two shook hands like old friends, except when Cheramie withdrew, he had an envelope in the palm of his hand. It was all pre-arranged and Judge Cheramie had just added five thousand dollars to his retirement account, compliments of CajunAmerica Bail Bonds.

Only a few yards away, a federal agent held a concealed camera that recorded the entire brief encounter and the exchange.

124

37

Matt had no idea what he was doing when he walked into the Best Buy on Veterans Memorial Boulevard. For all he knew about electronics, technology left him behind when the switch was made from beta to VHS tapes. He knew nothing about digital advances in video and audio recording. He belonged to the generation that communicated with two tin cans and a length of string. Lucky for him, there was a knowledgeable sales representative ready and willing to relieve him of his money.

By the time he left the store, his Visa card was some three thousand dollars heavier but he was thankful that he was able to hold the amount down to that; it could have been over three times that, the none too sympathetic sales rep had told him.

"I'm looking for some equipment to set up a surveillance system," he said when Frank walked up to him. Matt knew his name was Frank because his badge said so.

"You want motion sensors?" "Is that necessary?" Matt asked.

"Not unless you want to sit down and review video frame by frame for hours on end."

"No, I don't think I want to do that. How does a motion sensitive system work?"

"Just the way the name implies," Frank replied. "It isn't activated until there's motion in the area being monitored by the camera. Do you know how many cameras you're going to need?"

"What's the maximum?"

"Oh, we can go as high as sixteen, but most of our customers start out with four mini cams. They're easy to install and they can be connected to a hide server that you can put in a closet or a cabinet, out of sight. The server feeds the signal to a board that in turn stores the video to a hard drive that you can access." The sales rep may as well have been speaking in a foreign language as far as Matt was concerned. And in a sense, he was.

125

"What kind of price are we talking about here?" Matt asked for the first time, suddenly aware that what the sales rep was talking about sounded more expensive by the minute. He was right, of course.

"You can easily get as high as ten thousand dollars, depending on how sophisticated you want your surveillance system to be. What will you use it for?"

"I want to install it in an elderly lady's home up in Covington. She's been having trouble with intruders. Will I be able to retrieve the video from my home in Metairie?"

"Sure, you can use any computer with internet access, and in real time, too."

"What kind of time?"

"Real time. That means you can monitor the video live, as it occurs."

"What if I'm out for a while, can I come back and review what I missed?"

"Certainly. No problem. And you can watch all four cameras on the screen at once. You asked about the price. I believe with four cameras, you can keep your cost down to somewhere in the neighborhood of three thousand dollars."

"That's a pretty expensive neighborhood," Matt said as he realized he was about to bust his budget by a hundred percent. He'd figured fifteen hundred, tops.

Well, at least when this is over, I can install the system in my home and maybe get a break on my homeowner's insurance.

He wished he'd brought Ashleigh with him. *Hell, her* job *is with computers. She'd know exactly what we need for this. At least maybe she can help me set it up.*

Frank had assumed, incorrectly, that Matt would want the black and white surveillance equipment, but he opted instead for the more expensive color cameras, which kicked the final cost to a little over thirty-three hundred dollars before sales tax.

His car loaded with his suitcase and the new computer equipment, he next swung by Ashleigh's house to pick her up and the two set out across the Pontchartrain Causeway for Covington and Rose's house. Ashleigh said little as she read through the installation instructions on the drive across the lake. "Well, it looks easy enough," she finally said.

She had already called Rose and tossed the idea out to her and Rose had grabbed at the opportunity. She was certain it would expose the identity of the intruder. "I guess that means I won't be able to run around the house naked now," she joked.

Matt winced when Ashleigh passed Rose's comment on to him. "I hope she wouldn't anyway," he said. "That's a visual I didn't need."

"Well, you know Grandma Rose is kind of spunky, so don't you go setting up one of the cameras in her bedroom or her bathroom," Ashleigh said.

126

She took Matt's hand in hers as they rode. "I hope we're doing the right thing," she said.

"I really believe we are," he said. "I was thinking of installing one camera each in the living room, the dining room, the kitchen, and the back porch. The kitchen is where everything seems to take place. But I'll need to position one on the back porch so I can monitor the freezer-safe, since that's where she keeps her valuables. Depending on how this goes, I may add two or maybe even four more later for better angles. I may even use one camera for both the living room and dining room and put two in the kitchen."

38

J. François was beginning to experience mood swings. His enthusiasm over the upcoming trial on one day turned dark the next, giving way to new anxieties and deep funks that were occurring with greater frequency. The emotional lows were usually the result of some rumor leaked to him from courthouse employees. He wasn't too stupid to know that the judges would have him or anyone else killed if the enterprise began falling apart. Falling apart, he knew, meant his own personal and professional downfall. A nervous breakdown now would almost certainly be equivalent to a death sentence – his.

He spun around in his overstuffed desk chair to his computer keyboard and logged on. He typed for about twenty minutes, printed two copies of the document and signed both. He stuffed one in an envelope and sealed it. He saved it to a thumb drive and created a new document. This one was a letter to his own attorney telling him the sealed envelope was to be opened should he die under mysterious or violent circumstances. There were other instructions, as well. He signed it and folded it once, placing it and the already sealed envelope into another, larger envelope onto which he affixed an address label to his attorney. Finally, he folded the second copy of the original document, sealed it in an envelope, and locked it in his floor safe. He considered it his insurance policy.

39

Rose took a few minutes to get all the dead bolts unlocked but once she had the door open, she greeted Matt and Ashleigh with her accustomed enthusiasm and affection. "So, I'm going to be on TV?" she asked after giving each of them a gentle hug.

"Hi, Grandma," Ashleigh said.

"Hi, Rose, Matt said. "Not exactly television; you're going to be on my computer screen. But it's almost the same thing."

"You better watch your man, Ashleigh. If he watches me for long, I might just be taking him away from you." She was laughing and her eyes had their ever-present twinkle. Watching the older woman, Matt decided where Ashleigh got her laughing eyes.

"Well, just you try. I'd have to fight you for him," Ashleigh said.

When she returned from depositing the suitcase in the front bedroom, Ashleigh took Rose by both her wrinkled, gnarled hands. "Grandma, I have to ask you something and I want you to think carefully before you give me your answer."

"What is it dear?"

"Well, you know we're setting up the video cameras to try to solve the disappearances of your things. And the cameras are going to record anything that goes on here. They'll be documenting everything that happens."

"Yes, I know. That's why we're doing it, to catch whoever's taking my things."

"Right, right. It's just that…."

"Just what dear?" Rose looked puzzled.

"Well, I'm not saying they're going to do this, but what if the cameras show us that you're hiding the stuff yourself and then just forgetting where you put it?"

Rose stared up at Ashleigh as if her granddaughter had inexplicably lost her grip on reality. "Then I'd just know somebody tampered with the video."

Ashleigh looked at Matt who was still holding an armload of video surveillance equipment. "Okay," he said, "enough chit chat. Let's get started hooking this stuff up."

131

Matt and Ashleigh started working that afternoon while Rose busied herself in the kitchen cooking spaghetti and meatballs and whipping up one of her delicious banana puddings. It had become her specialty when the two visited because Matt loved her banana pudding so much, especially the meringue. Ninety minutes went by before their first break. Sweat was pouring into his eyes, making it difficult for him to focus as they labored with the camera mounts in Rose's stuffy home. They had the living room camera installed when they heard her call out to them from the kitchen.

"Ashleigh, Mitch, supper's ready."

"Man, was I ever ready to hear that," Matt said.

Ashleigh looked down from the stepladder where she had been running coaxial cable to the hide server they had placed on a shelf in a small closet. She giggled at Rose's insistence on calling Matt by the wrong name. "Then let's be quick about it, Mitch. There's still a lot of work to be done."

40

Judge Cheramie had the files of Jamal Alexander, D'Wayne Robinson, and Theron Washington spread out all over the top of his huge oak desk. The files of Deacon Watson, Lenny Stevens and Billy Boy Borque were piled on a nearby credenza. He had already combed through them once and now was trying to glean something from the final three that might tell him how all six men were connected and why someone – he still didn't know who – was so interested in the same files. As an attorney and judge, he considered himself skilled at being able to scan a legal document and find obscure statements and references in, say, a deposition, that might provide him with valuable insight. All lawyers do that, some better than others and that's why those can command higher fees. Charles Cheramie took a lot of pride in his uncanny ability to pick up any legal document and find some obscure nuance that might give him an edge – something that might have been overlooked by an opposing attorney.

Now, though, he was stumped. The only connecting link between the six men, the same link that any moron would find obvious, was the fact that each one had been represented by the same defense attorney, J. François Berthelot. Convinced he had missed some subtle point, he plowed into the three remaining files, determined to solve the mystery of the missing connection. He took a huge swallow of lukewarm coffee and grimaced. He hated coffee – bourbon was his preference – but he needed to stay alert and sober. He was beginning to entertain thoughts that J. François might even be behind the killings. He needed more coffee.

Judge Cheramie thought for a moment about calling in judges Lyle Bergen and Ray Sonnier to assist him but thought better of it. *They're already too nervous to be of any use. They'd just get in the way and ask a thousand stupid questions.* He pulled his notes to him and read then for the twentieth time. Jamal, D'Wayne, and Theron were the only blacks; their victim had been Sri Lankan. Deacon had killed a woman who only recently had moved back to New Orleans from Lake Charles but that attack occurred in another part of town, far from the Magazine Street convenience store. *No connection there.* Chad Moran was a nine-year-old boy who had been abducted, raped and killed by Lenny. He had been grabbed from a sidewalk in front of his home in a blue collar residential

133

area of town. That happened in still another section of the city. Finally, there was Steven Olsen, the tourist from Minneapolis who was robbed and stabbed to death by Billy Boy in the French Quarter, only half a block from hundreds of tourists.

Judge Cheramie read the notes again and again, trying to pull something from them. Nothing. No pattern, no connection other than J. François. The deaths of Deacon, Lenny, and Billy Boy had occurred in close proximity to the areas in which they had killed their victims and had it not been for Jamal, D'Wayne, and Theron having been killed on Esplanade instead of near the Magazine Street store, Cheramie might have taken notice. But the pattern had been broken at the outset with those three almost as if there had been some deliberate effort to deflect attention from any connection that might exist between the bizarre string of violent deaths. It was a hell of a way to spend a Saturday.

41

"You want to come in and monitor Rose for a few minutes?" Matt asked as they pulled into his drive in Metairie Sunday evening. They had just returned from Rose's.

"Yeah," Ashleigh said. "I'd like to see what we have after all the work we did this weekend. Besides, I have to go to the bathroom."

It took a few minutes to configure the software so that all four camera images could be displayed on the screen at once. Matt played around with the program some, alternating between full-screen single images and quarter-screen shots from all four cameras simultaneously. They laughed when they saw Rose look up directly into one of the cameras. She was moving her lips, talking, obviously under the mistaken assumption that there also was audio. "I wonder what's she's saying," Ashleigh said.

"Probably wondering who stole the microphone."

"That's not funny, Matt," Ashleigh admonished him, giving his arm a gentle shove. "You see anything yet?"

"Nope. We're not likely to while she's in the room with one of the cameras."

"What about the other rooms?" she asked.

"Well, the cameras are all motion activated. We won't see anything unless there's movement in the room. See, three of the screens are blank. We only see Rose."

"That's spooky."

They watched a little longer and then Matt got up and poured each of them some orange juice. "I'm going to run to the criminal clerk of court's office again tomorrow at noon to try and take another look at a couple of those files," he finally said. "I must have missed something the first time. You want to meet me there?"

"Sure, I'd like to see some of those records," she said. "I think they'd be interesting."

"Not really. It's all actually pretty boring, but I just want to be sure I haven't missed anything. Another set of eyes might help, though."

135

Bored already at watching Rose moving about in her home, activating first one camera and then another, Ashleigh said, "I guess I'd better be getting home to shower and get to bed. I'll see you tomorrow. What time do you want to meet?"

"I'll be there at twelve. The clerk's archives are on the ground floor and on the north end of the courthouse. You'll have to enter from the outside through a garage door and then it'll be the first door to the left. It's a small, crowded room."

They walked to her car together. She opened the door and turned to kiss him goodnight. "I'll pick up a couple of Whoppers on the say so I may be a few minutes late," she said. Matt closed her door as she started the engine. He watched her as she drove away and then went inside to prepare for his shower.

On his computer monitor, unseen to him, a pale, watery thin, indefinable image floated across the screen. The kitchen camera recorded the refrigerator door as it slowly swung open. The form, whatever it was, carried a quart of milk through the air to the sink and poured it down the drain. Matt wouldn't see all that until much later.

42

Matt unwrapped the sandwich he'd brought from home and shoved it into his mouth as he climbed into to the taxi. "Criminal court house, 2700 block of Tulane," he managed to mumble through a mouthful of his lunch. He checked his briefcase to be sure he had a pad and ball point pens.

A one-hour lunch break wouldn't give him much time, so he decided he'd start with Deacon Watson's case first. For some reason he couldn't explain, that was the one that intrigued him the most. Perhaps it was because there appeared to be no witnesses to his death or maybe it was because Deacon died at the gravesite of the woman he was accused of raping and murdering. *Why would he return to her grave like that?* He told himself that there might be something in the trial record that might explain why he was at Denise Fleming's gravesite. In his heart, however, he knew better; the police investigation never even made the connection between his death and where he was found. He knew he was on a quixotic quest, but he had to try.

The employee in the clerk of court's file room eyed Matt with suspicion when he shoved Deacon's file across the counter to him but Matt didn't notice. "Thanks," he said, taking the file and placing it on a cluttered table nearby. He pulled out a chair, sat down, and began leafing through the file. Then he remembered that Ashleigh was supposed to bring hamburgers. *Damn! I wish I hadn't eaten that sandwich now. She's gonna be mad if she brings me a Whopper and I don't eat it.* He glanced around but didn't see her anywhere. He did, however, notice when the employee looked back over his shoulder at him as he disappeared into an adjacent room filled with more dusty files. Matt heard a door close from somewhere in the back but attached no significance to the brief and otherwise inconsequential event.

He was engrossed in the file five minutes later when the door to the garage opened and two men walked up to his table, standing next to him without speaking for several seconds. Matt sensed their presence and looked up at the two, mostly out of curiosity. "Yes?" he said. "Can I help you?"

"Can we see some identification?" said one of the men, short, middle-aged, overweight, but muscular. Matt took in the thick neck and heavy jowls that rippled upward along the sides of his face and his cheeks, creating the appearance of pressure that seemed to almost squeeze his eyes shut. He had closely-cropped hair that might have passed for a flat top if he'd had enough hair on top of his head to support the concept.

The man was a good twenty years older than Matt and at least four inches shorter but still he felt intimidated by the older man's menacing demeanor. He hadn't even looked at the other man yet. "Identification?" he repeated, rising to his feet. "I'm sorry, who did you say you were?" Suddenly, he recognized the man as the same one he'd bumped into on his way out the last time he was here. He may have been fat, but he was quick, so quick, in fact that he shoved Matt back into his chair before he even had a chance to react. "Hey!" Matt yelled. "What're you doing? Who are you?" He thought he caught the glimpse of a gun under the man's coat when he was pushed down.

The second man spoke for the first time. "Orleans Parish Sheriff's Office. I'm Deputy Barnes and this is Detective Gilbert Arceneaux." Matt turned his gaze to the second man, Deputy Barnes and saw that he was holding his shield for him to see. Matt read the man's name: Gene Barnes. He was taller, younger, and leaner than his partner, but Matt could see the bulging muscles under his khaki shirt. The shirt was part of his deputy uniform, a dress code that Matt guessed wasn't enforced on detectives since Arceneaux was wearing slacks and a hopelessly out of style plaid sports coat. Barnes was also armed and made no effort to conceal his weapon. "I believe Detective Arceneaux asked for your identification," he said in a quiet but authoritative voice.

"Is there a particular reason that you require my identification? This is a public building and I'm a member of the public here to examine public rec--"

He never got to finish his sentence. Barnes slammed a huge fist into his midsection and Matt crumpled to the floor. Attorneys who were in the records room to examine files of their own scrambled to exit the premises and to forever thereafter deny, if asked, that they'd seen anything. Employees behind the counter did likewise, disappearing like rats into the rows of criminal records, out of sight and uninvolved.

Barnes and Arceneaux hauled Matt to his feet even as he struggled to suck air back into his lungs. It took him several long and painful attempts to regain the otherwise natural ability to breathe. "Now, about that identification," Arceneaux said.

Matt could only nod as he reached for his wallet and pulled out his driver's license. It didn't occur to him to show them his Supreme Court employee badge.

"Okay, Mr. Matthew Ramsey, we're gonna walk out of here real quiet like and go around front, walk up the steps, get on the elevator, and go upstairs. You don't want to make a scene, now do you?" Matt shook his head and the three, with him in the middle, walked out the door and into the dank garage. There was a coroner's white hearse parked in the entrance to the garage, but Matt didn't see a body inside. An attendant concentrated on cleaning the vehicle.

138

Arceneaux shoved him into the hot, bright sunshine and led him around to the front of the courthouse. For the first time, as he turned back toward Arceneaux, Matt noticed how grimy the depressing building at the corner of Broad and Tulane really was. The two-story sandstone building had not been sand blasted in years, probably decades, and the sooty black exterior stood in ugly contrast to the nearby district attorney's building and the traffic courthouse, themselves nothing to boast about.

Ashleigh had just parked her car in the parking lot across from the New Orleans Police Department's bicycle storage unit situated behind the criminal courthouse and was walking past a building that shared two occupants, the Night Court Lounge and a bail bond office. She was already looking at the white hearse parked in the garage door when she saw the three men exit the building. She thought she caught a quick movement by one of the men. It was a subtle move, but obvious enough to her that it appeared that the man had pushed another who stumbled slightly. She froze in mid-step. The man had his head down but looked back when he was shoved and when he turned back, he looked directly at her. It was Matt. Before either of them could react, he was directed around to the front of the courthouse.

Instantly realizing something was not right, she threw the bag with the Whoppers and drinks onto the sidewalk and started after the three men as they walked away. They were almost at the courthouse entrance by the time she reached the base of the front steps so she had to almost sprint up the steps to close the distance. Once inside, she blinked twice to adjust her eyes to the change in lighting. She threw her purse and keys into the plastic tray and placed it on the conveyor belt that would take it past the X-Ray machine as she walked through the metal detector. Luck was on her side when no alarm sounded and she quickly gathered her belongings as she scanned the first floor in search of the men. She saw them just as they entered an elevator and the door closed behind them. Besides the first floor, the courthouse has a basement with a parking garage and several offices, including a jury pool room, and a second floor, where the courtrooms are located. Ashleigh had to make a decision and she hoped it would be the right one. She walked as deliberately as her desperation would allow to a spiral staircase and started up to the second floor, praying she was guessing correctly.

She stopped when she heard the elevator door open, hoping her pounding heartbeat wouldn't give her away. She didn't move again until she heard men's voices and multiple footsteps moving away from her position on the stairway. *Thank God they turned right and not left.* The loud echo of their footsteps on the marble floor as they walked down the arched corridor reminded her to slip her shoes off so that her own footsteps wouldn't be heard by the men, whoever they were. Leaving her shoes on the second step, she crept into the corridor and moved to a nearby column. She flattened her body against the wall as she concealed herself behind the column. Slowly, she reached into her purse,

139

removed a compact, and opened it. She extended the mirror far enough past the edge of the column to see the men as they walked, holding Matt's arms between them. They stopped at a doorway and both men turned back and looked in her direction. Unable to see the small mirror and satisfied that no one was watching, Arceneaux opened the door and shoved Matt inside. The last sound she heard before they disappeared inside was one of the men saying, "Call Judge Cheramie."

Ashleigh waited a few minutes more before moving and was soon glad she did. She heard another door open and shut from nearer her vantage point. The sound of the closing door echoed in the hallway as she quickly re-opened the compact and thrust the mirror around the column just in time to see a smaller man scurrying down the hall to the door of the room that Matt and the two men entered earlier. She watched as he knocked once on the door. When it opened, he, like the other two men, looked from side to side, and then entered. When the door closed behind him, Ashleigh ventured out and started toward the door. As she approached it, she saw that it was a door to a courtroom. She observed another staircase in the middle of the corridor that led to the first floor. She eased past the door to position herself closer to that stairwell because of its closer proximity to the room where she was sure Matt was being held against his will by the other three men. As she walked past that door, she could hear muted voices but she forced herself to keep walking until she came to another column that she could hide behind in reasonable safety.

Just then she heard a shout. "God damn it, I want some answers! Who do you work for and why're you looking at those files?" When there was no immediate response, she heard a sound that could only be a fist striking flesh, followed by crashing furniture, probably a chair. She could hear Matt groaning and trying to say something but obviously he was in a lot of pain. She heard the door open but she couldn't get her compact out in time to see Arceneaux stick his head out but she could hear him speak from only a few feet away. "Keep it down in here," he said as he looked up and down the hallway. "We don't want nobody to hear us."

"Everybody's at lunch," said a voice that she took to be that of the third man. The door to the room closed and Ashleigh could still hear muffled but clearly excited voices coming from the room as she eased away from the safety of the column and moved toward the staircase. The maneuver took precious seconds, but she had no choice; she had to be sure no one heard her. She prayed silently that no one would come out of the room and she didn't dare to take a breath until she was halfway down the stairs to the first floor. But for the fact that Matt was still up there, she might have breathed more easily once she was safely outside. She knew he was still being held in that room and probably being beaten to a pulp, and for what reason she had no idea.

Back in the sizzling New Orleans sunshine, she sat down on a bus stop bench and tried to collect her thoughts. She knew she couldn't go back into the

140

courthouse for help; that was where the danger was. *Think, damn it, think! You've got to do something, find someone, but who?* Her heart pounded and her mind raced as the traffic noise, pedestrian chatter, and the endless motions of both whirled about her, making her dizzy.

Then it hit her. *Justice Gravois! Of course!* She jumped up from the bench and ran into the street, forcing a taxi to screech to a halt to avoid hitting her. "Jesus, lady!" the irate driver yelled. "You trying to get yourself killed, for Christ sake?"

Ignoring the driver, she flung open a rear door and reached into her purse, withdrawing a handful of twenties, she didn't know how many, nor did it matter to her. "Take this, all of it," she said to the startled passengers, a couple in town on their honeymoon for all she knew – or cared. "Just let me have this cab and you can get another one. It's an emergency or I wouldn't ask, okay?"

"Well, gee," said the man, "I'm not sure about this...."

"Get out of the damned cab! Don't you understand the word *emergency? Life or death?*" Ashleigh was screaming and the couple tumbled out of the taxi.

"We have our luggage in the trunk," the man said, almost afraid to speak.

"Get it out," she said to the driver. "I'll triple your fare."

"Quadruple it and you got a deal," said the cabbie, sensing a rare opportunity.

She didn't quibble. "You got it, you greedy bastard," she replied, scrambling into the back seat. "State Supreme Court building as quick as you can get me there. It's on Loyola, in the 300 block I think." For the first time, she noticed she was not wearing shoes. She'd left them on the spiral staircase. *Jesus! What'll Justice Gravois think?*

"I know where the Supreme Court building is, lady," the driver answered. "I do this for a living, y'know." The taxi was already pulling into traffic, leaving the bewildered couple behind, their luggage piled on the sidewalk around them, but one hundred sixty dollars richer. Pedestrians, momentarily curious at the spate of activity that played out in their midst, were already turning away as they resumed their daily routines.

Ashleigh was oblivious to it all. The only thing that mattered at the moment was getting help for Matt. *What were they doing to him? And why? What did they want?* Then she remembered why he had gone to the clerk's office. *The ghost stories! Those men up there aren't ghosts but they've got to be connected somehow to those men who were killed. Oh, God, they know Matt's looking at the records. They might kill him.*

"Please drive faster! I know a Supreme Court justice who'll fix your ticket!"

141

43

The intense pain in his mid-section told Matt in no uncertain terms that one or more of his ribs were broken. The blinding stabs of pain prohibited him from taking a normal breath. His ears were ringing and he was bleeding from his nose and mouth and his left eye was already swollen shut. He could still see the three men with his one good eye. The latest arrival looked to be in his mid-fifties and appeared to be distinguished enough. Even in his semi-conscious state, he knew the third man was no cop. His gray hair was neatly combed and his clothing was more expensive than that of the other two. He wasn't one to dirty his hands on one such as Matt. He was there to learn what he could; the others were the enforcers and so far, Matt would have to give them high marks on the performance of their duties.

When he swallowed he tasted blood. He focused as well as he could on the older man. He looked familiar. *I've seen him somewhere, but where? He looks like a professional; a doctor, maybe. Attorney? Or no.... Wait! A judge! That's it! Arceneaux said call Judge Cheramie, Charles Cheramie! Damn, what's he doing here?*

Now the older man was talking and Matt strained to hear him over the ringing in his ears. "We only want to know why you are so interested in Deason Watson," he said, walking across the room until he stood in front of Matt. "And why were you looking at the files on Lenny Stevens, William Borque, Jamal Alexander, D'Wayne Robinson, and Theron Washington last week? What's your interest in those cases?"

Matt did his best to sit up but when an involuntary groan escaped his throat, he slumped back in his chair. "I told you already," he mumbled. "I was exercising my right as a citizen to examine a public record. I was curious why they were all acquitted."

The older man, the man who Matt was now convinced was Judge Cheramie, bent down low, the palms of his hands resting on his knees. "These weren't the only men to be acquitted of crimes but they were all killed last week. Is that why you were curious?"

"I wouldn't know about that," Matt lied. "They were killed? How"

143

"We think you already know how. We want to know why you're so interested. You didn't just happen to pick those files at random. Do you think we're stupid?"

Matt wanted to answer but he knew better. He was in enough pain already.

Judge Cheramie stood up and looked around the room. He motioned for the other two to join him and they adjourned to a far corner. Matt could hear them talking but couldn't understand what they were saying. It gave him time to think and his first thoughts were of Ashleigh. *What happened to her? Where'd she go? God, she was cool the way she handled herself, by not giving herself away.* His thoughts were interrupted when the men returned and Judge Cheramie was again standing in front of him. "We're going to get you cleaned up and place you in a holding cell until you decide to talk."

"Am I being charged with anything?" Matt asked. "Don't I get a phone call? Aren't you violating a few of my rights here?"

"No, no, and yes," Cheramie said. "But we can't concern ourselves with that right now. You've got bigger problems."

44

Judge Gravois hurdled forward in his chair as if zapped by electric current. "They did *what?*" he said to Ashleigh. His pale blue eyes were open wide in a combination of incredulity and outrage.

Ashleigh sat across from him. "They have Matt in the criminal district courthouse and they're beating the hell out of him," she repeated.

"Who is 'they'? And why?"

"Two men. Three, actually," she said, "but the third doesn't look like a thug. The other two do. One was wearing a uniform, a sheriff's deputy, I think. The third one was a judge. Someone called him Judge Cheramie. They took him into a courtroom on the second floor. I listened outside the door while they were beating him."

Judge Gravois had heard enough. Without another word, he picked up the telephone and punched in a number. From across the desk, Ashleigh could hear someone answer. "This is Judge Gravois. Have a trooper meet me in the lobby in two minutes." He hung up the phone and started for the door. "Let's go," he said to Ashleigh.

The justice didn't wait for the elevator but chose the stairs instead. As he took the steps two at a time, Ashleigh, labored to keep up in her bare feet and marveled at the physical stamina of the man, whom she took to be at least in his sixties.

"Can you go in without a warrant? she panted."

"If there's probable cause," Judge Gravois said without looking back.

They burst through the door on the first floor and the justice spotted a state trooper in the foyer. "Let's go! You drive!"

Without a word, the trooper sprinted to catch up with the pair and led them to his unit. "Where to, sir?"

"Criminal District Court at Broad and Tulane."

Judge Gravois jumped into the front seat of the state police patrol car and Ashleigh climbed into the back. They rode in silence for nearly a block before Judge Gravois spoke. "Ashleigh, what's Matt's home address?"

Ashleigh gave him the address and the Supreme Court justice turned to the trooper. "Get some men over to that address and instruct them to allow no

145

one on the premises, and I mean *no one*. I don't care if they have a search warrant; have your men instructed that they're acting on authority of the Louisiana Supreme Court and any other warrants, writs, or court orders they might receive are automatically countermanded."

The trooper relayed the information by radio to a skeptical dispatcher. Only when he explained who his passenger was, did the order get the desired action and two troopers were dispatched to Matt's home. Judge Gravois turned around to face Ashleigh. "I don't know what they want out of Matt, but whatever it is, if they want it badly enough to abduct him and beat him, they probably want it badly enough to break into his home."

Ashleigh thought about his computer and the monitors in Rose's home.

Even with lights flashing and sirens wailing, the frightening task of negotiating traffic through the narrow New Orleans streets proved arduous.

45

The cuts and the bruised swellings weren't going anywhere for a while, no matter how diligently Deputy Barnes sponged Matt's battered face with a wet cloth to wipe away the blood. *Damn, I shouldn't have hit 'em in the face. The body, always the body; that doesn't show.* Detective Gilbert (pronounced Jo'bare) Arceneaux was sipping coffee and reading the sports section of the *Times-Picayune*, paying little attention to his partner's futile efforts to make Matt presentable. Though it hurt every time the deputy touched his face, Matt was too exhausted and sore to resist. In addition to broken ribs, his upper lip was split and his nose was probably broken. A tooth felt loose. His entire face was puffy.

His body gave an involuntary jerk when the door burst open, again sending pain shooting through his ribcage. "State police, no one move!" someone shouted. Matt tried to focus with his right eye and saw a gun being pointed in his direction. *Now what?*

Gilbert Arceneaux lumbered to his feet. For a split second he considered reaching for his gun but thought better of it when he saw the uniformed state trooper aiming his own weapon right at him. "Keep your hands where I can see them," the trooper demanded. Another state police officer followed him into the room, his weapon drawn.

"Sir, I need you to drop whatever you're holding and put your hands up," the first trooper said to Deputy Barnes. Both Arceneaux and Barnes did as they were told and the trooper took their weapons and looked around the room. "Secure," he shouted to someone in the hallway. He turned to Matt. "Are you okay, sir?" Matt could only stare at him with his one good eye. He turned his head when the door opened again as Judge Gravois walked into the room, followed by Ashleigh who ran straight to him. She was already crying. "My God, what'd they do to you?" she sobbed. She tried to caress his face but drew back when he winced. He wanted to say he was okay, but no words would come from his mouth.

"Where's Judge Cheramie?" demanded Judge Gravois of Arceneaux. When Arceneaux didn't respond, Gravois's fury erupted and he was in Arceneaux's face in a flash. "You listen to me you piece of garbage. There's nothing lower than a bad cop and I will personally see to it that you get an early

147

retirement at best and hopefully the Louisiana State Penitentiary, and I can promise you that Judge Cheramie is not going to be able to help you out of this one. Now I'm going to ask you again, where is he?"

"He went back to his office," Arceneaux said.

"Just so you know," Judge Gravois said to Arceneaux, "my name is Thomas Gravois and I am a justice of the Louisiana Supreme Court. The man you just beat to a pulp happens to be my law clerk and you'd better have a very good reason for your actions." He watched as Arceneaux blanched at that bit of news. The detective groped for his chair and plopped down in it, staring straight ahead, saying nothing. "Get these vermin out of here," Judge Gravois said to one of the troopers. "Book them on kidnapping, extortion, illegal arrest, assault, illegal parking, and whatever else you can think of. And someone get Matt here to an emergency room right away."

At that, Judge Gravois started toward Judge Cheramie's chambers. Turning to the trooper who had driven him, he said, "we have one more stop to make."

46

Judges' chambers in the Orleans Parish Criminal District Court are right off the courtrooms, behind and to the side of the judicial benches.

"May I help you?" the receptionist asked, looking up into Justice Gravois's angry face. Their sudden, unannounced entrance had startled her.

"We're here to see Judge Cheramie," he said without introducing himself.

"I'm sorry, sir, but he's due in court in a few minutes."

"This won't wait. Is he in chambers?" Gravois asked, moving past her desk and toward Cheramie's office.

"Sir, you can't go in there without an appointment!"

"I'm Supreme Court Justice Thomas Gravois and this man, as you can plainly see, is a state trooper and I believe we can." With those few words, he opened the door and he and the state trooper walked into the judge's office.

"Who the hell are you?" demanded Judge Cheramie, apparently unimpressed at the presence of the state trooper.

"Judge Cheramie, my name is Thomas Gravois of the Louisiana Supreme Court" he said for the third time within the past few minutes. "You just abducted my law clerk downstairs and beat him half to death right down the hall. Your deputies are already on their way to jail. And as you should know, on recommendation of the Judiciary Commission, the Louisiana Supreme Court may censure, suspend, remove from office, or involuntarily retire a judge for any willful misconduct relating to his official duty, willful and persistent failure to perform his duty, persistent and public conduct prejudicial to the administration of justice that brings the judicial office into disrepute, and conduct while in office which would constitute a felony, or conviction of a felony.

It was as if he were quoting verbatim from the powers and procedures of the Louisiana Supreme Court's Judiciary Commission, which he was.

"You, sir, have brought your judicial office into disrepute by committing a breach of ethics in personally participating in the questioning of a suspect, although I'm still a little hazy as to what Mr. Ramsey was suspected of doing. I'm not certain yet as to whether or not a felony has been committed but I intend

149

to find out and if there has, you will be indicted, tried and, I hope, convicted and sent to jail for a very long time.

"I'm telling you all this to say that I am personally going to see to it that the Judiciary Commission recommends your permanent removal from the bench and I hope I am the justice who will have the privilege to sign the papers. In the meantime, I am ordering that you be suspended without pay pending a full investigation of what has happened here today."

He had continued his verbal barrage uninterrupted and by the time he finished, Judge Cheramie was trembling but he never uttered a word in response. Judge Gravois finally said to his driver, "would you be so kind as to take Judge Cheramie into custody on the same charges as the other two, and then find out where they took my law clerk and drive me there?"

47

The two state troopers had no idea why they had been sent to Matt's Metairie home but they knew it must be important if a Supreme Court justice was involved. So, they were on higher alert than usual when the Orleans Parish deputies showed up. They were escorted by Jefferson Parish deputies because of the jurisdictional issue. When a warrant is issued for a jurisdiction outside the domicile of the issuing authority, the domicile jurisdiction, in this case the Jefferson Parish Sheriff's Office, issues its own search warrant on the basis of probable cause and accompanies the Orleans Parish officers. The deputies from both parishes exited their cars and exchanged curious glances when they saw the state troopers parked in the driveway.

"We have a warrant to search these premises," said one of the Orleans deputies before the troopers could ask.

"I'm sorry sir, but no one has authorization to be on this property," said one of the troopers, Lieutenant Aubrey Johnson. 'I'm going to have to ask you to stand down."

A Jefferson Parish deputy tensed for just a moment and then stepped forward, extending a sheet of paper. "This is a warrant that gives us authority to enter and search the premises," he said. "It's signed by Judge Charles Cheramie of the Orleans Criminal Court."

"Our verbal orders are from Louisiana State Supreme Court Justice Thomas Gravois and I'm afraid my judge trumps your judge," Lieutenant Johnson said.

The Jefferson deputy stopped in mid-step and then slowly pulled his warrant back. Looking at his counterpart from Orleans Parish, he said, "I've never encountered this situation before. I think you'd better call for instructions."

The Orleans deputy retreated to his vehicle and got on his radio. He talked for a moment and then waited. "They're checking with Judge Cheramie's office," he explained to no one in particular. When he returned he offered his apologies to the state police officers and the Jefferson Parish deputies. "We're sorry to have bothered you, gentlemen. It seems that Judge Cheramie has been relieved of his duties, so I guess that means our warrant is void, so our business here is over."

151

Without another word, the Orleans Parish deputies returned to their squad car and pulled away, leaving the two state troopers and the Jefferson Parish deputies staring at each other. Neither of the four had ever been involved in any activity in which a sitting judge was removed from office and neither had ever acted on direct orders of a State Supreme Court justice. They didn't know what to say or do in a situation as unprecedented as the one in which they now found themselves. Finally, one of the Jefferson deputies spoke. "Well, I guess we'll stand down, too."

Inside, Matt's computer was still busy monitoring and storing some extraordinary activity in Rose's home. Besides the container of milk, the motion-activated cameras recorded other items as they levitated across rooms and into cabinets and drawers. The items would be missed by Rose, of course, but she wouldn't bother even telling her children since none of them believed her anyway. There was only one person in whom she knew she could confide anymore: Ashleigh. *She and Mitch would soon get to the bottom of this and then she would know who was entering her house uninvited.*

48

"If you wanted the afternoon off, all you had to do was ask."

Matt tried but was in no condition to laugh at Judge Gravois's little joke. The justice found Matt in his room at Tulane Medical Center and now that he had time to look at him closely, he saw just how bad his law clerk really looked. He was already sedated and every action or word was met by a delayed reaction. Ashleigh stood beside his bed holding a glass of orange juice. She periodically inserted the straw between his lips and he took delicate sips, grimacing if the acidic juice found its way into a cut on his lips.

She nodded when Justice Gravois motioned for her to join him in the hallway outside Matt's room. "Excuse me, Matt, I'll be right back. Here's the call button in case you need a nurse. I'll be right outside." Matt tried to answer but again was unable to respond. The sedative was working and he was on the fast track to a deep sleep.

She and the justice walked together out the door, past the armed state trooper stationed in the hallway, and down to the end of the corridor where they stood next to a window and watched the traffic outside for a few moments. Ashleigh was the first to speak. "Judge Gravois, they might've killed Matt if you hadn't done what you did. Thank you so much."

The justice appeared much smaller than he had less than two hours before, Ashleigh thought. His pensiveness made her uneasy as she waited for him to reply. Finally, he did. "Ashleigh, we got very lucky this time. Whatever is going on over at criminal district court goes a lot deeper than either of us knows, including, I'm sure, Matt. I don't know what Matt was doing that got him beat to hell and back like that, but I'm sure it doesn't start or end with Judge Cheramie."

'What are you saying?" Ashleigh said, confused now.

"I'm saying that I'm afraid Matt might still be in some sort of ongoing danger. Until we can sort out what's going on, I don't where the danger is. I can't begin to fathom who else might be involved but if they tried once, they'll probably try again and next time we might not be there to help him."

"Oh dear God," Ashleigh whispered.

153

"Until we can find out what's going on, Matt's going to require armed protection twenty-four-seven and we're going to have to get him someplace where no one will know him and he'll be safe."

Tears were rolling down Ashleigh's cheeks as her mind raced. She thought for a moment, considering her options. She was hesitant to reveal the exact nature of Matt's investigation to Gravois for fear he'd think Matt was deranged and that the justice might even fire him. Finally, her fears for his safety and well-being got the better of her, winning out over her concern for his credibility with his boss. "Let's go down to the cafeteria for some coffee," she said. "We need to talk."

49

Justice Gravois was a short, stocky man with close-cropped gray hair and a deep tan, the product of his favorite pastime of deep sea fishing. He was accustomed to giving orders and having them carried out, as evidenced by events that had taken place over the past couple of hours and the way state police had responded to his directives. Now, though, he just sat and listened without interrupting as Ashleigh laid out the whole story.

When she finished, he leaned back in his chair and crossed his arms across his chest as he stared down at the floor for a full minute without speaking. "Ashleigh, that's a helluva story," he finally said, standing and walking over to refill his coffee cup. He returned to her table to find her sitting with her hands in her lap, looking around the cafeteria, wondering if she'd done the right thing telling him.

"Now here's the way I see it," he said when he rejoined her at the table. "Ghosts or no ghosts, Matt's spooked somebody, if you'll forgive the bad pun. I'm not even going to address the paranormal aspects of what's going on. I want the two of us to look at the practical side of things here. Whatever Matt has been investigating, he upset some people in very high positions, including a criminal court judge. I've never in my entire career witnessed any situation in which a judge participated in the questioning of a suspect. A judge, by definition, must remain above the fray. He must be totally and completely impartial. To do otherwise would be to irreparably prejudice a case, even if that case is ultimately tried before a completely different judge."

Justice Gravois took a long sip of coffee while Ashleigh continued to listen. "The presence of those two sheriff's deputies and the fact that they were beating Matt and questioning him in a courtroom instead of a police interrogation room also disturbs me a great deal," he said. "It mocks the very sanctity of a court of law. But the bottom line right now is we don't know what's going on or where this is leading. We don't know who's involved or what they may be involved in. There're just too many unanswered questions and I'm convinced we have to get Matt to a safe house, somewhere where only we and the state police know where to find him until we can get all this sorted out."

155

He stopped talking when an orderly walked by with a tray and then he looked across the table at Ashleigh. "Any suggestions?" he asked.

The question caught her off guard. "What?"

"You know Matt better than anyone. Do you know some place where the two of you like to go to get away, some place in Louisiana where we can provide protection?"

"Grandma Rose," she half mumbled to herself as if hesitant to suggest anything.

"I'm sorry?" Justice Gravois said.

"I – that is, my grandmother Rose lives in Covington. Maybe he could stay with her," Ashleigh said.

The Supreme Court justice stared in the direction of the cafeteria entrance for a moment. "That might work. We could give him round the clock state police protection that way. How do you think your grandmother will respond to such a request?"

"She loves Matt, but how do you know we can trust the state police here?" she asked. "We already know at least two sheriff's deputies are probably involved in whatever this is. Could it include state police, too?"

"New Orleans is in State Police Troop B," he said. "It's located out in Jefferson Parish and they're most likely not involved in anything in Orleans, but there's no need to risk it. Covington is in Troop L. It's located in Mandeville. I know the troop commander there and I can arrange for surveillance of your grandmother's house is she's willing."

Ashleigh, for the first time, thought of the consequences of bringing Rose into the mystery that now was growing exponentially. "When I mentioned my grandmother, it was just a thought," she said. "I have to explain the situation to her and see if she's willing to let Matt stay with her. I'll drive up to Covington tomorrow to talk to her."

"I understand," Justice Gravois said. "You talk it over with her. Tell her state police officers will see to it that no one not known to them will be allowed to approach her home. We'll have undercover agents stationed around her home and officers will be prepared for any eventuality. Here's my card. Call me as soon as you get an answer." He scribbled his cell phone number on the back of his business card.

Ashleigh had to stifle a laugh, despite the gravity of the situation. She imagined how Rose would react to her imagined intruder's continued tampering with her personal belongings with state police officers stationed right outside her doors. Then, for the first time in a while, she thought about the surveillance cameras. *I wonder if they've caught anything unusual yet. I bet Justice Gravois would love to know about that. He'd probably have Matt committed if he did.*

50

"You want Mitch to stay here with me?" Rose asked when Ashleigh finished explaining what had happened. "Honey, that boy can stay here anytime he wants to for as long as he wants. But you better not leave me alone with him."

"Grandma, this isn't a joking matter. They nearly killed Matt and they might try again. I'm asking you if he can hide here; it's not a social visit. There'll be state police right outside day and night. Are sure this is going to be okay with you?"

"Ashleigh, honey, if I'd known it was this easy to get those good-looking state troopers to hang around my house, I'd have beaten Mitch up myself," Rose said. "You bring him here and I'll take good care of him. I'll feed him good food and he'll be up and around in no time. Will you be staying here with us?"

She hadn't considered that possibility. She'd been too preoccupied with Matt's safety to think about what she would be doing while he was at Rose's or where she would stay. *Those two deputies saw me. What if they learn who I am, where I live?* She made a snap decision. People live in the Covington-Mandeville area and drive into New Orleans to work every day. "Yes, of course. You don't think I'm going to leave you alone with my man after what you said, do you?" she answered with more humor than she felt.

Ashleigh called Justice Gravois on his cell phone number as soon as she was in her car. "I'm headed back to the hospital now," she said. "Grandma said she would love to have Matt stay at her place. I'm going to be staying there with him."

Justice Gravois didn't get himself elected to the Louisiana Supreme Court by being stupid. He didn't relish the idea of having both his key witnesses isolated in the same remote location, exposed to the same as yet unknown danger. At the same time, he knew he could not object. If he did so, it would unnecessarily alert her to the existing potential exposure to peril. To do that would be to admit that he had knowingly put Ashleigh's grandmother in harm's way and there was no way he could do that without further upsetting Ashleigh. It was a situation that demanded all the tact he had learned as a lawyer and judge. He couldn't stress the importance of keeping Ashleigh safe from peril without alerting her to her grandmother's vulnerability.

"If you do that, we'll have a state trooper to take you to and from work," he said.

"I can't do that," she said. "I use my car for work and I'll need it every day."

Justice Gravois didn't respond.

"Are you there?" Ashleigh asked.

"Yes, I'm still here."

"What if I leave my car at my office and ride back and forth with the trooper?"

"We can't do that. If someone knows who you are and notices a routine like that, they could tamper with your vehicle while it's left unguarded."

"Well, I guess I'll just have to drive my car back and forth then," she said.

Justice Gravois relented reluctantly but only after getting Ashleigh to consent to allowing a trooper to ride with her and a second trooper to follow her to and from work and while making business calls.

"Is this what the President's family has to endure?" she asked. "Something like that," he said. "The Secret Service protects the President and his family. We have to protect our witnesses."

If his words were meant to placate her, they failed. For the first time the reality of being in physical danger sank in and she felt as if she no longer had any control over her own destiny. Only a couple of days before, she was leading a normal single working woman's lifestyle, one that was even dull in its routine. Now, though, events were spinning out of control and she felt helpless against the onrushing tide of events.

She drove straight to Tulane Medical Center and found Matt sitting up in his bed. He still hurt, but his head was clear now that he was no longer sedated.

"I hope you brought me a Whopper," he said by way of greeting.

"You know, it's not too early for you to get off this junk food," she said, handing him a sack containing a Whopper and a vanilla milkshake. She'd been trying for two years now to get him to eat more green vegetables and less red meat. For someone who'd grown up on a vegetable farm in north Louisiana where squash, beans, and okra were in abundance, he was quite the picky eater, much to Ashleigh's never-ending frustration.

He laid the burger on his tray and looked at Ashleigh. "I can't believe how cool you were at the courthouse," he said. "How did you know not to say anything when we came out of the archives office?"

"I'm not sure," she said. "I knew you were supposed to be alone and I didn't know those men with you. I just somehow sensed that something wasn't just right, so I decided to follow you."

"You followed us?"

"I took the stairs while you were on the elevator. I watched them take you into the courtroom and I saw Judge Cheramie go in after you. I took off my

158

shoes and walked past the door where you were and I heard them beating the hell out of you in there. That's when I ran back down the stairs and then went to Justice Gravois's office."

"Jesus, Ashleigh. You're something else, you know that?"

"I've been trying to tell you that for years. Did you know I left my shoes on the spiral staircase in the courthouse? I had to go to Justice Gravois's office in my stocking feet. That's so embarrassing. I wonder if I'll ever find those shoes." *Why do we think about such insignificant things at times like these?*

Ashleigh then brought Matt up to date on Justice Gravois's quick thinking in dispatching state troopers to Matt's home to protect his property. She didn't know about the confrontation between the troopers and the Orleans Parish sheriff's deputies, nor did she know that Gravois had personally relieved Judge Cheramie of his duties pending a full investigation. She then told him about Judge Gravois's insistence on moving Matt to a safe location with state police protection and of the decision that he would be the guest of Grandma Rose for the foreseeable future.

"I can't do that," Matt protested. "I have work to do at the office and I have to get back to investigating what's going on with these deaths."

Ashleigh flared in a rare display of temper. "Just who do you think is going to investigate your death?" she asked, standing next to his bed. "You listen to me, Matt. You've got to stop acting like some kind of TV private detective and charging off into areas you know nothing about. You already know now that it can be treacherous."

"You would be wise to listen to your lady, young man." It was the voice of Justice Gravois, who entered the room at that moment. They both turned to their visitor when he spoke. "She's right and you know it," he said. "You would be extremely prudent to stay away from where you're not wanted and let people we pay to do that type of work earn their keep. As for your job, you're not to worry about that. We've got plenty of people who can cover for you until it's safe for you to return. Hell, I can even do a little of my own research and writing if I have to. That'd surprise a few people."

Justice Gravois stayed long enough to update Matt on Judge Cheramie's status as a result of what had transpired in the courtroom the day before and on the appearance of the Orleans deputies at his home, assuring him at the same time that the deputies had been turned away by state police he'd personally ordered sent there.

"We've got to move all my computer equipment to Rose's house if I'm going to be staying there," Matt said. "I'll need to review what goes on at Rose's during the night while everyone's asleep."

"No, we don't," Ashleigh said. "We can use my laptop to monitor the cameras."

"We can do that with a laptop?"

159

"Matt, you need to join the Twenty-First Century. We can do just about anything with a laptop that can be done on a desktop, including wireless internet access. God, you're so out of touch with the rest of the world. Here's another news flash: you can even do that on your cell phone."

51

J. François skimmed through the record while he waited for Deke Morgan to be ushered into an empty room in the St. John the Baptist Parish courthouse in Edgard. Most times, he would have been allowed in his client's cell for the consultation, but crowded jail conditions prohibited that accommodation so the sheriff was kind enough to offer this room, hardly larger than a broom closet, but the best he had to offer.

This case was a challenge, but J. François was accustomed to challenges and he had every confidence he would prevail. There were graphic color photographs of the seventy-eight-year-old victim lying in a pool of his own blood in the middle of his living room.

He read over the eyewitness report. A neighbor reported seeing a strange man run out of Father Jeansonne's home, jump into his ancient Olds Ninety-Eight, and speed away, the report said. He was unable to identify Deke as the driver. The neighbor was an elderly man, himself in his mid-eighties. Surely, his vision was not what it once was. J. François was confident he could destroy the neighbor's testimony with little effort.

A more formidable challenge was the deputy sheriff who saw Father Jeansonne's car driven by someone he didn't know, a man he'd had never seen before. The deputy radioed in the car's license plate number to confirm that it was Jeansonne's and then pulled Deke over less than half an hour after the murder. Deke, stoned on crack, never admitted to the murder, probably because he truly could not remember committing the act. Car theft was a charge J. François probably couldn't beat but that was the least of his worries. His primary concern was getting his client off on the murder charge.

The prosecutor was going all out on this one, as much from public pressure as from any real sense of justice. Given the choice, prosecutors would rather try a defendant on a lesser charge because the chances of a conviction are much better. The decision to try a suspect on a first-degree murder charge is always a crap shoot. One dissenting vote on the jury is all it takes to see a capital murder case go down the drain. There would still be a conviction, but everyone would know the district attorney rolled the dice and failed. Such tactics in a white-hot case such as the upcoming trial of Deke Morgan could be politically explosive.

161

J. François welcomed the opportunity to take on the political power structure in St. John the Baptist Parish. Few people in the largely rural parish just upriver from New Orleans had ever heard of the great J. François and for the most part, they couldn't care less. There was a cold-blooded killer in their jail who they were certain had taken the life of an innocent old man, a priest at that, in a brutal, sadistic manner and there was no way Deke Morgan could ever be acquitted.

Oddly enough, J. François never moved for a change of venue, a tactic that was considered all but automatic for most defense attorneys in a small-town simmering with hatred for the defendant. But J. François was not most defense attorneys. The more volatile the situation, the more he seemed to relish the prospect of fighting the good fight on behalf of his downtrodden clients, men who had never been able to catch a break in their miserable lives. If no one else would be their advocate, then J. François was ready and willing to do so.

Deke entered the small room clad in the bright orange jailhouse uniform, his feet and wrists shackled to a belt around his waist. Despite his apparent lack of mobility, he nonetheless had two armed escorts, St. John sheriff's deputies. They helped Deke to a chair and then took up posts outside the room's closed door. They weren't allowed to listen to the attorney and client as they discussed the case and their strategy for the upcoming trial and besides, he wasn't going anywhere.

"Deke, it doesn't look good," J. François said in opening the session. "Hey, man, I don't want to hear that shit. You're my lawyer and I heard you're good. You gotta figure a way to get me out of this."

"Deke, they found your prints and your DNA all over the old priest's house. The only chance we have is to say you entered the house to burglarize it, thinking Father Jeansonne wasn't home. You found him lying on the floor beaten to death in a savage and heinous manner. Then you did something really stupid by picking up the bat you found lying next to him. You panicked, grabbed the keys you saw lying on the table, ran out, and jumped in the car and down the road you went. That about it?"

"Yeah," Deke said. "That sounds right."

"Only one problem with that story; how'd you get to his house? You had no car, so how'd you get there?"

Deke leaned over the table, getting as close to J. François as possible and answered in a slow, measured voice. "You told me I rode the ferry from Reserve, remember?"

"No, Deke, I don't remember coaching you at all. This has to be your story, not mine. When you answer that or any other question, you never look at me, got it?"

Deke nodded as he slumped back in his chair.

"Now then, how did you get to Reserve?

162

"I hitchhiked. I caught a ride with a trucker and he was spending the night at a truck stop, so I got out and started walking. I ended up at the Mississippi River just as the ferry was docking, so I decided to ride it to see what it was like."

"Where were you hitchhiking to, Deke?"

"I was trying to get to New Orleans from Houston."

"Houston? That where you're from?"

"No, man, I'm from Galveston but I'd been living in Houston for a few months."

"Why New Orleans?" J. François asked.

"I've always liked the place and I just wanted to go there."

"Did you have a job waiting for you there?"

"Nah, I was just gonna panhandle. I ain't worked in over a year."

"But you didn't kill Father Jeansonne?"

"No sir, I did not," Deke said. "I stole his car, that's all."

"All right, Deke, you seem to have your story down pretty well," J. François said. "I can't make any guarantees, but all we need is doubt in the mind of a couple of jurors and the rest usually takes care of itself. You stay with your story and you just might be out of prison in two to three years for car theft, unauthorized entry and a couple more minor offenses."

Deke was a prime candidate for J. François's enterprise.

163

52

"Grandma, it's Ashleigh and Matt. We're on your road, about a quarter-mile from your house." She called Rose before they arrived so that she could have the front door open for them. But Rose's solitary existence had long been drowning in a sea of paranoia so they still had to knock and wait for the alarm to be disabled and the three deadbolts to be opened one by one before the door at long last swung open, squeaking on protesting hinges as it did so.

The old woman looked and took a quick step backward, pressing her hand to her mouth. "Mitch, my word, look what they did to you! Oh, honey, get in this house and lie down. I'll get you some aspirin. Let me soak those cuts with some Epsom salts."

"It's okay, Rosie, I'm fine but you should've seen the other guy."

Still she persisted in getting him to the sofa and sitting down, afraid he might collapse any second from the intense pain from which he most surely must have been suffering. He didn't argue and sat down to humor her. Besides, his ribs still ached when he took a deep breath. *At least she's not concerned about my stomach this time.*

"He's fine now, Grandma," Ashleigh said. "He was beaten up pretty badly and he's still a little sore, but that was three days ago and he's a lot better now."

"Who did you tell me did this to him?" Rose asked her granddaughter, ignoring Matt for the moment.

"Two sheriff's deputies, with the blessings of a judge," Ashleigh said with a bite in her voice. She still felt bitter that people entrusted and charged with enforcing the law and protecting citizens could be capable of such an act of violence.

"How can that be?" Rose asked, as bewildered as Ashleigh was bitter.

"They were dirty, Grandma. Dirty men involved in a dirty business."

"What dirty business?"

"We don't know, yet, Rosie," Matt said from the sofa. "But they're somehow involved with six men who were recently killed and I'm going to find out what that involvement is. Then I figure we'll know what their business is."

165

"You're not going to do a damned thing," Ashleigh snapped. "You almost got yourself killed and you're not about to go digging around again."

"That's right, Mitch," Rose said. "You're just going to stay here and let us take care of you. You're in no condition to go chasing people, especially someone who might do something worse next time. There're times when you have to use your brains."

Matt didn't respond. He knew when to keep quiet and this was one of those times. The two women were in control of the moment and he understood that.

"We saw the state police when we drove up," Ashleigh said, changing the subject. "They have two unmarked SUVs across the road."

"I know," Rose said. "There's another car parked around back. They've been out there a couple of hours now. They must've known you were coming. I took them some coffee earlier and tomorrow Ashleigh and I'll bake them some fudge brownies."

53

Hours and days can crawl by when one has nothing to do with his time. It was for that reason that Matt didn't look forward to his stay at Rose's and his worst fears were soon confirmed as mere boredom soon turned to outright drudgery. He made up his mind to make the most of the situation, however, because he genuinely liked the old woman.

He also loved crossword puzzles so he brought a couple of books of them, but a man can spend only so many hours scribbling letters in squares before that activity, too, becomes just another form of tedium. Rose, for the most part, went about her daily activities with little conversation because neither of them had much to talk about while Ashleigh was at work. The state troopers were kind enough to agree to bring him a copy of the *Times Picayune* each morning but he required an hour at most to digest the day's news. Justice Gravois checked in daily but he refused to discuss activities in his office lest Matt might start worrying about his job so those conversations were far too short.

He had always looked forward to seeing Ashleigh, but never as much as now. There is, after all, only so much daytime television a man can take. He couldn't wait for her to get home from work each evening, even if it was Rose's home and not his own. Her arrival always elevated the mood around the house but at the same time, it served as a constant reminder to the couple that like Rose, they were also prisoners in her home now if for very different reasons. Rose refused to leave her home for fear someone would break in and take everything she owned, never mind the fact that her presence had so far failed to discourage all other heretofore unexplained activity.

Matt and Ashleigh couldn't go out to eat or to a movie for fear that the wrong person might see them and learn where they were hiding. At least Ashleigh was free to seek refuge each day in her work; Matt couldn't even look forward to that respite. It didn't take long for the walls to start closing in on him and because he was recovering from his injuries faster than expected, his desire to move about freely was even more intensified.

Out of options in ways in which to pass the time, he was desperate to talk about any subject by the fourth day of isolation. The thought of Ashleigh's laptop lying on the table in its black canvas case didn't cross his mind until he was

167

forced to consider more creative ways to occupy himself. Even then, it was she who brought the matter up over dinner the night before. "Why don't you go online and check on the surveillance system while I'm out tomorrow?" she asked.

He laid down his fork and looked at her. "Jeez, I haven't thought of that since back at the hospital. Good idea. I'll need you to set it up for me tonight so I can log on tomorrow morning. I've never even used a laptop, much less wireless internet."

Ashleigh gave him a look of mock scorn. "I can't believe you're so computer illiterate," she said. "A laptop is no different than any other computer and the wireless connection is already set up. All you have to do is log on with your password and you're in. I thought it was the woman who was supposed to need help with technical stuff."

"Your *job* is with computers," he said. "Mine is with writ applications and writing opinions. I read law books for precedents and I interpret laws and then I write opinions about how the law applies to a particular situation I just never had the time to learn computers. They scare me."

She laughed. "Well, if it makes you feel any better, I'd be intimidated by your job. I can't imagine having to conduct legal research and then author an opinion that's going to impact people's lives. I'll give you a crash course on the laptop after we eat and all you'll have to do in the morning is log on. I'll use the AC adaptor instead of the battery so we won't have to turn the computer off from now on."

In spite of Matt's apparent reluctance to make the full commitment to joining the information age, it took her less than twenty minutes to show him how to get up and running on the laptop. In the end, she was satisfied that he had a sufficient grasp of the basics to access the hard drive data and to pull the images from the four cameras up on the laptop screen.

As she went about cleaning up the dinner dishes in the kitchen, Rose pretended not to hear what was being said. But she heard every word and their conversation filled her with anticipation for what she was certain *Mitch* would find the following day. *We're finally going to get the bottom of all this and then people will quit shaking their heads and feeling sorry for me. Then we'll see who's crazy.*

She had no way of knowing it, but Matt drifted off to sleep with a head filled with apprehension and considerable doubt over what he might discover when he reviewed the data stored on his computer's hard drive the next day.

Ashleigh, lying next to him, harbored her own private thoughts. *I hope Grandma isn't humiliated too much by what the cameras show. I don't think I could forgive myself if she's hurt by this.*

54

J. François found out about Judge Cheramie when he arrived at work and opened his *Times Picayune*. He jerked the telephone receiver from its cradle to check his messages. None. That made sense. If Judge Cheramie had talked about, or even hinted at the existence of the enterprise, J. François's lines would be tapped as would those of Judges Ray Sonnier and Lyle Bergen and they would know that. He also knew Judge Cheramie wouldn't call because he had to know his own lines would be bugged by authorities as well and he had a deep distrust for cellular telephones because of the isolated but well-publicized occasions in which signals from celebrities' cell conversations were picked up by other cell phones and splashed all over the media.

J. François was reasonably certain that Judge Cheramie wouldn't talk or at least had not at this point and he was just as certain no one outside his felonious circle knew of the existence of the enterprise. The newspaper said only that he had been removed from office for "inappropriate" conduct. That could be just about anything. The story did not give details of that conduct so J. François knew nothing yet of Matt's beating at the hands of the deputies or of Judge Cheramie's participation in his questioning. In fact, because Matt's name was not mentioned in the newspaper story, J. François had yet to even learn of the existence of the State Supreme Court law clerk or of his activities.

Satisfied then that whatever Judge Cheramie had done to get himself relieved of his duties did not involve him, J. François dove into the morning's work. There were notes from his receptionist that a small-time drug dealer had called after being arrested over a residential break-in that had resulted in the fatal shooting of the homeowner. He wrote himself a note to visit the caller in jail for an initial consultation to determine if he could help the man. He was deeply involved in the pending trial of Deke Morgan but no lawyer is ever involved in only one case despite the way in which attorneys are portrayed on television and in the movies. Somehow, they manage to devote every ounce of energy to a single client or case. Any decent lawyer makes his living juggling several cases at once and J. François calculated that if he took this man as a client he would have three active cases, not including Deke's. He thought attorneys must have invented multi-tasking.

As the conspiracy of silence grew ever tighter among criminal courthouse participants, J. François, however unwittingly, found himself increasingly shut off from those who possessed the means to exclude him from their inner circle. These were people who would quickly ostracize anyone they thought might represent a potential liability to their reputations, their livelihoods, and their very freedom – people like J. François. It was a calculated move and a dangerous game, to say the least. They held in their hands the ability to help or hurt J. François but they had no way of knowing just how deadly an adversary he could be in return. They had cut the lines of communication without knowing about the sealed letter he'd mailed to his own attorney.

So, he blithely went about his daily routine of protecting the poor downtrodden, misunderstood felons from the evils perpetrated by onerous, lazy prosecutors willing and eager to pin any charge that would stick on his clients because they were convenient.

55

Mat had been pacing back and forth for over an hour when Ashleigh finally turned into the driveway. He bolted out the front door, never hearing the shrill beep, and ran to her car to meet her, unable to compel himself to wait until she was inside. He barely paused long enough to kiss her hello. "Hurry up," he said. "You've got to see this."

"What's up?" She asked. "You look pale."

"Just hurry and get inside."

He half pushed and half dragged her into the front door where they found themselves confronted by a glowering Rose. "Mitch, why did you open the front door without waiting for me to disable the alarm?" she said. "You triggered it and now the sheriff's office is going to be calling me to see if there's trouble." She had barely finished admonishing him when the telephone rang. "There, you see? I hope you're happy." She walked into the dining room to answer the phone and they could hear her explaining that she had forgotten and opened her front door before disabling the alarm.

"I'm sorry, Rose," Matt said when she returned to the living room. "I was in a hurry and completely forgot about the alarm. It won't happen again."

She turned and made her way back to the kitchen where she was preparing dinner for the three of them. "Dinner's almost ready so you two get washed up and ready to eat," she called back over her shoulder. Matt took Ashley's arm to steer her into the bedroom where the laptop was set up.

"Can it wait?" Ashley asked. "I've been on the road for over an hour and I have to go to the bathroom and then it's going to be time to eat. Why don't you wait until after dinner to show me?"

He groaned audibly at the prospect of having to wait any longer. He felt like a kid on Christmas Eve awaiting the annual visit from Santa Claus, excited and filled with eager anticipation and yet helpless to make the time go faster. He picked at his food, keeping his eyes on Ashleigh, trying to will her to eat faster. Then, to his horror, when she was finished, she started helping Rose clean the dishes. He almost felt as though she was torturing him on purpose.

After what seemed an eternity, the last dish was wiped dry and put away. She turned to him. "What did you want to show me?" she asked, appearing oblivious to his growing anxiety. In reality, she knew Matt had stumbled upon something significant on the laptop and she was just as excited as he but she managed to check her emotions in deference to her grandmother. She wanted to see what Matt had found before she revealed anything to Rose. It was the only way she knew to shelter her from the embarrassment that would almost certainly occur if the data stored on the hard drive showed anything other than an outside influence on events within Rose's house. If, however, the images showed that there were circumstances beyond Rose's control which warranted her attention, she would be allowed to view the recorded images for herself.

56

Matt couldn't believe it when he heard the knock at Rose's front door. *Now what?*

"Were you expecting anyone, Grandma?" Ashleigh asked, walking toward the front room.

"No, I don't have any idea who it could be."

Ashleigh stopped short before reaching for the door. "Who is it?"

"State police, Ma'am," a man's voice said.

She stepped back as Matt approached the door. "What's your name?" he asked. He had become friendly with the state police detail assigned to surveillance of Rose's home and he knew each trooper by name.

"Sergeant Timmons," the man answered. "Geoffrey Timmons."

"It's okay," Matt said. "I know him."

Rose moved toward the door as Matt and Ashleigh stepped back. As always, she attempted to block their view of the keypad as she punched in the code to disable the alarm. The door creaked on is oil-thirsty hinges to reveal the massive form of Sergeant Timmons, a broad-shouldered six-foot-four black officer. "I hate to bother you folks this time of night, but there's been a breach in security," he said. "We have reason to believe you may be in danger and we've been instructed to move you to safe quarters until we get the all-clear."

"What does that mean?" asked Rose, confused at the sudden intrusion. "It means someone who's not supposed to know found out I'm here," Matt said. His thoughts at the moment were more about the safety of Rose and Ashleigh than his own. *Damn. I knew I shouldn't have come here. This was a bad idea.*

"That's correct," Sergeant Timmons said. "We don't know where the security leak originated or even who's involved. If there's an error, we want it to be on the side of caution. We're going to get you folks settled in a motel in Slidell where we can keep closer watch on you and until we can get to the bottom of this. There's too much open space around your house and it would be more difficult to prevent penetration here."

Even as Matt cursed under his breath in anticipation of the relocation, Rose squared her shoulders and stood as erect as her small frame would allow.

173

"I'm not leaving my home and that's that," she said, looking up at Sergeant Timmons who towered over her by more than a foot.

"Ma'am, I hate to have to do this, but I have no choice," he said. "For your own safety and well-being, I'm going to have to insist." Somehow his voice didn't carry the confidence and authority that he hoped it would, however, and now he looked at Matt for backup, hoping that he could prevail on Rose to relent.

Matt caught his look and took over in the effort to dissuade Rose from digging in her heels. "Rosie, we're out of options here. They're still going to have officers watching the house but they just feel better if we're not here for a couple of days. We'll be back here as soon as they get this cleared up."

Sergeant Timmons was visually relieved to have Matt on his side. "That's correct, Ma'am, it's just for a couple of days and you'll be right back here."

"I haven't spent a night away from my home in almost thirty years," she said. "Are you sure it's going to be okay, Mitch?"

"I'd bet my life on it," he said, regretting in an instant the bad choice of words.

"It'll be fine, Grandma," Ashleigh said, her assurance even less certain and authoritative than the officer's. "We're going to be okay. It's just a routine procedure." Her attempt at assuaging Rose's concerns still rang hollow, but it was the best she could do under the circumstances. She was more than a little frightened. There followed several moments of awkward silence because each of the three had said all they knew to say to mollify the feisty octogenarian. It was she who finally broke the silence. "Two days. That's how long I'll give you to get all this mess cleared up. After that, we're coming back here, no matter what you say, you understand me?"

Sergeant Timmons found himself smiling at her spunk in spite of his best efforts not to. "Yes, Ma'am, two days and you're back here." He had no idea what his strategy would be if the security breach was not solved by her arbitrary deadline but for now it was all he had and he was relieved to get even that concession from her. They were packed in twenty minutes and in another fifteen minutes the three of them were in the back seats of two unmarked state police SUVs eastbound on I-12 to nearby Slidell. Rose, in the front vehicle and seated next to Ashleigh on the rear seat, kept a vice-like grip on her oversized purse into which she had packed her medicine and all twenty-four keys to her windows, doors, and her freezer. In the trailing car, the laptop computer rested on Matt's knees. He was still waiting to reveal his discovery to Ashleigh.

"What kind of breach were you talking about?" he asked Sergeant Timmons, who was driving.

Timmons glanced up at Matt through the rear-view mirror. Matt was struck at how gentle the eyes seemed for a man of such size and strength. Of all the troopers assigned to watch Rose's house, he had become friendlier and more comfortable with Timmons than with any of the others, mainly because of the

174

trooper's easy-going manner and genuine affability. He'd also observed that Timmons commanded the respect of his fellow officers. The two had passed several hours in idle conversation.

"I don't know that I'm supposed to tell you this," he said, "but we believe someone who was in the courthouse the day they worked you over spotted your girlfriend when she called on a law office to make a presentation on some computer software. Our sources believe they followed her to Mrs. Melancon's home here in Covington."

"Who was it? Do you know?"

"We think we have a pretty good idea. We believe it was one of the three who beat you up."

"Only two beat me up," Matt corrected the trooper.

"Right," Timmons said. "The other one was the judge who participated in the questioning. Anyway, they're all out on bail and they all ran for their attorneys. One of their lawyers apparently works for the firm where your girlfriend was making a call and one of those three was there to see his attorney and spotted your lady."

"You don't know which one it was?"

"No, because we didn't have a wiretap on the cell phone he was using. It looks like he got a new phone because he suspected we were monitoring him, which we were. But he made the mistake of calling another guy that does have a phone tap and we listened to them planning to break into Mrs. Melancon's home and kill all three of you."

"Who was the guy you had the phone tap on?" Matt asked.

"Just some street dealer we've been after," Timmons said. "He was a guy who we arrested some time back for running a drug ring that extended from Biloxi to Morgan City. Actually, he's a sleazeball private detective and he killed a guy in a drug deal that went south. We thought we had a good case but he goes out and hires this lawyer who got him off like he's done for so many oth---"

"J. François Berthelot?" Matt interrupted.

"Yeah, I believe that was his name. How'd you know that?"

"Jesus, that's it! J. François is in this up to his neck!"

"In what up to his neck?" trooper Timmons asked, suddenly intrigued.

For the rest of the ride to Slidell, Matt filled Timmons in on J. François and his relationship to the dead men and how they'd died in apparent attempts at duplicating the crimes for which J. François had obtained their acquittals. He even told him about Deacon's dying near the grave of his victim, Denise Fleming.

175

57

Timmons was correct on most of his theory except for his speculation on who had made the call to Travis Whitten, the man whose telephone was tapped by authorities who were hoping to learn more about his widespread drug operation. The call had not come from either of the deputies or from Judge Charles Cheramie. They were far too smart to make poor judgment calls like that. The fiasco involving Matt was quite sufficient when it came to making stupid mistakes. The call had come from an attorney who had been drawn into their web because of his affection for the latest designer drug – crystal meth. Robert Vennet was so new to the enterprise that he was flying well below the radar of investigators. No one suspected him or, for that matter, even knew of his existence.

When Robert Vennet made his call to Travis Whitten, the eavesdroppers had no idea who it was who was calling their suspect. It was just a disembodied voice who kept the connection open only long enough to convey his information to Whitten before hanging up and discarding the cell phone after just the one call.

"Travis Whitten?" the monitors heard Vennet say when Whitten answered his cellphone.

"Yeah?"

"There's a woman named Ashleigh Templet. She's in computer applications and she has a boyfriend named Matt Ramsey who's been getting a little too nosy. It looks like he's gone into hiding and they're staying with his girlfriend's grandmother, a Rose Melancon, in Covington. His girlfriend, this Ashleigh Templet, is the only one who leaves and goes to work. You think you can take care of a little business with them?"

"Shouldn't be too difficult," Whitten said. "Tell me a little about her."

As quickly as he could, Vennet described Ashleigh, gave Whitten the name of the company for whom she worked and a description of her dark green Chevy Malibu so that he could follow her and learn where Rose's house was. "This needs to be done quickly, quietly, and neatly," he said. "No loose ends."

"Don't worry about it," Whitten said. "It's as good as done."

177

"One thing more," Vennet said. "Since they've left Jefferson Parish and are staying in Covington, there's a good chance there're police officers hanging around the grandmother's house."

"Unless they have night-vision goggles, they might as well be blind," the private detective said.

58

"That's a helluva story," said trooper Timmons when Matt had finished. "What do you think is the connection between these dead men and their victims? This Deacon Watson is interesting. Why would he go to her grave and get himself killed there?

"A guy acts like he's bending down to grab something that ain't there and gets eaten alive by pit bulldogs. That's exactly why I don't want no mean dogs at my house. My wife's Pomeranian is enough dog for me. Then you got that fool that runs out in the street and gets hit by a car and ends up getting kicked in the head by a mule. That's humiliating. Nobody should have that as the cause of death on his autopsy report.

"I'll tell you what I think," Timmons continued. "I think it sounds like you been snooping around some supernatural stuff but the guys who whupped up on you weren't supernatural anything. They were real warm-blooded men and they're scared of something you might find out. They're scared enough to send somebody to Mrs. Melancon's home to try and kill all of you. I don't think you have anything to worry about from any ghosts, the undead, or whatever you want to call 'em. Your problems are with live men with guns and knives and you would be wise to tread very carefully."

"You sound like Ashleigh," Matt said.

"Well, maybe you should listen to her."

179

59

Travis Whitten was a walking caricature, right down to his dark clothing, greasepaint-blackened face, and latex rubber gloves. He made his way through the wooded area east of Rose Melancon's home. It was the one side of the house obscured from the view of the state police surveillance team. This was the easy part; the difficulty would be gaining access to the house without waking the occupants. He'd done jobs like this before so he wasn't nervous. He was always cautious, making no hasty movements that might give him away. It was a simple task for him to pick the lock and in a matter of seconds, he was inside the house. He noticed the stove light was on in the kitchen and table lamps emitted soft lighting in the dining and living rooms, giving the three rooms a shadowy aura – just enough light for the cameras.

The security system didn't concern him; he would do what needed to be done in less than a minute and two minutes after everyone was dead, long before the sheriff's department could respond to the alarm, he would be well on his way through the woods back to his car parked in the brush less than half a mile away.

Whitten made his way in the semi-darkness across the kitchen to the dining room and on into the front room. His first objective was Matt and Ashleigh. He knew most people in older homes like this one had their bedrooms near the kitchen in the rear of their houses so he assumed correctly that the couple's bedroom would be toward the front. He would take care of them first.

He stood motionless in the living room for perhaps three seconds before stepping into the doorway and firing into the room with his silencer-equipped automatic pistol. He got off six rounds before turning on his flashlight. He was careful not to wave the light around so as to alert the police surveillance team. Instead, he kept the light pointed to the floor in order to give off just enough light for him to survey the room. He cursed to himself when he saw the bullet-riddled but empty bed. *What the hell? Of all damn times for them to be away! That dumb ass said he never left the house!*

He was still confused as he backed out of the bedroom into the living room when, with no warning, the bright ceiling fan lights came on. He froze in his tracks, expecting to be confronted by one of the occupants but he saw no one. It didn't take him long to decide to vacate the premises. Knowing the sheriff's

181

office would soon be responding to the alarm, he realized his time was short; the mission had to be aborted. The telephone was already ringing. That would be the sheriff's office, unaware of the state police surveillance team's presence, calling to check on the alarm. If there was no answer, a deputy would be dispatched to Rose's house. But that was the least of his worries now.

He started toward the rear of the house, intending to exit the same way he came in but as he started into the dining room, the ceiling lights in that room came on, causing him to take two quick steps backward. Just then, the living room went dark, causing him to spin in that direction. He saw no one but when he turned back, he was confronted by an old man, tall and frail-looking, with thinning hair, who stood blocking the doorway into the dining room. The apparition was not armed nor did he speak as Whitten raised his pistol and fired three quick bursts. The old man disappeared but immediately reappeared beside Whitten, who let a guttural sound escape from somewhere deep in his throat. He nearly fell down as he tried to get away from the man. *What the hell is he doing here? Nobody said anything about him. How'd I miss him?*

Even as he stumbled toward the kitchen in his haste to get out of the house, he forgot all about the state police outside. He was far more concerned with what he found inside the house than anything – or anyone – who might be outside. He was stumbling into the dining room now, hell bent on getting through the kitchen and out the back door. He was six feet from the kitchen when that room's lights came on, again revealing the old man blocking the doorway just as he had the dining room door moments earlier. Whitten more nearly lurched than stepped backward. If he couldn't escape the way he came in, then he'd take his chances with the front door, state police be damned.

He spun in the direction of the living room just as those lights came on again, illuminating the old man as he stood in the front doorway. The would-be assassin spun from front to back to front again, each time finding himself confronted by the unspeaking specter. His temples were pounding now and he was feeling clammy all over when he felt a stabbing pain in his chest and between his shoulder blades. The pain overwhelmed him as he clutched his chest. He groped for a dining room chair, knocking it over.

Unable to withstand the piercing pain in his chest, he went down with the chair and as he did so, he saw the old man once more. This time, however, he appeared to be floating in mid-air and he no longer appeared as a mortal being but as a semi-transparent figure. Whitten's last terrifying thought was that he seemed to be able to see the door behind the old man, as if he were looking right through him. Then the man was gone, replaced by a shadow that dissipated into a shapeless, indefinable form that floated through the ceiling.

In the same instant that the silhouette disappeared, Whitten took his last tortured breath and lay still on Rose's linoleum dining room floor. State police surveillance team members, seeing the lights go on and off in the house and knowing no one was home, sprang into action and burst through the front door

182

where they found his body before it was cold. Sheriff's deputies arrived seven minutes later in response to the alarm.

60

The rooms were comfortable enough, but it wasn't home and Rose was not happy. State police had rented adjoining rooms – one for Ashleigh and Rose and the other for Matt. A common door between the rooms was unlocked so that the occupants had access to each other without having to step outside. State troopers took up positions in rooms to the left and right of theirs as well as in the parking lot.

Matt's priority was getting the laptop powered up so that he could show Ashleigh the images of the objects floating through the air in Rose's home. He was fascinated at what he'd found and after waiting all day to share his discovery with Ashleigh, he was bursting with excitement and impatient to bring the images up. Ashleigh sat on the bed to his left and gasped audibly each time some object made its way from one point in Rose's home to another, defying gravity and several laws of physics in the process.

They reviewed data stored on the hard drive for about forty minutes, most of which was nothing more than Rose moving about inside her home. There were, however sufficient inexplicable occurrences for them to know they were witnessing something mysterious – baffling events that should not be possible and which were certainly beyond the realm of physical science. Moreover, none of the events ever occurred while Rose was in any of the rooms where they took place. They happened only when she left the room.

"Matt, this means Grandma's not imagining things," Ashleigh said at last. They're real, they're really happening."

"Of course, they're really happening," said Rose who had just entered from the adjacent room. "I've been trying to tell that to everyone who would listen for years." Matt and Ashleigh looked up at her and were struck by her calm demeanor. There was no surprise in her face or her voice, only the self-satisfaction of one who had at long last been vindicated. "Let me take a look at what you have there," she said, sitting down on the bed to Matt's right. Together, the three of them viewed the data from the beginning. They watched for another hour, the cameras revealing a few events during the final twenty minutes that Matt and Ashleigh didn't get to during their initial review.

185

For the entire time, Rose never showed any surprise, nor did she gloat. Instead, she only seemed relieved that the long-running mystery had been solved, at least in part. The disappearance of items in her home was more understandable now, if not the manner in which they had been moved about.

"You know what I'd like to see?" she said, breaking the silence. "I'd like to see what's going on right now. Can you do that?"

Matt wanted to respond in the affirmative but he didn't remember how to access the cameras in real time. He was glad Ashleigh was there when she came to his rescue. "Of course, Grandma, that's simple." She typed in a couple of commands and the monitor went blank for an instant before an image reappeared. It took a moment for Matt and Ashleigh to come to the realization that there should have been no picture unless there was activity in the room and they were looking at the interior of the living room. They exchanged quick glances but said nothing to Rose who at first didn't fully comprehend the significance of what they were seeing. That quickly became clear to her when the form of Travis Whitten appeared in the upper left corner of the screen.

"Who is that?" she said when she saw the intruder.

No one answered her as all three watched transfixed as Whitten raised an automatic pistol. Because there was no sound, they couldn't hear, but they saw the subtle recoil of the pistol as he fired six shots into the front bedroom. They watched him as he first shined his flashlight at the floor and then as he backed out of the bedroom doorway into the living room. He came into sharper focus when the living room lights suddenly came on, causing him to freeze in his tracks and then begin walking at a fast pace toward the dining room – and the camera mounted on the wall so that it looked into the living room from the vantage point above the dining room door. The trio watched as he stopped and stepped back two steps. They were unable to detect the form that blocked his access to the dining room because of the camera angle but they knew he saw something when he fired three shots in the general direction of the camera.

Ashleigh typed in another command and the screen instantly divided into four squares, each representing an image from one of the cameras. On the living room image, they saw an eerie image appear next to the shooter who promptly stumbled in his desperation to get away from the image.

"Jake!" Rose said, breaking the silence.

"What, Grandma?" said an incredulous Ashleigh. Before Rose could answer, they saw that the dining room light suddenly illuminated that room and that camera showed the translucent image of an old man standing in the path of the now panicky would-be killer.

"It's Jake. I recognize him." After several moments, she added in a quiet voice, "Don't you see he's protecting our house?"

Ashleigh peered intently at the screen and even though it'd been twelve years since she had seen her grandfather, she found herself in agreement with her grandmother. "Oh my God," she whispered. "Oh God." She shivered as Matt

186

slipped his arm around her shoulder and pulled her gently to him. Tears appeared in Ashleigh's eyes and rolled freely down her cheeks. Matt couldn't think of anything to say, so he just held her.

They continued watching, mesmerized by the scene unfolding before their eyes. The kitchen light was on now and the man, whoever he was, had discarded any pretense of caution as he sought a way out of the house. He started for the front door only to find the image of the old man again blocking his access to an exit. The would-be assassin turned back toward the kitchen and then again to the front of the house and back again. Then, abruptly, he grabbed his chest and stumbled. Wordlessly, they watched on the dining room camera as he lurched to grab a chair and then as both and he and the chair crashed to the floor.

The living room camera simultaneously recorded the image of Jake as it evaporated and floated upward, toward the ceiling but neither Matt nor Ashleigh saw that. Only Rose was watching that quadrant of the laptop screen. For the first time during the entire series of events, she let an audible sob escape. Ashleigh tore her eyes from the screen long enough to embrace her grandmother and then the three of them continued watching until state police officers broke down the front door and found the lifeless body of Travis Whitten. They were still watching when St. Tammany Parish Sheriff's deputies arrived in response to the alarm that Whitten triggered when he first entered the house only minutes before.

Without a word, Rose stood and walked back to her room. Matt and Ashleigh, unable to believe what they'd just witnessed, re-ran the entire sequence again, freeze framing some images in order to study them more closely. They were about to watch for a third time when there was a light knock on the motel room door.

Matt walked to the door. "Yes?" he said.

"It's Geoffrey Timmons," said a voice from outside the door.

Matt opened the door. "Sergeant, you've got to see this," he said.

"Maybe later," the trooper said, "but first I have some news."

"We already know."

"Know what?"

Matt pulled him into the room and closed the door. "Look at this," he said as Ashleigh re-started the sequence from the hard drive for the officer.

"Damn," was all Timmons could say when it was over. "You were watching that in real time?"

"Yeah, and let me tell you, it's a creepy feeling to see something like that as it's happening. Any idea who he is?"

"His name was Travis Whitten," Timmons said.

"Is he the private detective you were telling me about?"

"Yep, that's him all right. Apparently, he was there to kill all three of you. You saw him pump those shots into that room. Was that your bedroom?"

"Yeah, it was," Ashleigh said. "I don't know if I can ever sleep in there again."

187

Timmons smiled. "Well, at least you're safe here. As far as we have reason to believe, he was the only operative and no one knows where you are right now. We'll keep you here a few days until we're certain it's safe for you to return."

"Good luck trying to keep Rose here any longer," Matt said.

61

Long after a somewhat dazed Timmons returned to his post in the parking lot, Matt and Ashleigh sat together on the side of Matt's bed and watched the video over and over, scrutinizing every nuance of every significant frame, trying to make sense of it all. Matt, after reviewing the objects moving through the air and Whitten's reaction to the appearance of the apparition, was now more certain than ever there was some paranormal force at work in Rose's home.

Ashleigh was just as convinced that the force was her grandfather and that his appearance was no coincidence. "Grandma's right. He's protecting her," she said.

"Tormenting would be more accurate," Matt said. "Look what he's been doing to her all these years. By moving her things around, he's got her believing people are breaking into her home and stealing her possessions. That's a long way from protection."

"What about what he did tonight?" she asked.

"He was protecting his *own* turf and, in the process, protecting *her*," Matt said. "Look, Ashleigh, no matter what rationale you may use, you can't get away from what he's been doing to her. She's estranged from everyone in her family except you because of him. Maybe he was only teasing her all this time but look at the toll it's taken on her. She's a recluse, afraid to leave her own home because of what he's done."

Ashleigh stiffened. "Matt, that's a cold-hearted thing to say. You never knew my grandfather. You certainly don't know him well enough to say that about him."

"I know your grandmother," he said. "I love her very much and I can see what he's been doing to her through the years. You can see it too, if you'll just look at the video with an open mind. The only thing I see here that could be described as cold-hearted is what he's been doing to Rose. Now the only thing we have to do now is find out why he would want to do this to her. There has to be a reason."

Angry now, she didn't want to talk to him anymore. She made him leave so she could watch the videos once more, alone. He walked outside and Sergeant Timmons exited his patrol car and approached him. "Matt, you shouldn't be out here like this."

189

"Mind if I sit in your car with you, then?"

"Fine by me as long as you don't mind listening to talk radio. I love to listen to all those lonely people out there who have nothing better to do than to call some talk show host and regurgitate the same thing he's been telling them for three hours."

"What?"

"Do you ever listen to these shows?" Timmons asked. "Politics or sports, it doesn't matter; the listeners who call in all just basically repeat the same thing the host has been saying. They've never have an original idea and if someone does get past the call screener with one – an original thought, that is – the host always cuts 'em off. No disagreement allowed with these guys. It's hysterical and it keeps me from going to sleep." Then he turned serious. "What's wrong? You and your lady have a fight?"

"No, not really," Matt said. "But I need to talk to you, to get some feedback on some theories I'm working on. Do you have a few minutes?"

62

The telephone on Justice Gravois's desk interrupted his thoughts as he struggled to write the opinion on the catastrophic auto accident that had left the young boy a quadriplegic. Normally, it would have been Matt who wrote the opinion on behalf of Justice Gravois, but since he was out for an indefinite period, Gravois did his best to take up the slack without placing additional burdens on an already overworked staff. So, it was with slight irritability in his voice that he answered the phone.

"Yes?"

"Justice Gravois, there's someone here to see you," said his receptionist.

"I'm too busy to see anyone right now. Does he have an appointment?"

"No sir, but they're two men here from the U.S. Attorney's office and they say it's important. They're pretty adamant."

"The U.S. Attorney's office?" *What could they want?*

Despite the controversy over the bail bond arrangements at the criminal district courthouse, Justice Gravois was so far out of that loop he might as well have been hunting pheasant in South Dakota. He was only vaguely aware of events that occurred outside the State Supreme Court's jurisdiction. He'd heard occasional reports of complaints from district court but attributed them to political sour grapes and because the feds had done a good job of keeping a lid on their probe, he was surprised to get a visit from them. "Well, I guess you'd better let them in," he said, moving his law books and papers to the side of his desk.

The two men were both about six feet tall and each appeared to be in his late thirties or early forties. Neither of them smiled as they introduced themselves to the Supreme Court Justice. Neither did they accord him the respect that a subordinate would normally show a Supreme Court justice. That was because neither of them considered themselves as subordinate, even if they were on his turf.

"Justice Gravois, my name is Anthony Lockett," said the first man to enter the office. "This is Wilson Tircuit and we're with the Eastern District U.S. Attorney's office here in New Orleans."

"I'm vaguely aware where the Eastern District is," Justice Gravois said without smiling. His sarcasm had a biting edge to it and he was a bit put off by

191

the notion that the man thought it necessary to explain to a State Supreme Court justice where the U.S. Attorney's office was. His tone put the visitor on the defensive before they could even state their business. He remained seated and didn't offer his hand in greeting. "What can I do for you?" he asked. They sat across from the justice without being asked to do so.

"Justice Gravois, we understand you're conducting an inquiry into the activities of Orleans Criminal District Judge Charles Cheramie," Lockett said.

Thomas Gravois leaned back in his chair and laced his fingers across his chest. "I'm not sure I'm at liberty to discuss an ongoing investigation by this office – not even with representatives of the U.S. Attorney's office," he said. "Why do you ask?"

"Justice Gravois, we're here to ask that you cease and desist in your investigation immediately. This is to be considered a formal request from the U.S. Attorney's Office."

Justice Gravois sat up straight, suddenly intrigued. "You guys conducting an investigation?" he asked.

"I'm afraid we're not at liberty do discuss that," Lockett said.

"Well now, it looks like tit for tat, doesn't it?" Gravois said. "I don't tell you what I'm doing and you don't tell me what you're doing. Isn't that just typical for the bureaucracy? It's no damned wonder the taxpayers are fed up with their government. The FBI and CIA don't share information, the DEA and FBI don't share information, law enforcement computers aren't compatible, and we don't share our information with each other, and everyone stays in the dark. I can't imagine why people are jaded."

The two visitors glanced at each other and then Lockett spoke again. "Justice Gravois, I'm afraid we're going to have to insist on ---"

"You're going to insist on nothing," Justice Gravois said, standing now and drawing himself fully erect. "Gentlemen, I have my job to do and I don't believe anything I'm doing will have any effect on the feds unless my investigation evolves into a civil rights violation and if it does, I'll be sure and let you know."

"I'm afraid you don't appreciate the gravity of the situation," Lockett said.

"No sir, it's you who doesn't understand," Gravois spat back. "I'm not going to give you the satisfaction of answering your question but you obviously have done your homework and already know what you know. But I am not about to relinquish my authority nor do I intend to knuckle under to you just because you have the balls to barge in here and try to intimidate me with your laminated federal I.D. badges. If you're conducting an investigation, I'll try to stay out of your way, but you sure as hell better stay out of my way – if I'm conducting an investigation, that is. Good day gentlemen."

The two remained seated, making no move to leave and Gravois's blood pressure was escalating quickly when Tircuit spoke for the first time. "Justice

Gravois, you mentioned something a moment ago that is a real problem. You were correct to say that the lack of cooperation among agencies hampers progress."

"Your point?" The Supreme Court justice's face was still red, but he eased himself back into his chair.

"If we provide you with some of the details of our investigation, can we be assured that our information won't leave this room?" Tircuit asked.

"Certainly. I've already said I have no intention to impede your investigation."

The two visitors again exchanged quick glances before Tircuit continued. "Justice Gravois, the U.S. Attorney's office and the FBI have been conducting an investigation of the criminal district court in New Orleans for several months. We have developed information that indicates a number of New Orleans attorneys, a bail bond company, and several criminal court judges are implicated in a complex scheme to siphon off more than half-a-million dollars in bail bond money over a period of several years."

Gravois let out a slow whistle. "Jesus," he said. "Half-a-million dollars?"

"That's what we've been able to confirm so far," Tircuit said. "It could go a lot higher before it's over. We haven't gone to the grand jury yet, but we believe there may be as many as a dozen to eighteen people involved. We've already applied some pressure and we believe we have some targets of the investigation ready to flip. If they do, their testimony will be crucial."

"That brings us to our reason for being here," said Lockett. "It's imperative that you not take action that would be detrimental to our investigation before our case is fully developed."

"You know you could have said that at the beginning and I would've offered you a drink instead of getting my dander up," Gravois said.

"I apologize for my approach, but we have to be very careful."

"Gentlemen, I appreciate your position and I certainly don't want to step on your toes but I hope you can understand my situation. I have a state district court judge who took part in beating a man who wasn't a suspect in any crime. The man was my law clerk and I take personal umbrage at his being worked over."

"Your law clerk? We didn't know anything about that," Tircuit said.

"It really shouldn't matter who was beaten," said Gravois. "It was at least inappropriate and at most illegal for a judge to take part in ex parte questioning of an individual, let alone participate in beating him half to death. My job as a State Supreme Court justice is to remove the man from the bench and to refer the matter to the Judiciary Commission with a recommendation for permanent removal and disbarment. There could even be a prison sentence. But that shouldn't interfere with your investigation."

"Except that the man you removed and that you're trying to send to prison is one of the primary targets of our investigation," Tircuit said.

Gravois sank back in his chair. "Holy shit."

193

63

By now, J. François knew all about the events that led to Judge Charles Cheramie's suspension from the bench. Moreover, he now knew who Matt Ramsey was and he knew Matt had been nosing around the trial records of his late clients. What he did not know was why. *What the hell's a Supreme Court law clerk doing going through those records? How could Charlie have been so stupid?*

Paranoia had J. François firmly in his grips, thanks to the untimely deaths of his clients/enterprise employees. The mysterious sightings and subsequent disappearances of the four beings at his home on two separate occasions were bad enough. Now a law clerk had somehow managed to get a criminal court judge suspended because the damned judge panicked over the clerk's examination of the trial records of six of J. François's clients. *Why was he investigating those cases? What is he looking for?*

The notorious criminal defense lawyer still had not communicated with Judge Cheramie or his judicial colleagues, Lyle Bergen and Ray Sonnier. He understood, though, that this was the time to keep a low profile in order to lessen the risk of exposure. The enterprise shut down for the foreseeable future, at least until Judge Cheramie's fate could be decided by the Judicial Commission. Every phase of the enterprise's operations – especially drugs and prostitution – simply went underground. One couldn't even get a traffic ticket fixed now; too many people were watching.

The news media, led by WWL-TV and the *Times-Picayune,* received several unconfirmed reports that something was awry in the criminal district courthouse and reporters began their preliminary snooping. As is often the case, though, the media get lazy while becoming too close to those they cover. Reporters didn't have a clue as to what they were looking for or where to look. They didn't get help from the courthouse crowd. The entire scene evolved into a comical farce of judges, lawyers, and deputies ducking into doorways when any of them saw a reporter approaching. The media never caught on and, in the end, they mostly ended up interviewing each other for questionable leads that never seemed to pan out.

Confusion, mistrust, and suspicion were not limited to the fertile mind of J. François and the news media. Uncertainty became the order of the day as lawyers, judges, law enforcement officers, and even parish jail inmates found themselves caught up in the frenzy swirling through and around the criminal courthouse, making it the most likely place in the city for the hottest new rumor.

There was the omnipresent undercurrent of misinformation exchanged freely within the legal community and theories abounded as to the identity of the mysterious Matt Ramsey. No one was buying into the story that he was a law clerk for the Louisiana Supreme Court. Even those who knew the story about his occupation to be true, some who had attended law school with him, suspected something murkier, something far more sinister and ominous. Some said he was a narc on undercover assignment for the DEA. Hell no, others argued; he was working for ATF or the FBI. Another, smaller contingent even claimed to know for certain he was a member of a rival group of lawyers from the Mississippi Gulf Coast that was trying to move in on the enterprise's operations and that events were building toward a major turf war.

Clerking was just a cover to conceal his real intent, one rumor had it. Conjecture begat speculation, creating unprecedented chaos in the already tainted New Orleans legal profession. Distracted judges, even those uninvolved in the enterprise, could only half listen as they presided over trials. Attorneys couldn't concentrate on pending litigation or criminal proceedings lest they miss out on the latest gossip. *Who the hell is this Matt Ramsey guy? Where is he? What's his next move? Who's his next target?*

Justice Thomas Gravois, already frustrated at the widespread lack of cooperation encountered at the criminal district courthouse, became more determined than ever to build a case for the permanent removal of Judge Cheramie from office, even if it meant knocking down some very old stone walls at the courthouse. At the same time, however, he knew it was crucial that he temper his anger and personal involvement in the probe with professional restraint. To do otherwise would almost certainly undermine the results of his investigation and that of the U.S. Attorney's office as well. Privately, he felt that his hands were tied and he feared he might get no more than a temporary suspension or worse, a simple reprimand unless one of the deputies could be persuaded to plea bargain. For now, that was where he was concentrating his efforts. He would let the federal investigation run its course and trust that justice would be done.

A greater priority was keeping Matt and Ashleigh and Ashleigh's grandmother Rose alive and well. They survived one attempt on their lives and that near miss was enough. The stakes were high and there was no margin for error.

196

64

"You've got to give your lady some room," Timmons was saying as the talk show host ranted on in the background, spewing his latest conspiracy theory about Congress, Islam, illegal immigration and anything else that he thought went against America's and his – mostly his – best interests. His favorite targets were, as always, Democrats. "She's got some complex issues to deal with right now. On the one hand, she loves and wants to protect her grandmother. On the other, she's in denial but she recognizes a pattern of torment that she believes her grandfather's ghost is perpetuating against Rose. That's a tough conflict to come to terms with and she's going to need your support."

The stereotype of all Louisiana State Troopers as sex-crazed woman chasers didn't seem to apply to Timmons and Matt was grateful for the chance to speak openly with someone who wouldn't laugh at him. "So, what do you think of my theory?" he asked. "Unofficially, of course."

"Matt, you know I'm not going to stick my neck out that far. If I tell my troop commander there's a ghost in Rose's home, I'd be laughed right out of Troop L. I hope you understand I can't endorse a proposition like that openly. But unofficially, I can tell you privately and confidentially that after watching the video, there was definitely *something* in that house. When I say 'something,' I don't mean something physical. That's obvious. Whatever it was that I saw, that you and Ashleigh saw, was something that can't been felt, held, or controlled. I've read a little about paranormal events and this falls within the parameters of similar events where ghosts supposedly remained near places where they'd died because of some unfulfilled wish or something else that wouldn't let them rest peacefully after their deaths."

"Unfulfilled wish?" What're you talking about?"

"In some cases, the person may have died violently and his ghost is unable to leave the area where he died because of the way in which he died," Timmons said. "It may be seeking vengeance. In other instances, there may be some unfinished business and the ghost is hanging around in pursuit of some kind of closure. You said Jake died a natural death, so that leaves only one other thing that could be keeping him around."

197

Matt stared out the front windshield without speaking as he recalled everything Ashleigh and Rose had ever told him about Jake. It took nearly a full minute before it struck him. "The ashes!" he said, still staring straight ahead.

"What?" Sergeant Timmons asked.

"Jesus! I can't believe no one's thought of it before now." Slack-jawed, he turned to Timmons. "Jake wanted his ashes scattered over his vegetable garden because he loved working there. Instead, Rose told Ashleigh and me she keeps the ashes in a box on her fireplace mantle. He wants his ashes taken to his garden and that's why he's moving things around in the house. He's pissed at her for not honoring his wish."

"I didn't even hear that, Matt," the trooper said. "I can't sanction your theory in my capacity as an officer of the law, but if I were you, I'd get Rose to get those ashes the hell out of her house and into the garden, the sooner the better. But I didn't tell you that."

65

Matt found Ashleigh asleep on his bed when he returned to his room three hours later. The laptop was still on but the screen had gone blank. He moved the wireless mouse just enough to cause the screen to come to life again. The hard drive data was still activated and the images of Travis Whitten's break-in were still playing. Matt again watched the intruder as he fired shots into Ashleigh's bedroom and as he encountered what appeared to be the human-like figure that Rose identified as her late husband Jake Melancon. Finally, he watched as Whitten suffered an apparent heart attack and died on Rose's dining room floor. He'd already lost count of how many times he'd watched the scene and each time he was as fascinated as he had been when he watched it in real time.

Whitten was collapsing onto the floor again, along with the chair he had grabbled, when Ashleigh roused and sat up on the bed slowly beside Matt. Placing her hand on his knee, she spoke quietly so as not to disturb Rose in the adjoining room. "I thought a lot about what you said and I think you may be onto something. I don't know what it is, but after watching all the videos of things that were moved around, I tried to come up with a logical explanation, but I couldn't."

Matt tried to quiet her, but she continued. "After thinking back on all the things that've disappeared over the years and trying to put it all into context, to gain some perspective from it all, I can see why you say Jake is cruel. Then, when I saw that man in Grandma's house tonight, when I saw him trying to get away from Grandpa Jake, it just all seemed to come together. He *was* being sadistic in the way he's torturing Grandma. That leaves two questions: why was he doing it and what can be done about it?"

Matt was still watching the video. "I think I have the answer to both of those questions but first, I've changed my mind about his being evil," he said. "I spent the last three hours talking with Geoffrey Timmons and he's a pretty sharp guy. He told me something that made a lot of sense of what's been a completely senseless situation."

"What?" Ashleigh asked.

199

"He said he's studied paranormal events and there's a common thread that seems to be found whenever a ghost hangs around like Jake has and causes mischief."

"Mischief? I wouldn't call this mischief," she said.

"You're right, it's not. Sergeant Timmons said ghosts are rarely violent. It's usually an emptiness of some type created by something incomplete like an unfulfilled promise that causes them to stay on and move things around the way he's been doing."

Ashleigh said nothing. She just looked at Matt and waited for him to continue.

"Don't you remember Rose telling us that Jake wanted his ashes spread in his garden?" he asked. "She told us she couldn't bring herself to do that and that she keeps his ashes in that box on the man---"

"On the mantle," she said, finishing his sentence for him. "Oh, my God, Matt, could it be something that simple? Is that the bottom line to all this?"

"I don't know about any bottom line, but it's a place to start," he said, "if we can convince Rose to get rid of the ashes, that is."

66

Robert Vennet now had reason to worry. A phone call told him about Whitten's death, though the caller knew only that it was caused by a heart attack. The news came from a driver for the funeral home sent to pick up Whitten's body. He told someone and the story eventually hit the streets and Vennet got the phone call. Worse than the news of Whitten's death was the knowledge that he'd failed to carry out his assignment because the targets, Matt Ramsey, his girlfriend and her grandmother weren't home.

Now that authorities knew of Whitten's apparent motives after finding his gun a few feet from his body, there was too much heat to risk another attempt. The conspirators had no way of knowing that law enforcement authorities had learned of the plot before Whitten ever set foot on Rose's property only to die – of natural causes, of all things – in the home of the intended victims. It was only a matter of time now before the trail would lead to Judge Charles Cheramie and eventually, to the co-conspirators.

J. François also had plenty to keep his mind occupied. It was bad enough that Judge Cheramie got directly involved in the beating of Matt Ramsey, but now the botched killings further threatened the enterprise and its principals. He wasn't sure who had set up the bungled assassination attempt, but it appeared to have Judge Cheramie's fingerprints all over it. He was more convinced than ever that he'd taken the right action in sending the sealed letter to his attorney. As a contingency plan, the letter's contents couldn't protect him but if he went down, he was not going down alone. Nor was his the only letter written concerning affairs of the Orleans Parish Criminal District Court.

His letter and the attempts to kill Matt, Ashleigh, and Rose were acts of desperation, to be sure. The first enterprise players received their letters from the U.S. Justice Department officially informing them they were targets of a federal investigation. That sent everyone scrambling to their respective lawyers to learn if a deal could be struck with prosecutors before indictments came down. Fighting, they knew, wasn't an option for most of them; they had operated too openly for too long. The Honorable Charles Cheramie was among the first to get such a letter, along with fellow judges Ray Sonnier and Lyle Bergen, and infamous criminal defense lawyer J. François Berthelot, III. Like the hooker who could see and feel

201

the encroachment of age and gravity upon her once-unblemished body, they knew time was the enemy.

———————————

J. François received his letter not as an attorney, but in his capacity as owner of CajunAmerica Bail Bonds. The feds, it seemed, considered it prudent to check corporate records at the Secretary of State's office in Baton Rouge and when they did, the connection was made to J. François who remained defiant and unready to cut a deal just yet. He felt he was clever and slick enough to evade prosecution and if not, certainly there would be no conviction. Too many times he'd proved himself just too damned smart for thick-headed prosecutors who found it necessary to belly up to the public trough in order to earn a living because they couldn't make it in private practice.

Bust a few low-level street dealers, some hard luck prostitutes, a few petty thieves and they think they're invincible. Prosecute a couple of crack-head murder cases, brag about an inflated conviction rate, and run for re-election on the money raised from extorting campaign contributions from fellow members of the bar. Yeah, that's how you become a crime buster. The day I can't out maneuver those dumbasses is the day we'll all be too old to play anymore.

J. François was making a fatal mistake in the legal profession: he was underestimating his adversaries. These weren't prosecutors who built their careers busting prostitutes, thieves, or even murderers. Nor were they running for office. These were experts in white collar crime. They knew what they were doing and they had gone about their investigation methodically and doggedly. Federal prosecutors, situated in their offices across town from J. François, were confident in the case they were building.

J. François had been fearful of wiretaps since Matt was beaten half to death in the courthouse and was wary of using his office telephone. He would have been better off had his paranoia kicked in several months earlier. The FBI had been busy in those months and now had hundreds of hours of video and audio recordings to wade through. The tapes were from clandestine surveillance and eavesdropping equipment installed in the offices of the three Orleans Parish judges, as well as judges in Jefferson and St. Bernard Parishes, CajunAmerica Bail Bonds, J. François, and on the residential telephones of each.

67

The laptop screen was blank again, thanks to the screen saver, when the first slivers of sunlight wedged their way through the motel room curtains that somehow didn't close completely. Not that it mattered, because Matt and Ashleigh had fallen sleep in each other's arms, still fully clothed. They'd watched the computer screen until they lost count, mesmerized at the sight of Travis Whitten as he first tried to kill them in their bed, then as he encountered what they both had finally agreed was the image of Jake Melancon, and finally, as he died on the linoleum covered floor of Rose's dining room.

They also came to terms, after hours of quiet discussion, with the fact that Jake wanted something done that was never carried out, and finally they decided between them that what Jake wanted was to have his ashes scattered in his garden. It seemed so obvious to them finally, and they were still discussing how they would be able to convince Rose to carry out his wishes when, exhausted, they laid back on the bed and fell asleep.

That was only three hours earlier, and now the sun's early light forced Matt to blink and to try and turn away from the bright glare. His movements caused Ashleigh to stir and then awaken. Still groggy, she struggled to sit up. "God, I'm half dead. What time is it?"

Matt squinted as he held his watch up only inches from his face. "Seven thirty-five. You hungry?"

"Starved," she said. "Do they have a continental breakfast here?"

"They should. Most motels these days do. Do you want to walk down to the desk with me and grab something?"

"Yeah, coffee and then more coffee. I'll bring something back to the room for Grandma Rose."

Matt was already on his cell phone. He listened to it as it rang twice. "Geoffrey," he said when Sergeant Timmons answered, "we're going down to grab some breakfast. You want us to bring you something?"

Timmons, who'd been awake the entire night listening to the radio talk shows, laughed. "Don't you two ever sleep? Tell you what; I'll walk down to the office with you. I don't like the idea of letting you out of my sight. We have another unit out here and they can watch the rooms while we're gone."

He joined Matt and Ashleigh when they emerged from their room and the three strolled together.

"I've been doing a little thinking about your theory," Timmons said.

"And what did you decide?" Matt asked.

"Before I answer that, let me ask you, do you still think that was Rose's late husband on that videotape?"

"There's not a doubt in our minds," Ashleigh said before Matt could formulate his own response.

"Okay, then my next question is what do you think he's trying to do?"

This time it was Matt who answered. "We both think he's been trying to get Rose to make good on her promise to scatter his ashes in his vegetable garden. He said before he died that was what he wanted done with them."

"That's consistent with what I've read about the paranormal. They – ghosts, that is – usually stick around after their deaths only for the purpose of trying to complete unfinished business. They can't communicate in normal ways, so they try to get their messages across by other means."

"In this case, it's been by moving things around in Rose's home and even hiding objects," Matt said.

"Right," added Ashleigh. "These disappearances have been going on just since Grandpa Jake died."

"Exactly," Sergeant Timmons said. "So, what are you two going to do about it?"

"We've got to convince Grandma Rose to carry out his last wish," Ashleigh said.

"Let me ask you something," Matt said to the state trooper. "If Jake's been hanging around in an effort to have his wishes carried out, what about the others?"

"What about them?" Timmons said.

"They were all killed violently by street criminals," Matt said. "Robberies, rapes, muggings, abductions, it didn't seem to matter. Now, each one of the people tried for those crimes – tried and acquitted, I should point out – have died violent deaths of their own and in each case, witnesses say they saw these thugs behaving erratically just before they were killed. All except Deacon Watson, that is. There were no witnesses to his death, but he was killed next to the grave of the woman he was accused and acquitted of raping and murdering."

"So?" Timmons said as he slowed his pace. "What's your point?"

"Could it be that these men were all killed as a result of attempts by the ghosts of their victims to seek some kind of revenge for their own deaths?" Matt asked.

Both men had stopped walking now and had turned to face each other as Ashleigh watch wide-eyed, wondering where the conversation was going.

"Jesus, Matt, that's pretty deep," Timmons said. "First thing, keep in mind that ghosts rarely take direct action in committing violent acts on humans."

"Exactly! These people weren't killed by ghosts! They killed themselves!"

"Why would they do that?"

"They saw the ghosts of people they'd killed and they were scared shitless and panicked. Look at the three guys in the car. They acted like they were trying to rob someone at that convenience store and then they tore out of there like a bat out of hell and right down the road, they run head-on into a garbage truck. Then there's this guy Lenny who jumps a fence into a yard with two dogs that tear him to shreds. Billy Boy runs into the path of a taxi and is knocked into the rear hooves of a mule that kicks him in the head. All of these are the acts of people who're not acting rationally.

"Don't you see? They were scared half to death and did irrational things out of fear that got themselves killed and the ghosts of their victims didn't have to lay a hand on them!"

"What about the guy in the cemetery?" Timmons asked.

"Nobody knows for sure how he died," Matt answered somewhat defensively. "It was a trauma to the head, but there were no witnesses. But we do know he died violently at the grave of his alleged victim."

"Don't get all lathered up," Timmons said. "I'm just being the devil's advocate here to see how well you've constructed your theory. If it helps any, I feel kinda the way you do. I'm not entirely convinced those men's deaths were accidental. But now, let me ask you something else. Didn't you tell me that all six of those men were defended by the same attorney?"

"Yeah, some guy named Berthelot, but what's that got...." Matt stopped talking mid-sentence and it took a moment for him to get his voice back.

"You don't think....Oh, shit, we've got to warn him."

"Warn who? The attorney, this Berthelot guy? Matt, slow down a minute. What're you going to tell him? You can't just walk up to him and say, 'Excuse me, counselor, but I think they're ghosts who're coming to get you and you might be in danger.' They'll laugh you right into the East Louisiana Mental Hospital."

"I don't care what he thinks or what he says. We have to warn him." "What you mean 'we,' paleface. I'm not sticking my neck out on this one. I already told you that. I'd never be able to live it down."

"I understand and that's fine," Matt said. "But I've got to try."

"You might consider just who it is you're trying to help here. He's a guy who's made his career putting bad people back on the street. Are you sure you want to try to help someone like him who's probably just going to laugh at you?"

"I won't be able to face myself in the mirror if I don't," Matt said.

"Matt, Sergeant Timmons is right," Ashleigh said speaking for the first time since the conversation had taken this turn. "Forget this idea. There's no good to be gained from it."

205

"I'm sorry, Ashleigh. I appreciate what you're both trying to do for me, but I can't let this happen. I'm going to try to warn him."

Breakfast was forgotten for the moment as the three stood on the parking lot discussing a course of action. Sergeant Timmons looked to his left and right to be sure no one was listening or watching. "Matt, you're not under house arrest, so I can't stop you. But do me a big favor. Wait until I go off shift and I'll ride with you just to hang back and be sure nothing goes wrong. There may still be someone out there who wants to hurt you and I don't want that to happen."

"I promise," said Matt, relieved to have Timmons volunteer to accompany him.

"You know Justice Gravois's going to be really pissed at you."

"Yeah, well I'll deal with that later."

"I still think you're both being stupid," Ashleigh said. "But I won't try to talk you out of it. Just be careful, Matt. That's all I ask."

"I will. I'm just going to tell him what I think and get the hell out. It'll be up to him to decide how he wants to handle it.

"By the way, weren't we going to get breakfast? I'm starving."

The three walked into the motel lobby and loaded up on waffles, blueberry muffins, bacon, coffee, and orange juice. They didn't leave until they'd had several cups of coffee and then Ashleigh got food and drink to take back to Rose in her room.

"I have an idea, Matt," said Sergeant Timmons as they walked back to the rooms. "Why don't you take this lawyer Berthelot your computer and let him watch the little episode in Rose's home. That might make him at least listen to what you have to say."

"That's a great idea," Matt said. "I hadn't thought of that."

68

Sergeant Geoffrey Timmons was driving west in the typically heavy I-10 traffic while Matt placed a call to his friend in the New Orleans Police Department. "I have another quick favor," he said when his friend answered. "I need the phone number for a New Orleans attorney. His name's J. François Berthelot." He waited for a few minutes. "The Third? Yeah, that's him. What's the number?" Matt jotted down the number and thanked his friend before disconnecting the call. He dialed the number he'd just been given.

"Mr. Berthelot, please."

"I'm sorry," the indifferent female voice on the other end said, "Mr. Berthelot isn't in the office."

"When do you expect him?" Matt asked.

"He's in Edgard in St. John Parish in trial this week."

Matt thanked her and ended the call. Then he turned to Sergeant Timmons. "Looks like we're not going into New Orleans after all. He's in trial in Edgard."

"No problem," said Timmons.

69

J. François was as confident as could be expected, given all the distractions of dead clients and a federal investigation when he headed out of New Orleans through Metairie and Kenner in Jefferson Parish en route to Edgard in St. John the Baptist Parish. He reflected briefly on his empty house as he passed through Kenner, but he didn't dwell on it or on the four beings he'd encountered there. He hadn't seen them again and he long ago attributed the eerie sightings to stress. He had a lot going on and he was determined to move forward, federal investigation and fatalities be damned. He was far too busy to let something as trivial as nervous tension disrupt his routine.

He was determined to arrive early in order to avoid the hordes of reporters who were certain to be on hand for such an emotionally-charged trial. It isn't every day, after all, that an elderly priest is brutally murdered in his small- town home. He'd heard rumors that network television news was keeping an eye on this trial.

He wanted time to make his final trail preparations without the distraction of the media circus that was bound to accompany the trial. He'd left his client, Deke Morgan, with specific instructions to shower and shave and to appear in court in the cheap suit J. François purchased for him. They'd gone over Deke's story countless times until he was sure his client could repeat without it sounding like a recitation. It was critical that nothing appear as if it had been rehearsed.

His cruise control was set on sixty as he made his way west on I-10, across the southern tip of Lake Pontchartrain and into St. John. He exited at LaPlace and headed straight for the Mississippi River where he waited impatiently for the ferry to take him and his vehicle to the west bank of the river. Once across, he drove off the ferry and found himself virtually in downtown Edgard, such as it was.

A world away from New Orleans less than twenty-five miles downriver, Edgard is small by any applicable standards and as with most small towns, the citizens are a close-knit lot who don't take easily to outsiders, especially an outsider accused of killing a priest – or his lawyer. That public mood was a factor that would make the jury selection critical and he wanted to go over the jury

209

venire with his hired-gun expert again to get an idea of which ones he would want to dismiss.

Less than forty minutes behind, Matt and Geoffrey Timmons made their way toward the same Edgard courthouse.

The state trooper negotiated his way through Metairie and Kenner, taking the exact route taken only minutes earlier by the attorney. Like J. François, they took the LaPlace exit and headed for the ferry landing on the Mississippi. For reasons he couldn't understand, Matt experienced a recurring sense of foreboding that he found himself unable to shake. *What do I say to Berthelot? What's going to be his reaction?* He cradled his laptop to his stomach. It held the only real evidence he had that might convince J. François that his life could be in danger. *What am I going to do if he doesn't believe me or worse, if he laughs at me?* He shrugged silently. *I'll do what I can. The rest is up to him and it won't be my problem.*

70

The offices of the U.S. Attorney in downtown New Orleans were alive with activity. Clerks had been busy typing transcripts of taped conversations all week long and were just now finishing their final drafts. The lead attorney in the investigation sat at a long table in a richly-appointed conference room across from his supervisor and three FBI agents who had been working on the Operation Dishonor probe for the past several months. Stacks of documents were piled on the table, each stack representing a key element of the ongoing operation. Even as the documents were passed around the table, clerks continued to enter with some new transcript or another shred of evidence from subpoenaed bank documents and telephone receipts. Upon depositing the new papers and leaving the room, that clerk would be replaced by another with still more papers.

It had been going on this way for days and the participants were beginning to suffer eyestrain from poring over so many papers. Finally, the supervisor tossed a folder onto the table. His name was Victor Carlotti. A veteran of more than twenty years with the Justice Department, he was an integral part of the U.S. Attorney's office, one of those anonymous behind-the-scenes grunts without whom little gets done. "What's our bottom line, gentlemen?" he asked, leaning back in his chair and rubbing his temples that were throbbing from four days of non-stop analysis of the evidence before him. "Do we have enough hard evidence to take before a grand jury?"

Jamie Maestri, the lead investigator, was first to speak. "I've gone before grand juries with a lot less evidence and gotten indictments," he said.

"Indictments, yes," Carlotti said, "but that ain't enough. I gotta have a rock-solid guarantee that we're gonna to come away from this with convictions. These aren't some Colombian drug smugglers we're looking at here. These are judges, three from Orleans, one each from St. Bernard, Jefferson, and St. John. These are attorneys who not only have reputations in New Orleans but are pretty damned influential. If we can't put these guys away, it's our collective asses. They'll come back and bury us." Carlotti was standing now, pacing around the room, stopping at and locking eyes with each man at the table. He ignored the lone woman sitting at the end of the table. "I'll ask my question again. Do we have sufficient hard evidence to move to the next level?"

211

Each man shifted in his chair and refused for the moment to make eye contact with anyone else. Finally, someone cleared his throat. It was Maestri. "Vic, you know as well as anyone here there're no guarantees. We take our best shot and hope we get a jury with a modicum of common sense that can decipher the evidence we give them and weigh that against the rhetoric the defense spews out. It's always been that way."

"I'm sorry, Jamie, I ain't buyin' that bill of goods," Carlotti said. "I don't want to come away from a major trial that's gonna attract national attention with egg all over my face. I will not go into this if we're going to become a national embarrassment the way the first couple of Edwards trials did or the way Jim Garrison did."

The first reference was to former Louisiana Governor Edwin Edwards who was twice indicted under the federal Racketeer Influenced and Corrupt Organization, or RICO, statute and subsequently made federal prosecutors look silly before finally being convicted on the third try. The second was the ill-fated attempt by the former New Orleans district attorney to tie New Orleans businessman Clay Shaw to the assassination of President Kennedy. "I will not have this office become a laughingstock. If I don't get the answers I want, we'll walk away from this right now."

More squirming and group preoccupation with the polished cherry wood table top. After what seemed an inordinately long pause, a feminine voice spoke with more authority than Maestri had been able to muster. "If you want a guarantee, boss, go work for Sears." Seven heads turned in unison to stare at Jessica Beauchamp, the Assistant U.S. Attorney who'd had the temerity to address her supervisor in such a manner.

"What did you say?" Carlotti said as first his neck and then his entire face turned crimson.

"I said if you're seriously interested in doing a public service on behalf of the citizens of Louisiana's Eastern District, if you're serious about seeing that justice is administered fairly and impartially, do what you swore to do when you took your oath of office. But if you're more interested in the political implications, you can just keep chasing some poor schmuck who's raking a few dollars off the top at his job at the bank, or some tax cheat who doesn't have the political clout to make your life miserable. As for the egg, if we lose, just remember it'll be on our faces, too, not just yours."

"You're way outta line Miss Beauchamp!" Veins stood out on his neck.

"*Mrs*. Beauchamp," she corrected him. "And yes sir, I realize I stuck my nose out a tad but I thought that's what we do here. You hired us to do our jobs but now that push has come to shove, you're vacillating. We're either good enough or we're not and I personally resent the implication that I've not done my homework. I've sacrificed my marriage and time with my family with the hours I've put into this investigation and I'll be damned if I'm going to go through all that just so you can wash your hands of it because you're concerned about the

212

political repercussions. I can't speak for everyone here, but I know we have plenty of evidence to get an indictment. But as every one of you is aware, there's no way we can know for certain going in that we'll come away with even a single conviction." She tossed her pen and legal pad onto the table. "So much for the noble champions of justice," she said, making no effort to conceal her disgust.

Carlotti looked as though he'd been struck in the face with a cold bucket of water. He was unaccustomed to subordinates speaking to him in this manner and he didn't know quite how to respond. Acutely mindful of harassment claims, he'd always been on his best behavior toward women and minorities but this was something new. She'd laid down the gauntlet and now he had to respond. "Mrs. Beauchamp, you've raised some valid points and I won't try to claim otherwise," he said. "But as you are aware, we don't live in a perfect world and I was merely relating the realities as they exist. I was in no way trying to imply that we should walk away from a fight, especially when we are right. I can understand your frustration. We're all frustrated. We've all put in some long hours and nerves and tempers are somewhat frayed."

He was trying to be tactful, to play the diplomat, but no one was buying it. He was desperate now to save face and still maintain his authority, but one by one, the others now spoke up to support their colleague. "Jessie's right," said Maestri. "There are times when you have to roll the dice and this is one of those times. There are no guarantees when you're dealing with a jury. Can you say for certain that Oswald would've been convicted if he'd lived? No, you cannot, but it's clear to all of us that these people are involved in a system of racketeering, collusion, bribery, graft, embezzlement, and God knows what else. We've built a helluva case, if I do say so myself, and I feel we should move forward with it."

Just that quickly, the others in the conference room seemed to all seemed to summon heretofore hidden courage and as one, they stood up to their boss in support of Beauchamp and what they'd found in their investigation. They agreed that they had no choice but to proceed aggressively.

"I believe we should take this to the grand jury and the sooner the better," said one. "Just from what I've seen in these reports here today, these judges are looking at more than two hundred years and fines of more than two million dollars under the RICO statute for racketeering, public bribery, mail fraud, extortion, and various other offenses and I, for one, feel that they're no better than anyone else. Let the evidence speak for itself in getting the indictments and again in the trials."

Another drew himself up and, looking directly at Carlotti, spoke in measured tones, as if weighing each word. "Vic, I know the pressure you're under here but that pressure is no greater than that felt by the rest of us. If there are to be political ramifications in this investigation, then I feel that should place an even greater burden on us to do our jobs as charged with no consideration given to those factors. So, we're looking at six judges and a handful of lawyers. So what? Without trying to sound too moralistic, I personally believe that

213

corruption in the judiciary is worse than corruption in any other branch of government."

The room then grew quiet as Carlotti looked from face to face. While he didn't like insubordination, he did admire backbone and self-confidence, and most of all, unity. "Well, I guess you've all said what I wanted to hear," he said. To get convictions, I have to have conviction from my people and you've shown it here today. Let's get ready to go to the grand jury and let's get our RICO indictments."

71

J. François Berthelot heaved his heavy frame into the hard, wooden chair at the defense table and opened his briefcase. Except for a lone sheriff's deputy serving as the bailiff, he was by himself in the stuffy courtroom. His expert on the jury pool had not arrived yet. The ancient courthouse air conditioning system wasn't helping much in the stifling south Louisiana heat and humidity, so he removed his seersucker suit coat and draped it over the vacant chair next to him. The chair would be occupied by Deke Morgan later, but it was only quarter to nine and the trial wasn't set to start until ten so for now, it was just J. François and the deputy, neither of whom spoke to the other.

The seasoned criminal defense attorney extracted a thick folder from his heavy briefcase which he then let fall to the floor with a heavy plop that reverberated in the empty courtroom. It may have been more accurate to call it a satchel, but attorneys called them briefcases, though its size more resembled a small valise than a briefcase.

The deputy, well past retirement age, ambled past the lawyer as he went about setting up microphones that were more for the use of the court reporter than for anyone who might be attending the trial. The microphones were not tied into a public-address system but were instead patched directly into the court reporter's earphones. With experienced efficiency, he went about testing each of the microphones. Satisfied that they were working properly, he checked to be sure the judge had a pitcher of ice water and a glass. That was the one part of his job he didn't dare ignore for fear of incurring a self-important judge's wrath.

American and Louisiana state flags adorned either side of the bench where the judge would sit as he presided over the sure-to-be emotion-fraught trial that had gripped this small community. There were fourteen chairs in the jury box, twelve for the jurors and two for alternates in case a juror had to be excused during the course of the trial.

J. François was oblivious to it all. He'd been through the same procedure too many times to remember. Instead, he busied himself going over his notes and the bill of information that formally charged Deke with the priest's grisly murder. He was surprisingly confident that he could win this case. The arresting deputies, so overzealous in their efforts to make the arrest, had overlooked several details, including forgetting to read Deke his Miranda Rights until over a full day after he'd been arrested, by at first refusing to allow him to call an attorney, and by continuing to grill him long after he'd requested an attorney. Any one of these omissions was sufficient to gain a retrial on appeal, but J. François was counting on more egregious errors that included deputies' wiping down the crime scene before necessary lab work could be performed that might lead authorities to the "real" killer. In the final analysis, all the prosecution had to go on was the priest's car that Deke was driving. Car theft is a long way from a capital murder offense and J. François Berthelot was primed for a good fight.

He was in middle of his file review when he first noticed a soft rustling that was too close to be the deputy who was on the other side of the courtroom. It was almost like a soft breeze, except that he sensed it more than felt it. It sent a slight shiver down his spine, but he ignored it and went back to his reading. He had turned his full attention back to the papers in his hands when a gust of wind sent the papers flying across the courtroom. He lunged forward in an effort to grab some of the papers, wondering at the same time what idiot had left the door open. He glanced around and found that all the doors to the courtroom were closed.

Cursing under his breath, he got down on his hands and knees. The deputy, seeing what had happened came over to help and together, they soon gathered all the strewn documents. He thanked the deputy who was still holding a handful of papers. As he took them from the bailiff, he turned back toward the table. That's when he saw the young boy. He was standing behind the chair in which J. François had just been sitting. He started to ask the boy what he was doing inside the railing that separates the principals in a trial from the spectators but then he recognized him and his heart nearly stopped. It was the same boy that he'd seen in his garage and in his driveway.

Letting out a loud grunt, he spun to his right and saw a sad faced man he took to be an Indian, but who in reality was Sri Lankan. "Who the hell are you?" he shouted. "What're you doing here?"

"What?" the deputy asked, wondering who J. François was talking to. He saw no one.

"Get them out of here!" J. François yelled even as a beautiful young woman appeared less than a dozen feet in front of him.

"Who?"

"Them! Get 'em out of here!" the attorney screamed as he whirled around to face the deputy only to see yet another figure of a man standing behind the deputy. "Him!"

"There's no one here but us," the deputy said, now growing concerned over the attorney's state of mind. He tried to be a subtle as possible as he unsnapped the holster that held his pistol that probably hadn't been fired in years.

"Get him out I said" J. François repeated, pointing to the figure standing behind the deputy who made the unforgivable error of looking behind him to see

216

where the lawyer was pointing, turning his back to him in the process. J. François grabbed the deputy's pistol and pushed the overmatched old man down in the process as he fired two quick shots at the figure that had been standing there but now was gone.

Two state troopers detailed to the courthouse for security for the trial, heard the crash of the chair when the deputy fell onto it, knocking it against the judge's bench, in turn causing the pitcher of water to crash to the floor. They were already headed for the courtroom when they heard the shots and they pulled their own weapons as they approached. At one trooper's signal, both men burst through the door and dove to the floor behind the back row of spectator benches and popped up to see what was going on.

J. François, in an uncontrolled state of hysteria, was spinning from one of the images to the other trying to decide which one to shoot next when he heard the commotion of the troopers' crashing into the courtroom. In a single, panic- driven motion, he turned and fired three bursts in the direction of the troopers just as the first one through the door rolled into the aisle and came up in a squatting position and fired once, then twice. By now the second trooper was firing at the already dying J. François but both troopers kept firing until their weapons were empty. He was hit eight times, once in the head, once in the leg, and the remaining six times in the upper torso. Any one of seven bullet wounds pumped into the lawyer would have been fatal.

In the corner, a dazed deputy, embarrassed that he'd allowed someone to seize his weapon, struggled to his feet, grateful to still be alive. "Who the hell was he shooting at?" he asked no one in particular.

As the two troopers cautiously approached the dead lawyer, one of them asked the deputy if he was all right. "I'm fine," he replied. "I just fell over a chair when he pushed me, but I'm not hurt."

"Were the two of you arguing?" the same trooper asked.

"No. I was helping him pick up some papers that blew off the table when he started acting like he saw somebody. He started turning this way and that, yelling at them and for me to get 'em out of here. Then, he grabbed my gun and started shooting."

"We'll need to run lab tests to see what he was on," the second trooper said.

"I don't think he was on anything," the deputy said, rubbing a bump on his head. "He was the defense attorney for today's trial."

"J. François Berthelot?" the first trooper said. "Oh, damn."

Matt and Geoffrey Timmons, having heard the shooting as they ran into the courthouse, knew before they arrived what they'd find when they entered the courtroom. They stood for several minutes, watching in silence and listening to the exchange between the deputy and the troopers. Then, without a word between them, they turned and walked back to Timmon's vehicle and drove back to Slidell. Matt felt sick to his stomach but Timmons was thinking that J. François

217

deserved no better fate. But mostly, he was just happy the man he was assigned to protect was safe. He'd grown to think of Matt as a friend.

72

J. François's death stunned members of the Justice Department's special task force. Besides the three New Orleans judges, he was a primary target of the ongoing investigation. They were equally surprised when, six days after his death, J. François's legal counsel walked into the U.S. Attorney's office and asked to see Victor Carlotti. At first, Carlotti sent word he was too busy to meet with anyone at the moment. But when word came back from the receptionist who the visitor was, the entire office swung into action.

Carlotti appeared in the lobby in a matter of just a few seconds to greet the lawyer, who identified himself as Ted Rowland. Carlotti had never heard of him, but he invited him back to his office nevertheless. "Can I offer you a drink?" he said to his guest when he was seated.

Rowland, appearing almost shy and definitely ill at ease, declined. "Mr. Carlotti, I represented Mr. Berthelot, mainly in business matters. I was his attorney for many years but I never represented him in criminal matters. This is new to turf for me."

"Okay," said Carlotti, pouring himself a drink. "What brings you here today?"

"Several weeks ago, Mr. Berthelot felt that his life might be in danger, so he wrote a letter and sealed it in an envelope and gave it to me to keep," Rowland said. "He gave me written instructions that no one was to see the letter unless he died violently or under mysterious circumstances. I believe his death meets both those criteria. In the event of his death by violent means, I was to deliver this letter to you personally." He extended his letter of instructions from J. François to Carlotti with his right hand while holding the still sealed envelope in his left. Carlotti read the instructions carefully and looked up from the paper at Rowland who now was holding the envelope out for Carlotti to take.

As Carlotti took the envelope, Rowland rose to his feet. "I believe my work on behalf of Mr. Berthelot is complete, so if you don't mind, I'll say goodbye."

"You don't know what this says?" Carlotti asked, taking a sip of his drink.

"No sir, I don't."

219

"You're not curious?"

"No sir, I am not in the least. My instructions were to deliver it. I've done that. To tell you the truth, Mr. Carlotti, I was seriously considering withdrawing my services as Mr. Berthelot's legal counsel when he was killed. I don't know what all he was involved in and I don't believe it was something I'd care to know about."

"You're probably right, Mr. Rowland. Thank you for bringing this by."

He waited until he was certain that Rowland was gone before he opened the letter.

He scanned it quickly the first time but then he read it again and then a third time. He laid the letter on his desk and picked up the telephone. He dialed an inter-office extension number and when Jamie Maestri answered he said, "Get into my office right now and bring Jessica Beauchamp with you. We just got our guarantee."

73

"It's so good to finally get back in my own house."

Rose was making her way up the sidewalk to her front door as Matt, Ashleigh, and Sergeant Geoffrey Timmons trailed behind, pushing aside the overhanging azaleas as they walked. The cat that had scampered away from Matt and Ashleigh on an earlier visit, emboldened by hunger, greeted them with loud mewls as she arched her back to rub against Rose's leg.

Displaying a burst of energy she hadn't felt in years, Rose took the three steps to her porch unaided. She already had her key ring out and was ready to unlock the three dead bolts. It took her only an instant to see that the door, destroyed when the state police officers found it necessary to break it down to get to would-be assassin Travis Whitten, had been replaced. The locks were the same but she was nevertheless convinced that someone must to have had keys made in order to replace them on the new door. "I have to have my locks changed again," she said as she turned the keys one by one and opened the door.

The old house, as could be expected, was hot and musty from being closed and unoccupied for nearly four days in the overbearing south Louisiana summer heat and humidity. "Come on in now," Rose said impatiently. "I have to de-activate the alarm before the sheriff's office calls. The other three entered with luggage and stood by as Rose positioned herself between them and the keypad on the alarm. She keyed in the numbers to de-activate the device and only then did she turn around to survey her home. "Let's just see what those bullets did in this room," she said, opening the door to the front bedroom. "Well, that doesn't look too awfully bad," she said when she saw the room. Matt and Ashleigh peered over her shoulders and they saw that there was no damage to the wall. All the bullets fired by Whitten had gone directly into the mattress – right where they normally would have been lying had they been in the bed. "It looks like I'll have to replace the mattress," was all Rose said.

"Don't worry about that," Ashleigh said. "We'll replace the mattress. The important thing is no one was hurt in all this."

Rose walked across the living room to turn on a window air conditioning unit and didn't respond to Ashleigh's observation. She turned and started toward

221

the kitchen but stopped abruptly just before reaching the spot on the dining room floor where Whitten had fallen and died. "I'll have to replace this linoleum, too," she said, almost to herself.

Sergeant Timmons placed Rose's suitcase on the living room floor. "If you folks don't need me for anything else, I'll be in my patrol car. We're going to have officers sitting outside for a couple of days to be sure everything's okay. Matt, you have my cell number. Call me if you need anything."

"Thanks for everything you've done, Sergeant," Ashleigh said.

"We'll keep in touch," Matt added. "Thanks again."

When he was gone, Matt and Ashleigh looked at each other. "I guess we need to discuss this with Grandma Rose now," Ashleigh said.

"I guess now's as good a time as any," he replied.

Together they walked into the kitchen where they found Rose sitting at the table, holding a glass of ice water. They sat across the table from her. "Grandma, we need to talk to you about something," Ashleigh said.

"I know, dear," the old woman said. "It's time we put Jake's ashes in the garden the way he wanted me to."

Ashleigh's mouth dropped open. "You knew we were going to say that?"

"These old eyes and ears don't miss much, honey. I've heard the two of you talk. You thought I was asleep but I listened to you that night at the motel while you stayed up most of the night watching the video. Besides, I've seen the video, too. I might be old, but I'm not stupid. And best of all, I know I'm not crazy like everyone seems to think."

"I never once thought you were crazy, Grandma," Ashleigh said, fighting back tears. "We just wanted what's best for your peace of mind."

"I know you did. That's why I enjoy having you and Mitch visit me. I wish you'd come more often than you do because you're the only ones in the family who didn't try to say I was losing my mind."

Rose stood and looked around. "Jake," she said, looking toward the ceiling, "I know you're still here and I still love you even though you've worried me half to death for twelve years now. You've been more trouble dead than you ever were alive so I'm going to spread your ashes in your precious garden first thing tomorrow and then I want you to *leave me the hell alone!*" They allowed themselves a nervous laugh as the lights flickered twice. "I guess *that* told him," she said with all the defiance she could muster.

222

74

"What I am about to divulge to you right now must remain in this room for the time being," Victor Carlotti said. The two assistants he had summoned to his office had never seen him so excited. "Details of what this letter contains will be made known at the proper time, but for now I have to have your word that nothing will be said about it until I can ascertain its authenticity. Are we agreed?"

The others nodded their agreement. "Of course, Victor," said Jamie Maestri.

"Certainly," said Jessica Beauchamp.

Both continued to look puzzled and by now their curiosity was so aroused they would probably have agreed to strip naked and run down the hall singing *Itsy Bitsy Spider* to learn the contents of the seven-page latter lying in front of the task force leader.

Carlotti reached into a desk drawer and removed two Photostat copies of the letter and gave a copy to each of them. "I want these back before you leave here but first I want to you to take your time and read it very carefully."

Both assistant U.S. Attorneys read without speaking. Beauchamp finished first but waited for Maestri. "Where the hell did this come from?" Maestri asked when he finished.

"You're not going to believe this, but the attorney for the late J. François Berthelot dropped this in our lap less than a half-hour ago.

"You're not serious," said Beauchamp.

"Yes, I am. He walked in here without an appointment and handed me a sealed envelope. He said he was acting on written instructions from his client. He even had the letter of instructions from J. François telling him to deliver the sealed envelope to us in the event of his untimely demise."

"How much validity do you give this?" said Jamie Maestri.

Carlotti leaned forward and picked up the original copy of the letter from his desk. Holding it up, he looked at his two assistants. "Why would anyone do something like this if it weren't true? This guy was afraid; he wrote it six weeks before we went public and you know we kept a tight lid on the investigation. He anticipated something bad happening. There was no reason for him to say all this,

223

to implicate all these people unless he knew he was in danger – and unless it was all true. He was writing this to protect himself from his partners. The timing on this letter is crucial."

Maestri stood up and walked to a window. "But this letter implicates the same people in activities we weren't even aware of. They weren't satisfied with the bail bond scam, they had to get greedy. Can you imagine their running a drug and prostitution ring using acquitted felons as their gofers? And J. François was right in the middle of it just like we thought."

Carlotti smiled at the other two. "All I can say is we've got our proverbial smoking gun. Juries love that crap. Christmas comes early this year."

75

Judge Charles Cheramie, the wily veteran of more than twenty years on the Orleans Parish Criminal District Court bench and twenty more before that as a practicing attorney, resorted to the most basic of animal instincts – survival – when he got the furtive telephone call. Indictments had been issued for his arrest, the caller said, on multiple counts of malfeasance, bribery, drug dealing, prostitution, racketeering, extortion, and misuse of public funds. Federal marshals were on their way to bring him in.

Rather than taking the dignified measure of turning himself into authorities, he decided to run. An unwise decision, to be sure, but it was one made on the fly and seemingly rational at the time. He unlocked his credenza, retrieved his passport, and emptied stacks of bundled one hundred-dollar bills into a leather briefcase and without a word to his receptionist, left for the parking garage. Pulling out from the garage, he headed for Louis Armstrong International Airport. He didn't know where he would go, but he knew it was time to leave. At the moment, Grand Cayman or even South America or Mexico seemed terribly attractive options. Venezuela was even better; it had no extradition treaty with the U.S.

His departure beat the arrival of marshals, armed with a warrant, by less than five minutes. It took authorities less time than it did Judge Cheramie to think of the airport. His photo went out to airport authorities with instructions to detain him at all costs. New Orleans police patrols were put on alert to watch for his dark blue Infiniti M45 Sport. State police and sheriff's deputies from both Orleans and Jefferson Parish were directed to I-10 to look for his car.

Sergeant Stuart Wiggins was on patrol in the downtown area of New Orleans, along with his young, inexperienced partner, a criminal justice graduate who, like Wiggins so many years before, thought he could change the world for the better through a career in law enforcement. Many were the times that Wiggins wanted to scream at the gregarious young officer that the real world was so different from what he'd been taught at Southeastern Louisiana University, far removed from Hammond or any other college town. *That was theory; this is the real world.* But he'd held his tongue even as he simmered in his own discontent and grew more and more jaded with his career choice with each passing day.

The radio was crackling with the alert and description of Judge Cheramie's vehicle – but not his name – when the Infiniti flashed by on Tulane barely slowing for a red light at Jeff Davis Parkway before barreling through the intersection, nearly causing several collisions. Wiggins hit his siren and lights as he pulled in behind the speeding vehicle, reaching for his radio as he did so. "Affirmative on that Infiniti," he said. "I have him in sight westbound on Tulane at Jeff Davis. He just blew a red light, so I may need backup."

A second and then a third patrol car responded to Wiggins, letting him know they were in the area and were closing off Tulane ahead of the fleeing vehicle but as it turned out, that wasn't necessary. Judge Cheramie, apparently aware that he wasn't going anywhere and continued flight would just delay the inevitable, slowed and pulled into a fast food parking lot. "Keep your hands where I can see them and exit the vehicle slowly," Wiggins instructed over his public-address system. He watched as the driver's side door opened and then his jaw dropped in disbelief.

He grabbed his radio microphone. "I have the suspect," he said. "Other than running a red light and reckless driving, what do we want him for?"

"Unlawful flight to avoid prosecution for now," the dispatcher answered, causing Wiggins to do a double take as he stared at the radio as if he thought it had somehow malfunctioned.

"Ten-four," he finally said. He didn't know the circumstances and he didn't really care. All he could think about at the moment was the contempt citation Judge Cheramie had slapped him with only a few weeks before. More than being held in contempt and fined, the pompous lecture to which he'd been subjected had left a lingering feeling of rancor and bitterness toward the legal profession in general, the judiciary in particular, and for New Orleans, and the inhabitants of its netherworld.

There are those rare moments in life when the stars and planets are in perfect alignment and all is right in the world, and while he didn't know why Judge Cheramie was wanted, he intended to enjoy this moment to its fullest. He would learn soon enough what kind of trouble the judge was in, but for now, Stuart Wiggins, Sergeant, New Orleans Police Department, wouldn't trade careers with anyone on earth. "You have the right to remain silent," he said as he approached the suspect who was already bent over the Infiniti's hood and was being handcuffed by his young partner.

226

76

The wedding was a simple affair because they wouldn't have it any other way.

The indictments, sixteen in all, totaling more than a hundred criminal counts, had come down more than a year before. Fourteen entered guilty pleas to lesser charges after negotiations with prosecutors and some of them testified against the two holdouts. Judge Charles Cheramie and a judge from St. Bernard Parish thought they could beat the charges and decided to fight back. It was a bad decision for both. They were tried separately and their trials lasted almost two months each. In the end, juries convicted Judge Cheramie on eight counts of criminal racketeering and mail fraud charges. The other judge was convicted on six similar counts. Each received lengthy prison sentences and substantial fines for their trouble. And in what seemed like overkill, each was removed from office, their licenses to practice law suspended.

Once their lives returned to normal, Matt and Ashleigh decided it was time to make lifelong commitments to each other.

Rose's living room served as the chapel since there were fewer than a dozen guests. Geoffrey Timmons was best man and the hulking state trooper cut a splendid figure in his dress blue uniform. The matron of honor was Ashleigh's mother, Rebecca, who flew in for the wedding, as did her three sisters. It was their first time back in Rose's home in years and all six women – mother, daughters, and granddaughter – couldn't have been happier.

The bride wore a modest short-sleeved pink blouse accented by white pants and matching white sneakers. The groom wore his best khaki Dockers and a Kelly green knit shirt complete with the Tulane University logo. Rose was in her element as she watched Matt and her granddaughter exchange vows.

After the wedding, officiated by Louisiana Supreme Court Justice Thomas Gravois, everyone adjourned to the reception hall, in this case, Rose's kitchen. She had catered the entire affair because she insisted. For the first time ever, she consented to allowing one person, Rebecca, to assist her in preparing enough banana pudding and iced tea for everyone in lieu of wedding cake and punch.

"There's plenty of pudding and tea for seconds," Rose called out over the idle conversation of the guests and most of them took her up on her offer.

"This is the first wedding I've officiated in many, many years," Justice Gravois said to Sergeant Timmons. "I believe the last time was when I was a first-term city judge back in New Iberia."

Sergeant Timmons laughed. "Well, this wasn't exactly your traditional wedding. This wasn't my first time to stand as best man, but it was my first time in dress uniform. I was tickled to do this for Matt. Did you know he tried to warn that attorney just before he was killed?"

"Yes, I did," Justice Gravois said. "Rose told me all about it. But that doesn't surprise me. Matt's the kind of person who would do that even though the guy was a real scumbag and didn't deserve a heads up."

"Yes sir, I learned to like the guy while I was guarding him."

"He's a good, steady law clerk," the Supreme Court justice said, "and he's going to make a helluva lawyer whenever he decides to goes into private practice. I don't look forward to the prospect of trying to replace him."

Their conversation was interrupted when the newlywed couple approached from across the room. "Justice Gravois, I want to thank you for doing this for us. We really appreciate it."

"And I really appreciate your help the day they tried to kill Matt," Ashleigh said. "You saved his life."

"No, my dear, you saved his life. If you hadn't done what you did, we probably wouldn't be standing here."

Matt put his arm around Ashleigh and pulled her closer. "She's pretty special. She was so cool when she saw them taking me away. You should have been there."

"She wasn't too shabby when she came into my office that day in her bare feet," Gravois said. "*You* should have been there for *that* performance."

All four laughed. Then Matt turned to Sergeant Timmons. "Geoffrey, I want to thank you, too, for everything you did for us," Matt said.

"No problem, Matt, that's my job."

"I'm not just talking about the guard detail. I'm talking about your taking the time to listen to my theory and helping me to put all the pieces together. You really helped bring things into focus."

"Any time, Matt," Timmons said. "By the way, I was just getting ready to tell Justice Gravois when you walked up that I was in Baton Rouge yesterday and I read in *The Advocate* some guy up there was killed in a weird altercation with undercover narcotic agents."

"How do you mean?" Matt asked.

"Some politician's son got himself killed in a shootout. He was arrested nearly two years ago for shooting and killing a state police undercover narcotics agent in a sting operation that went bad. Because of who he was, he got acquitted. It really pissed off a lot of state police officers. His daddy went out and hired some

228

hotshot lawyer from Lafayette who has a reputation for confusing juries and getting favorable verdicts for sleaze bag defendants."

"You've got to be kidding," Matt said.

"No, I'm not. And that's not all. This time, Baton Rouge undercover agents were on a stakeout waiting for a dealer to show when this kid walked up and started talking to a brick wall on a dark street corner in north Baton Rouge. Then he starts talking louder and waving his arms around like he's really upset at someone, except no one's there. The agents are naturally curious and they're watching the kid because they recognized him from before. They're waiting for him to make one false move so they can bust him. Then, all of a sudden, no warning, the kid starts arguing and screaming at the wall. He draws a gun and pumps two rounds into the brick wall of a vacant building. He's still holding the gun when the agents yell at him to drop it. But then he turns on them and raises his weapon. They open up on him and drop him right there on the sidewalk."

"They killed him?" Matt asked.

"They don't get any deader."

"Who was his attorney?"

"I didn't catch his name," Timmons said. "The guys at Troop A told me he has a reputation of defending bad guys and getting them off. He's done the same thing for other felons. Every cop in Baton Rouge and Lafayette hates his guts."

Matt was peering into his glass of iced tea and didn't respond at first. Finally, he looked up at Timmons. "Interesting," he said.

There was a pause at first before the others caught the significance of his pensive reaction to Timmons's story.

"Oh, *hell* no, Matt," the trooper said. "Don't even *think* about it."

"Sergeant, I can't believe you *told* him that!" Ashleigh said, visibly upset with their best man.

Justice Gravois was just as concerned and he decided to step in. "Matt, don't bother about asking for time off. I need you too much at the office and I can't be running all the way to Baton Rouge or Lafayette to pull your fat out of the fire."

Matt laughed. "I wouldn't think of it, sir. I'm a family man now. I have responsibilities. I'll be happy to let someone else chase that ghost story. I specialize in ghosts of the Crescent City."

Then he stared at Sergeant Timmons with a peculiar look in his eyes that revealed far more than was intended.

"You say he was talking to a brick wall and then he shot it?"

o0o

229